MW01709344

DANGEROUS CARGO

A gripping crime thriller full of twists

PAULINE ROWSON

The Art Marvik Mysteries Book 2

JOFFE BOOKS

Revised edition 2023
Joffe Books, London
www.joffebooks.com

First published by Fathom in Great Britain in 2020

This paperback edition was first published
in Great Britain in 2023

Cover art by Dee Dee Book Covers

ISBN: 978-1-80405-822-0

CHAPTER ONE

Friday

Marvik surveyed the road in the drizzling dusk of the chill March evening. There were two cars parked in front of the bank of trees and shrubs that rose to his left. Nobody was sitting in them and there was no traffic on the narrow road leading up from the small Dorset coastal town of Swanage towards the lifeboat station. No signs of life either in the houses on his right but as he turned and made for the lifeboat station he caught the deep throb of a motorbike in the distance. It gradually faded. Nothing wrong in that except a motorbike had passed him twice as he'd walked through the town. The registration number had been obscured by mud and even though Marvik hadn't been able to see the rider's face because of the tinted visor he knew it was the same motorbike by the rider's clothes and his build; it was also the same make, a powerful Honda. Maybe the rider was just cruising. Maybe he was looking for somewhere. Or maybe he was looking for someone. Him.

He turned on to the tarmacked track by the lifeboat station and made towards the shallow shore where his tender lay. His thoughts slipped back to the great echoing church on the eastern outskirts of the town where he had that day attended the funeral of a man he didn't know. There had been only five mourners and a clearly embarrassed vicar who'd had to relay the life of Bradley Pulford to his remaining relatives, except there was no life to relay. Pulford had appeared in Swanage in July 1989 and had vanished from it in January 1991, or rather, that was when he had been reported missing. During that time he'd worked as a fisherman on Matthew and Adam Killbeck's boat, had got involved with Matthew's niece, Stacey, and had left behind a son, Jensen. Nothing was known about Bradley Pulford before 1989 or after 1991, or more precisely the Bradley Pulford who had been cremated that afternoon because, according to Detective Chief Superintendent Philip Crowder of the National Intelligence Marine Squad, Bradley Pulford had died in 1959. So why had someone taken his identity? It was a question that Marvik and his former Marine colleague, Shaun Strathen, had been detailed to find the answers to.

He pushed his tender into the sea and leapt on board, noting in the rapidly diminishing twilight that a boat had anchored up not far from his during his absence. The tender's outboard spluttered into life and he pointed it towards his large, sturdy motor cruiser anchored to the right of Swanage Pier, recalling his conversation with Crowder earlier that day on his boat at the Hamble. Crowder had swivelled round his laptop computer and he and Strathen had studied the photographs of the decomposed body of the Bradley Pulford washed up in Freshwater Bay on the Isle of Wight on the twenty-eighth of January. The sea life had made inroads into it and what remained of the flesh was greenish black. That didn't mean it had been submerged for long — nature acted fast in cold sea water on the English coast in winter, as both he and Shaun knew. The forensic pathologist had estimated that the corpse had been in the sea for between three to four days. The fact that it had washed up on the Isle of Wight also didn't mean the man had entered the sea there or even from the mainland at Portsmouth five miles across the Solent. The tides and current could have brought him from as far afield as Brighton on the east coast or Dorset to the west. Marvik recalled Crowder's words: 'The autopsy couldn't determine the exact cause of death but there were signs of blunt force trauma to the skull which could have been caused by the body being battered against rocks or an underwater structure. DNA taken from the corpse was matched against that filed on the missing persons register. It threw up Jensen Killbeck, whose birth certificate states he was born to Stacey Killbeck and Bradley Pulford in June 1990 in Swanage, Dorset. Jensen Killbeck was informed of his father's death via a relative, Matthew Killbeck. Jensen claimed he'd never had any contact with his father and had never seen him. The family agreed to arrange the funeral. It takes place this afternoon in St Paul's Church, Swanage. You need to be there, Marvik.'

Crowder hadn't said why but as Marvik drew level with his motor cruiser, silenced the engine and secured the tender to his boat, he knew his job and Strathen's was to find out just who the dead man really was, why he'd been killed and who had killed him.

Ordinarily such matters would have been down to the police Major Crime Team, not two former Royal Marine commandos and civilians such as him and Strathen, but as far as the police were concerned the case had been signed off as accidental death or suicide, and a relative located. The fact that Crowder's National Intelligence Marine Squad were now involved, and hence them, meant Pulford's death was far from resolved and, what's more, it had international ramifications. It also meant Crowder knew a hell of a lot more about the body on the beach than he was letting on. But that was par for the course. Secrecy was one of the essential elements of their missions, because whoever was behind the crime was not only dangerous and desperate enough to kill many times to protect himself but was also in a position of power and influence to make sure he didn't get caught. If Crowder dug too deeply into police files and asked too many questions he could alert the target. Marvik's role, aided by Strathen — a genius on gathering and analysing information

— was to act as bait to force the target into the open. The motorbike incident might be coincidence — it might be nothing — but on the other hand, it could be the first stage in forcing the target to show his hand.

Marvik checked the anchors were holding at the helm and called Strathen.

'I was beginning to think you'd struck lucky and had gone off with one of the mourners,' Strathen said, answering on the second ring.

'One was in her mid-seventies, the other early twenties, fair-haired, plump with a surly expression and clearly very protective though not necessarily in love with her fiancé, Jensen Killbeck.'

'Bradley Pulford's son. What's he like?'

'Scrawny, sulky, brown gelled hair, dark, suspicious eyes. But maybe he looks that way at everyone and not just a stranger who turns up with a scarred face. He hardly uttered a word. But then none of them were exactly gushing. I don't think Jensen's silence was caused by grief either, not because it was stiff upper lip time but because he simply didn't care. He seemed to be genuinely bored by the whole thing. Aside from Jensen and his fiancé, Keely, there was Matthew Killbeck, his wife, Mary and their son, Adam, and that was it.'

'Bradley Pulford wasn't the most loved of men then,' Strathen said with cynicism.

'No, and they were only there out of a sense of duty. Matthew Killbeck said Pulford, despite buggering off and leaving his niece to raise their son, deserved a proper Christian service, although none of them followed the hearse to the crematorium.'

It had been a dismal service, dignified only by the robust singing of 'Eternal Father, Strong to Save' by the broad-shouldered man in his mid-seventies, Matthew Killbeck, and his son beside him in his late forties, Adam Killbeck. The vicar had done his best to raise a tuneful note but his voice, like his body, was thin and his expression bewildered and pained rather than sorrowful. Marvik couldn't help noting the relief on his careworn features as the short service came to an end with the Lord's Prayer. The coffin, a plain affair, had rested on a trestle table in front of the altar, beside the pulpit. There were no flowers or photographs on or around it. The undertakers had placed it there and left the church. None of the mourners had approached it after the service. All had simply turned their back on it, much as Pulford had turned his back on them in November 1990 when Matthew said he had taken off. They hadn't even waited for the coffin to be placed in the hearse to be transported to the crematorium. Outside, Matthew Killbeck had invited Marvik to join them for a drink in a nearby pub.

'Probably curious to know why you were there,' Strathen said.

Marvik recalled the man's keen yet tired grey eyes in a ruddy, weatherworn face etched with age and the ravages of the sea. On introducing himself, Marvik had taken Killbeck's rough hand in his, noting his strength. He'd seized on the invitation. It had been exactly what he'd wished for. He wasn't there to pay his respects to a man he'd never known, or to enjoy the splendours of the Dorset coast.

It had been a strange wake and Marvik hadn't been impervious to the strained atmosphere as they had sat around the table in the corner of the pub that was more a wine bar than traditional hostelry. It didn't look as though it was the Killbecks' natural habitat. It was too trendy, too expensive and the clientele, with the exception of the Killbecks in their black, ordinary chain-store clothes and himself in his casual clothes and waterproof jacket, reflected that. There was a well-dressed couple in their late sixties at a table in the window eating a meal, two women in their mid-thirties making rapid inroads into a second bottle of white wine and getting very noisy, and a couple of elderly men at the bar, one nursing a whisky and reading the newspaper, the other hunched over a glass of red wine, reading something on his phone.

Marvik said, 'Adam Killbeck didn't seem too keen on me being there. Jensen and Keely weren't bothered whether I was there or not as long as they had a drink in front of them, and I doubt if Mary Killbeck even knew why she was at the church. A sweet lady but clearly suffering from some kind of dementia. She kept mumbling from the scriptures about Jesus rising up from the dead, not surprising seeing as we'd been in church at a funeral service. Matthew said the least he could do was buy me a drink for coming all the way to attend a stranger's funeral.'

'Did he buy the story about you witnessing Pulford's body being found?'

'He looked ready to accept it but Adam Killbeck wasn't convinced. I think that's just his manner, though — he's naturally cautious and sceptical. I didn't get much out of him except for a few grunts and hostile looks. He's not the talkative type — probably spends too much time at sea. But Matthew told me that Pulford had worked on the fishing boat with him, his brother Leonard, Adam and another man, Joshua Nunton, from July 1989 until November 1990 before vanishing.'

'Why did they wait until January 1991 to report him missing?'

'They thought he'd come back. I got the impression they'd have preferred not have reported it at all but Stacey insisted. Matthew probably didn't want the police poking their noses into the family's affairs. Not that the police did much poking, Matthew said. It was filed and forgotten. He said he was flabbergasted when a copper came knocking on his door two weeks ago and said they'd found him. Leonard died in 1995, while Stacey died six years ago of a brain tumour.'

'Maybe they didn't want the cops involved because they were up to something illegal — smuggling, for example, under the cover of fishing.'

'I think it was just a fisherman's natural mistrust of anything to do with authority. I asked if they had any idea why Pulford had taken off. Matthew said they thought the responsibility of being a father had been too much for him. I pumped them for background but not too hard. I didn't want to push it, not only because Jensen was there and I didn't think either Adam or Matthew would say much in front of him, but also because Mary Killbeck got more and more agitated and distressed the longer we were there and Matthew became very keen for me to drink up and leave.' Marvik fleetingly recalled her frightened, fragile face and Matthew Killbeck's worried countenance as he tried to soothe her. 'Matthew said that Pulford told them he'd worked as a fisherman before, that his parents were dead and he'd gone to sea as soon as he was sixteen. He just showed up one day on the shore and asked if they could do with an extra pair of hands. He never said where he was from, but Matthew thought it was somewhere on the south coast because he seemed to know it well. That's about all I could get. I passed on my condolences, said it must have been a tough time for Jensen but he shrugged and said not really, because he had never known his father. What have you got on the real Bradley Pulford?'

'Not much. He was born in London in December 1939 and died in August 1959. His death certificate says he died of blunt force trauma to the brain, much like our recent corpse, but that covers a multitude of things: it could have been a road accident, a fall, someone striking him with a fist or crowbar, even an insect bite causing him to black out and strike his head as he fell. His death was registered in Singapore, though, which is interesting. I've no idea what he was doing there. Crowder might know but he probably wouldn't tell us even if we asked. It might be relevant, or on the other hand it might not.'

'Our recent corpse could have been that Bradley Pulford's son who decided to take his father's name.' Marvik knew the thought would already have occurred to Strathen.

'I'm checking it out, but if the Bradley Pulford from 1939 didn't marry — I can't find any record that he did — and if he wasn't named on a birth certificate by the mother as being the father, then there's very little way of finding out.'

'I'll get a description from the Killbecks of the Pulford who showed up here in 1989, or better still a photograph.'

'Are you thinking the son, if it was him washed up in Freshwater Bay, could have been born to a woman in Singapore? A Malay, Eurasian or Chinese?'

'Just an idea.' Marvik scanned the shore in the drizzling rain. Nothing was stirring. Lights were twinkling from the town across the bay and on the pier to his right.

He said, 'This man who used to fish with them, Joshua Nunton — he might be able to tell us more about the Pulford who showed up here in 1989. I'll see if I can get his contact details tomorrow.'

Marvik rang off and descended into the galley, where he made a coffee and something to eat. The wind was rising and the boat was rocking and bucking but the movement didn't disturb him or his stomach. He'd survived in far worse conditions.

He pushed away memories of his days in the Special Boat Services and mentally replayed his conversation that afternoon with the mourners — except none of them seemed to be in mourning — searching for something in their words that could give him more on Bradley Pulford, but there seemed little. Perhaps, as Matthew Killbeck had said, Pulford simply hadn't wanted the responsibilities of parenthood and had taken off — it wasn't unheard of. Marvik's parents had done much the same thing although they had waited until he was eleven before dumping him in an expensive English boarding school. Before then he'd spent years happily travelling with them on their marine archaeological expeditions. Once packed off to school, though, he had hardly seen them. There had always been some excuse.

He shut off his feelings of bitterness and returned his mind to Jensen Killbeck, who at twenty-four seemed immature. Still, that wasn't a sin. But by his age Marvik had seen and experienced more in his life in the Marines than Jensen ever would. He missed those adrenaline-filled days and the life the services had given him. But they were over. He hoped that working for Crowder would go some way to filling the gap. This was his second mission for the National Intelligence

Marine Squad and there was no room for failure. The word hadn't existed in Marvik's vocabulary in the Marines, but in civilian life he hadn't fared quite so well.

Soon his mind was replaying that fatal mission working as a private maritime security operative when he'd let a man die. It had been last July. His job had been to protect Harry Salcombe and his luxury yacht from pirates in the Indian Ocean, and although he'd taken all the right decisions as the pirate boat approached, his colleague on that boat, Lee Addington, had engaged the pirates. They'd returned fire. Harry Salcombe had got a bullet in the chest, Marvik in his shoulder and had struck his head as he'd fallen. He'd woken up in hospital some days later.

Crowder's arrival on the scene in February, when he'd been at his lowest ebb, had given him another chance, and Marvik wasn't about to throw it away. Strathen, too, injured during the conflict in Afghanistan, which had left him with a prosthetic left leg, was also keen to show his worth. They'd succeeded on their first assignment and Marvik's mind flicked back to the woman he'd met during it, Helen Shannon, with her purple hair, her blunt manner and her courage. The thought of her made him smile before he recalled the emotional pain etched on her narrow face, the bewilderment in her green eyes and their parting conversation, full of anger and bitterness on her part. He'd turned her world inside out by discovering her sister's killer, and in so doing had exposed raw emotions she'd preferred not to have faced. He knew how tough that could be. Or did he? He'd chosen to bury his.

Roughly, he pushed such thoughts aside and brought his mind back to the present. Accomplishing the mission was all that mattered and he was determined to make damn sure he and Strathen would. So far he'd gained little information but his appearance and questions had prompted a reaction — the man on the motorbike, which he hadn't yet mentioned to Strathen. He would, though.

He slept lightly, his senses attuned for any unusual sounds. He didn't think he was in danger on the boat but he wasn't ruling it out. At five, an hour before high tide, he was on deck watching the shore for signs of Matthew and Adam Killbeck's arrival. He'd discovered earlier that the red-and-white fishing vessel on the shore was theirs. They would go out on the tide but it was almost seven before he saw a battered pick-up truck turn on to the shingle bay and park close to the fishing boat. Adam Killbeck climbed out of the driver's cab; the man with him wasn't Matthew but Jensen.

Marvik locked the boat, climbed into his tender and headed for the shore. The sound of his boat approaching caused Adam to look up. A surprised expression crossed his rugged, tanned face before it was swiftly replaced with his customary suspicion.

'You still here?' he greeted Marvik grumpily as Marvik pulled the tender up on to the shore. A bleary-eyed Jensen nodded a greeting at Marvik and headed for the truck, pulling out his mobile phone as he went.

'Is it just the two of you?' Marvik asked.

'Dad's too old to go out now,' Adam answered, heading back to the truck.

Marvik followed him. 'What about the other man your father mentioned yesterday — Joshua Nunton?'

'He left years ago.'

'After Bradley?'

'Yeah.' Adam rounded on him, his eyes wary and mistrustful.

'Why did he leave?'

'No idea.'

'Where can I find him?'

Adam's mouth tightened. 'Don't know. We've got work to do.'

Marvik considered asking him for his father's address but knew that Adam wouldn't give it to him. He was clearly out of sorts, even more so than the previous day. Whether that was because of Marvik's questions and continued presence or a row with Jensen or his father, Marvik didn't know. He did know that Adam had lived alone since his divorce fifteen years ago. Maybe he had a girlfriend and they'd argued. Whatever the reason, Adam wasn't going to say anything more about Bradley Pulford, perhaps because he had nothing more to say.

Marvik watched them for a while longer in their waders loading up the fishing boat, the seagulls cawing and diving around them. Adam must have been about the same age as Jensen was now when Pulford had shown up in 1989. Maybe he hadn't taken much notice of him, although Marvik would have thought that working together on the boat would have forged some kind of relationship between them. But that relationship could have been one of hatred and envy, especially if Adam had resented Pulford muscling in on the family.

He turned but instead of heading for the town struck up towards Peveril Point. Would Adam call his father and tell him he'd been asking more questions? It was possible. But Marvik wasn't bothered about that. As he reached the small, white brick and wooden National Coastwatch station on the Point the wind carried up to him the unmistakable deep diesel throb of a fishing boat from the bay below. He watched it chug past his boat and out to sea.

Turning, Marvik struck out west towards Durlston Head. He had two hours to kill before the undertakers opened and he could obtain Matthew Killbeck's address. Then he'd see what more he could extract from him about Bradley Pulford.

CHAPTER TWO

The small, semi-detached house was situated halfway down a long, curving road of similar properties positioned on the edge of the town to the east and not far from the echoing church of the previous day. Many of the properties were in a poor state of repair and many boasted rusting and half-dismantled cars on the paved forecourts. Not Matthew Killbeck's, though. His was one of only a few that still retained a small front garden that was neat with some shrubs dotted around a tidy square of grass. The house also looked well-cared-for with clean net curtains at the windows. The funeral director had remembered Marvik among the mourners. 'Hardly difficult to forget, sir,' he'd said, 'there being so few.' Marvik had spun him a yarn about knowing Pulford while working abroad and, although he'd joined the Killbecks for drinks, he didn't have Matthew Killbeck's address and he wanted to call on him before leaving Swanage. He'd asked what was happening to the ashes and was told they were to be scattered in the Garden of Remembrance. That didn't surprise Marvik — after what he'd heard from the Killbecks he could hardly see them taking them out to sea and dispersing them, or putting them on their mantelpiece.

He pressed his finger on the bell and heard its chimes ring out tunefully. There was no movement behind the frosted glass of the front door. Marvik rang again. He hoped Matthew and his frail wife weren't out as it would mean a delay, but with relief he saw a figure approaching which, by its bearing and tread, he recognized as Matthew Killbeck.

The door opened and Marvik registered surprise in the elderly man's eyes before they narrowed with suspicion. Obviously Adam hadn't called his father to say he was still around asking questions. Marvik thought Matthew looked more drawn than he remembered from yesterday. Peremptorily, he said, 'I want to talk to you about Bradley Pulford.'

'Why? I've nothing more to say about him.' Matthew Killbeck made to close the door when a querulous voice called out from behind him. Marvik recognized it as Mary's.

'I'm busy,' Killbeck snapped at Marvik.

'I won't take up much of your time.' Marvik held Matthew's stare as if to say *if you don't talk to me now I'll be back.*

'Matthew, where are you?'

Killbeck looked pained. He tossed an anxious glance over his shoulder and then, scowling at Marvik, said roughly, 'Come in. Wait there.'

Killbeck disappeared into a room on Marvik's left, leaving him to survey the narrow hallway and stairs in front of him with its worn light green carpet and anaglypta cream wallpaper that looked as though it had been painted over many times. There was a blue vase of brightly coloured silk flowers on a small table to his right. He noted the flowers were dusty, as was the barometer on the wall above it. It registered rain.

Marvik could hear Killbeck talking softly to his wife. Ignoring his instructions to stay put, Marvik stepped into the tiny, overheated and over-furnished living room, crammed with ornaments, and smiled a greeting at Mary, who studied him with concerned confusion. Killbeck glowered and was about to speak when Mary said, 'You're not Mr Howard.'

Killbeck answered before Marvik could. 'She thinks you're the plumber who's come to fit a bathroom.'

But Mary seemed to have other ideas. 'Have you come about the dead?' and quickly intoned in a quavering, fearful voice, 'The Lord said, "We tell you that we who are still alive, who are left till the coming of the Lord, will certainly not precede those who have fallen asleep." Did I get it right, Matthew?' she appealed to him with frightened eyes.

'Yes, dear, it's perfect. Now let me talk to Mr Marvik.' He jerked his head at Marvik to get out and said gruffly, 'We'll talk in the kitchen.'

It was small and, like the hall and garden, clean and tidy on the surface, but if he looked deeper Marvik could see there was dust and dirt on and among the red units and stained yellow Formica worktop. A door to the right of the window above the scratched stainless-steel sink gave on to a small yard. Opposite them was another door, through which Marvik could see the bathroom. Matthew Killbeck caught him looking.

'We had it installed in 1976. Mary forgets things.'

'She seemed to be very good at quoting the Bible.'

'She was raised in what they call a God-fearing house. She had to learn great passages from the Bible as a child and if she forgot them she'd be punished. Her dementia makes her remember those days and brings back the terror,' Killbeck curtly explained. Marvik could see how the strain of looking after his wife was getting to him. Abruptly, Killbeck said, 'Are you a policeman?'

'Should I be one?'

Killbeck shrugged as though he didn't care but his eyes said something else.

'I'm not a police officer but I would like to know more about Bradley Pulford.'

'Why? What's he got to do with you?'

'How did he arrive here in 1989?' Marvik asked, avoiding the question.

Killbeck gave a weary sigh. 'Like I said yesterday, he just showed up on the shore as we were bringing the boat in and asked if we needed any help. He said he'd fished before and needed a job. I agreed to give him a go.'

'Why?'

'Things were different in 1989. In those days we could always do with an extra hand. The market for fish wasn't as bad as it is now and there weren't so many regulations and quotas. Adam's got a tough time.'

'Did Pulford look as though he could handle himself?'

'He was fit, if that's what you mean.'

'Fair? Dark-haired?

'Darkish hair, blueish eyes.'

'Foreign looking?'

'No.'

'But good looking?'

'Depends on what you class as good looking.'

'Stacey thought he was.'

'Yeah.' Killbeck sniffed. He didn't invite Marvik to sit at the small wooden table pressed up against the wall or offer him refreshments. After a moment, Killbeck continued, 'He was different to the local lads — more worldly.'

'Older than them?'

'By ten years.'

'Then you know his birthday.'

'No. Stacey was twenty-two and he said he was thirty-two.'

'But you never saw any paperwork to confirm that, a birth certificate or medical card?'

'No. Why should I have? Look, why are you interested in him? All that stuff yesterday about finding his body on the beach was bullshit, wasn't it?' Then an idea suddenly occurred to Killbeck. His eyes narrowed. 'He's got a wife and she's sent you. You're a private detective. You want to know if he's got any money. Well, he hasn't and neither have we. Pulford left nothing behind him except a broken-hearted girl and a son he didn't give a shit about.'

Did Pulford have a wife? Marvik didn't know. 'I've not come from any wife or relative. I'm trying to find out if he had any.' Marvik didn't deny he was a private detective — let Killbeck think that.

'Then bloody good luck to you, but if you find them don't come back to tell us. We don't want to know. Jensen's done well enough without any of Pulford's relatives for the last twenty-four years and that's the way we like it. Now is that all because I've got to see to Mary.'

But Marvik wasn't going to let him go that easily. 'What did you talk about on the boat?'

'Nothing. We fished.'

Marvik didn't believe that for a minute. 'Pulford could have had a criminal record. He could have just come out of prison or he could have been on the run from the law.'

'He could have come from Timbuktu for all I knew or cared. I didn't ask him and he didn't say.'

'He must have told Stacey something about his background.'

'Well, you can't ask her, can you? She's dead,' he said sharply, and then seemed to regret his flash of temper and harsh words. More evenly, but still with an edge of acrimony in his voice, he said, 'Stacey was just glad to have him around. She wouldn't have cared if he'd had a wife or was a mass bloody murderer on the run.'

'You didn't like him.'

'I didn't say that,' Killbeck said defensively, running a hand through his fine grey hair. 'But what he did to Stacey was cruel. She was a kind, trusting, caring girl.'

'And he took advantage of that and of her.'

'I knew he wouldn't stay around — he was a drifter. I've come across them many times. They take on work here and there on the boats, working their passage around the country or around the world but neither Leonard, my brother — Stacey's father — nor Stacey could see that. She thought he was here for good. Leonard was working on the boat with me and Adam. He asked Bradley if he had anywhere to stay and he said he hadn't. Leonard's wife was dead — there was only him and Stacey. Bradley soon moved from the put-you-up in the front room into Stacey's bed, making life much more comfortable for himself. Leonard wasn't averse to the relationship. Bradley was very likeable. He had the knack of being able to get on with anyone.'

But not you, thought Marvik, or perhaps the years had soured Matthew Killbeck's views, understandably so given that his niece had been left devastated by Pulford's desertion and with a child to raise.

'Did Pulford have any luggage when he arrived?'

'Only a rucksack, like yours.'

'And papers? Means of identification?'

'I didn't ask to see his passport,' Matthew snapped. 'I took him on as casual labour.'

And that meant both Killbeck and Bradley Pulford had avoided paying any tax or national insurance. 'For two years!'

'You're not from the Inland Revenue, are you? After all these years you can't be after me for tax dodging?' he cried incredulously. 'Bradley's dead — does it matter?'

It mattered to Crowder and therefore to Marvik.

'Was he ever sick?'

'No.'

So no medical records at a local doctor's surgery or the hospital.

'Matthew?' Mary called out.

Killbeck looked troubled. 'I can't tell you any more about him.' He made to move but Marvik stayed put, blocking his way.

'Does Jensen have anything of his father's?'

'No. Like I said, he took off leaving nothing.'

'What about photographs?'

'He hated them. Wouldn't have his picture taken, not even with his son. Stacey took one once and he tore it up.'

That sounded as though Pulford had something to hide. He *had* been on the run. But why and from whom? That was what Marvik was hoping to discover.

'What did he do when he wasn't out fishing or making love to Stacey?'

'Not much. He wasn't sociable. He went out walking.'

'Where?'

Killbeck shrugged. 'Along the coastal paths.'

'Matthew, where are you?'

'Coming, dear,' he called back to his wife. To Marvik, he said, 'There's nothing more I can tell you about him. And I'd prefer not to know. Jensen's better off that way too. So leave us be.' He brushed past Marvik and marched to the front door which he threw open, leaving Marvik in no doubt that the interview was over. Perhaps Matthew Killbeck didn't know any more about Bradley Pulford or if he did he saw no reason to relay it to a man he'd only just met. Either way, Marvik didn't think he'd get anything further from him or his son. But there was someone who might be more forthcoming. On the threshold he asked where he could get hold of Joshua Nunton.

Killbeck looked taken aback. 'Why do you want to know that?'

'He was on the boat with you and Leonard. He might know more about Bradley.'

A fleeting expression crossed Killbeck's face that Marvik couldn't quite interpret. 'I don't know where he is. He took off one day and never came back.'

'Seems to have been catching.'

Matthew shifted. 'It was to do with Bradley. Before he showed up Stacey was sweet on Josh. When Bradley left Josh thought he'd take up again with Stacey only she wasn't having it. She always thought Bradley would come back. Josh took it hard. He went off and that was it.'

'He never said where he was going?'

'No.'

'And no one's seen him or been in contact with him since?'

'No.'

'What about his family?'

'He doesn't have any. That's all I can tell you,' and with that, the door closed firmly on Marvik.

He headed back to town mulling over what he'd learned. It didn't seem much. He couldn't even trust the answers Matthew had given him or the information Pulford had supposedly revealed to the Killbecks. Would a man say so little about himself and his past? Probably if he was ashamed of it or running from it. Marvik never spoke of his past and he didn't mean his service in the Marines, which he wasn't permitted to speak about and didn't want to anyway, but the years before he had joined up were locked inside him. They were no one's business but his and anyone enquiring about his parents' expeditions, their papers or their past was referred to his solicitor. Perhaps Pulford had been in the services. He might even have been in intelligence on an assignment here and had adopted the cover of a fisherman with the Killbecks. That would certainly fit. Once his mission had been completed, he'd left. Or possibly he'd been in danger or about to be exposed, hence the rapid departure. It had been too risky for him to return until January. And even then someone had targeted him. But what in 1989 and 1990 could possibly have been happening here, in this quiet seaside town in England that could have warranted an undercover assignment? And why take the name of Bradley Pulford?

He rang Strathen and relayed the outcome of his conversation with Matthew. 'Bradley could easily have lied about his age to Stacey. But if he didn't that puts him as being born in 1957, which makes his age not far off the pathologist's estimate of the dead man's. Not that that gets us anywhere.' He said nothing about his theory of Pulford possibly working undercover. He would, but only when he had greater privacy — not that anyone was listening in or following him as he entered the bustling High Street. 'It's strange that two men connected with the Killbecks both took off at the same time,' he added.

'And I've got another coincidence for you. The real Bradley Pulford — or rather the one who died in 1959 — is buried in the church graveyard at Steepleridge.'

Marvik was taken aback but maybe it wasn't so unexpected. Steepleridge was only nine miles to the west. 'So the Pulford of 1989 could have come from around here.'

'Or he just saw the name in the graveyard and picked it at random.'

That fitted too because, according to Matthew Killbeck, he never saw any of Pulford's identity papers. Except that

Steepleridge was only a hamlet and hardly on the route to anywhere unless you counted the coastal path and the neighbouring army range. Did that tie in with his recent thinking that Pulford could have been working undercover? Could he have been army intelligence?

The Ministry of Defence owned vast tracts of land to the west of Steepleridge including the lost village of Tyneham, so-called because its occupants had been evacuated in 1943 when the area had been used for the D-Day preparations in the Second World War. They'd never returned. The empty village, the scattered ruined buildings and land around it were used for armed forces training and only accessible to the public at certain times. Both he and Strathen had been involved on exercises there.

'How did you discover he was buried at Steepleridge?' Marvik asked, catching the sound of a motorbike but it was a different one from that of yesterday. He weaved his way around two mothers with pushchairs.

'There are databases that give the details of where individuals are buried. I started with a search of the Dorset coast beginning with Swanage, given that's where the phoney one showed up in 1989, and then worked out westwards. I didn't expect to find a Bradley Pulford but there he is. Someone brought him back from Singapore and deposited him there but there's no one registered with that name living in Steepleridge, or in the surrounding district, either now or back in 1959 when he died. And no other Pulfords listed as being buried or cremated around there.'

'I'll head there now.'

'And I'll see what I can get on Joshua Nunton.'

Marvik wasn't sure what a gravestone could tell him — very little, he thought — but someone in the hamlet might remember the Bradley Pulford buried beneath it. Even if they did, he knew it might not have any bearing on their mission, just that the man washed up on the Isle of Wight beach in January had taken a fancy to that name on his way to Swanage to work as a fisherman for the Killbecks.

CHAPTER THREE

The taxi deposited him at the northern edge of the hamlet of Steepleridge and Marvik set out along the tree-lined country lane to where he could see the square church tower on a slight knoll to the south-west. Behind him rose the Purbeck Downs and around him rolling open farmland was punctuated by the occasional hedgerow, clumps of trees and roaming sheep. Five miles to the south was the sea. He couldn't see it from here but there was a luminous silver glow in the distance that belied its presence. The lane was deserted, as were many of the grey Purbeck stone cottages, interspersed with the white Portland stoned ones and some thatched whitewashed properties that dated back to the 1600s. The pub was one such building but here, at least, there were signs of life. In front of it were parked several expensive cars. He might strike lucky and find one or more of the older customers propping up the bar who might remember the original Bradley Pulford — it was a small enough place for everyone to know everyone — but he didn't think anyone would recall a man from 1989 who had passed this way and perhaps stopped to study the grave or ask about its occupant. *If* he had.

The twelfth-century church was set back off the road and approached via an ancient lychgate with a sign proclaiming it was the Church of St Michael and that services were held at nine fifteen every Sunday. It was rare that he attended church and then only when on service in the Marines, or to funerals and on a couple of occasions to colleagues' weddings. His non-attendance didn't mean he didn't believe. Part of him would like to. He'd witnessed enough death and carnage to hope that somewhere there was something better than the huge cock-up they all made of their lives but he wasn't sure, and thinking about it only led him to bouts of unease. David Treagust, the navy chaplain, was the closest Marvik had come to God, and that was without him ever even mentioning Him.

The church was surrounded by gravestones, most of them ancient, ivy-clad, leaning and illegible. He had no idea where the Pulford of 1959 was buried so he began to quarter it methodically. He was alone but even if anyone was watching him they'd think he was looking from idle curiosity or researching family history. There were some large family plots which spanned the generations from the 1800s to the 1960s and there was an elaborate memorial to the Wellmore family who had obviously been the big shots in these parts. The last one he could see having been buried here was in 1933. There was no grave with the name of Bradley Pulford in front of the church or on its eastern flank, so Marvik headed for the rear where he noted the tombstones were more recent.

He scoured the names and memorials on the headstones and soon found what he was seeking. It was in the second to last row that bordered a field, sandwiched between the grave of Elizabeth Jilley, born 1905 died 1958, and George Gurney, born 1938 died 1959. The grass around all the graves had been cut. There were no flowers on Bradley Pulford's grave, or the others in the row, but that was hardly surprising given the length of time they'd been dead. Someone, though, had cared for the young man who had died in Singapore in 1959 because his headstone wasn't the bland basic statement as displayed on his neighbours. Marvik read the inscription with interest.

'Like as the waves make towards the pebbled shore, so do our minutes hasten to their end.' And beneath it another: 'I am standing upon the seashore. A ship at my side spreads her white sails to the morning breeze and starts for the blue ocean.'

He considered this. So this Bradley Pulford had had an affinity with the sea, like the one who had shown up along the coast in 1989. Perhaps they *were* father and son. Had this Pulford been a fisherman like the Killbecks? But he couldn't have been fishing in Singapore when he died. And it was highly doubtful he'd have been there on holiday in 1959 when only the wealthy took holidays to exotic places, and the Singapore of the fifties had not been on the holiday itinerary with the trouble there had been in Malaya.

Marvik took a photograph of the headstone with his mobile phone and made his way around to the front of the church where he almost collided with a woman emerging from it. Hastily, he apologized.

'No need.' She smiled at him. 'I was miles away. I should have looked where I was going. Have you come to view the church?'

'No, the graveyard.'

She cocked a quizzical eyebrow at him. She was in her early sixties, smartly dressed in a navy-blue coat, with a patterned scarf at her neck. Her hair was short and silver blonde.

'Do you have a relative buried here?' she enquired politely.

'No, just someone I was told about recently and I was curious,' he hedged, weighing up how much to tell her. 'Bradley Pulford. He died in Singapore in 1959.'

'Oh, Bradley, yes.'

Surprised, he said, 'You knew him?'

'Of him. I'm not quite that old.'

'I'm sorry. I didn't mean—'

But she waved aside his apology. 'I'm Irene Templeton, the church warden.'

'Art Marvik.' He returned her smile.

'Steepleridge is a very small place, as you can see, Mr Marvik. Everyone knew everyone in 1959 when Bradley died. I was only five years old. It's very different now with so many of our old cottages and outlying houses occupied by second homeowners who come down from London for the occasional weekend, in the summer holidays and at Christmas, which is usually the only time you see them at the church services. The church in 1959 was the lynchpin of the community, like the pub and the village shop, the latter sadly gone, and in the fifties and sixties nearly everyone went to church. There wasn't a great deal to do on a Sunday except worship and walk. Now there are so many more demands on everyone's time, and of course so much competition.'

'Do you know how Bradley died?'

'Only that it was an accident on board a ship.'

'He was in the navy?'

'No. It was on a cargo ship. I remember Bradley was evacuated here from London as a baby with his mother in 1940. A year later she returned to London to meet her husband, who had a forty-eight-hour pass, and they were both killed in an air raid. Bradley was adopted by the couple who had billeted him and his mother.'

'Are they still alive?'

'John and Alice Seacombe — no, they died a long time ago. They farmed one of Sir Ambrose Shale's farms. He used to own a great deal of land around here.'

Marvik knew the name because the Ministry of Defence land adjoined the Shale estate. 'What made Bradley go to sea?'

'Adventure? Escape?' She shrugged.

There came the impatient tooting of a car horn. Marvik followed her glance to the road where he could see a bulky, balding, cross-looking man in an Audi. Her husband, he assumed.

'Is there anyone I could speak to about Bradley? Anyone who might remember him?'

'Most of them have either died, left the village or have sadly got dementia.'

The toot sounded again, this time even louder and more frequent. She cast it an anxious and troubled look. 'I'm sorry — I have to go.'

So, dead end on that score but then he hadn't really expected much, although he had learned some new information.

He headed for the pub, hoping that one of its regulars might recall Bradley Pulford but the moment he entered the hostelry built in 1640, as the stone to the right of the door proclaimed, he knew he'd find no ageing local propping up this bar. The inside had clearly seen several revamps since it was built and, apart from the old flagstone floor and the large inglenook fireplace complete with log fire, its latest reincarnation resembled the trendy bar in Swanage he'd been inside yesterday after the funeral.

The clientele looked to be of the same ilk and, judging by their accents and dress, they were what Irene Templeton had referred to as 'second homeowners'.

Marvik bought a non-alcoholic beer from a barmaid who looked more like sixteen than eighteen and enquired if they ever got any locals in. 'Elderly ones, I mean,' he quickly added when she looked at him askance as if to say who do you think all these people are then? She still didn't seem to understand the question but fetched the landlord, who proceeded to tell him how he'd spent a fortune on renovating the place, added boutique en-suite bed and breakfast accommodation, recruited a top-class chef and was pleased to say he'd completely turned the place around from the dim hovel it had once been, all horse brasses, hunting pictures, patterned carpets and mahogany. If there were any elderly drinkers left in the hamlet then Marvik thought they must imbibe at home because, at the prices this place charged, he would too.

Outside, he hesitated before calling a taxi, thinking that he'd prefer to walk back to Swanage and work off some excess energy. But the decision lay with Strathen and what he had unearthed and whether it needed prompt action. Marvik called him and relayed what he'd learned.

Strathen said, 'If the accident was on board a British ship then it will be listed in the Registry of Shipping and Seamen. It holds details of deaths at sea from 1939 to 1995, including those that occurred in overseas ports. But I won't be able to get access to it until Tuesday. The files are held at the National Archives at Kew and they're closed on Mondays. I can't access the files via the Internet, but I'll do a bit of browsing in case someone's put something out there. I can't find anything on Joshua Nunton. His death isn't registered so for all I know he could have been committed to a psychiatric hospital or emigrated. He could even have been killed and his body never discovered. Or he could have died more recently, such as two months ago.'

'You think he could be the body washed up at Freshwater Bay on the Isle of Wight?' asked Marvik, heading back down the village street in the direction of the sea.

'Why not? The DNA matched Jensen's but how do we know that Jensen is really the phoney Bradley Pulford's son? He could be Joshua's kid. Theory one: Stacey was putting it about, keeping both Joshua Nunton and our phoney Pulford happy. Pulford found out, killed Nunton then took off in a panic after burying or disposing of the body. Theory two: Nunton killed Pulford because he was jealous. Then he took off and the DNA proving that Jensen is related to the remains found on the Isle of Wight show that he is in fact related to Joshua Nunton and not Pulford. The Killbecks could even be involved in Pulford's murder. They hated him muscling in, disturbing the rhythm of their lives. Or perhaps he discovered them smuggling or fiddling their fish quota and threatened to tell. Perhaps they didn't want an outsider marrying the fair Stacey. They arranged it between them and ditched Pulford's body in the English Channel. And we've only got Crowder's word that the body washed up on the Isle of Wight is that of a man who went by the name of Bradley Pulford. How does he know that for sure? I doubt any ID the man had been carrying would have survived. And if the Killbecks discovered that Nunton was returning to confess his sins maybe they decided one more murder wouldn't matter. They didn't want to be implicated. They could have arranged to meet him and dumped his body overboard from their fishing boat in January.'

Marvik considered this. 'The Killbecks are clearly uneasy about something. But that doesn't make them killers.' Had Adam Killbeck been the man on the motorbike, though, who had followed him yesterday? 'I'll email you the picture of Bradley's headstone,' he continued. 'There's an interesting inscription on it. Someone thought enough of him to shell out for an expensive memorial — it could have been his adoptive parents, John and Alice Seacombe. The woman I spoke to at the church said they died some time ago but I didn't get the chance to ask her when she had an impatient husband waiting for her.'

'I'll check it out.'

Marvik rang off and made for the coastal path eastwards back to Swanage. His photographic memory conjured up the inscription word for word. 'Like as the waves make towards the pebbled shore, so do our minutes hasten to their end.' It sounded familiar. He searched his memory for it. He was certain he'd heard it before. Yes, he had. At another funeral — that of a former Marine colleague. It was Shakespeare. He frowned, puzzled. It was a literary quotation, which was perhaps surprising for the Seacombes, a farming couple, although that was a gross presumption because for all he knew they might have had a love of literature and the works of the Bard. And the other inscription on the gravestone: 'I am standing upon the seashore. A ship at my side spreads her white sails to the morning breeze and starts for the blue ocean.' Where was that text from? Did it matter?

Perhaps the sea had been Bradley's first love; it had certainly been almost his last. Maybe he'd always had a hankering to be on it, as Marvik had. It was in his blood and maybe Bradley's real father, the one who had died in the Blitz, had been on leave from the navy.

With athletic ease, Marvik hiked along the top of the hills and then cut down on to the coastal path. It was mid-afternoon and he could see a fishing boat out to sea and a leisure cruiser heading west towards Portland and Weymouth. The sky was overcast and the sea choppy with the rising wind. He marched onwards, thinking over what he and Strathen had gleaned so far, but none of it made any sense. There were too many gaps and they would continue to flounder unless Strathen could throw up some leads or Crowder gave them more information.

It was just after five when he reached the bay. The Killbecks' fishing boat was there but there was no sign of them or their pick-up truck. He headed into the town and found a small Italian restaurant. While he waited for his pasta to arrive he thought of the inscription on the headstone and took out his phone, where he entered the text into the search engine. It was the opening lines of a poem entitled 'Gone from My Sight' by Henry van Dyke, an American professor, poet and clergyman who had died in 1933. Maybe the Seacombes had got it from a book of funeral poems from the library. Perhaps the works of Van Dyke were a favourite of theirs, as was Shakespeare, or perhaps the vicar had suggested it. Or perhaps the title 'Gone from My Sight' was the real message the Seacombes had wanted to convey.

He replaced his phone and attacked his meal, noting that there were only a handful of customers in the restaurant and no one remotely interested in him. Why should they be? But he recalled the motorbike which he was almost certain had been stalking him yesterday. Could he have been mistaken? Maybe, because there had been no sign of anyone following him today. But perhaps that was because the motorbike rider had been Adam Killbeck and he had been out fishing all day. The build was right from the glimpses he'd had of the rider, who had been tall and lean. But Marvik thought Adam more broad-shouldered than the man he'd seen. And he'd witnessed that brief look of surprise on Adam's features this morning when he had alighted from his tender on the shore before suspicion had set in. So maybe Adam hadn't known he'd arrived at Swanage by boat.

It was dark and drizzling by the time Marvik left the restaurant and made his way through the almost deserted streets. As he turned into the road that led parallel to the bay and eventually to the lifeboat station, he considered the image of Bradley Pulford that Matthew Killbeck had drawn for him earlier that day and the emotions he'd exhibited when speaking of Pulford: resentment, anger, hatred even. Maybe Shaun was right and the Killbecks had killed him, if not in 1990 then more recently, in January.

Through his thoughts he caught the sound of a motorbike and one whose engine he instantly recognized. He dashed a glance over his shoulder and his heart quickened. Yes, there it was cruising slowly some distance behind him, and he was certain it was the same one that had stalked him yesterday. Astride it was a darkly clad figure, the face hidden by the visor, but Marvik could swear it was the same rider. He picked up his pace. The road was deserted both ahead and behind. He swiftly calculated that he had another three hundred yards before the entrance to the lifeboat station and the shore. Glancing back, the motorbike was keeping pace with him but still holding back. Marvik knew why. The rider was judging it perfectly — there would be a moment when no one would witness what he was about to do and that moment would soon be here. It would come when he turned down towards the lifeboat and he'd be alone in the dark close to the shore.

Adrenaline surged through his veins but instead of instinctively breaking into a run he forced himself to maintain the same walking pace. Although he was fast and fit, he wasn't as fast as that motorbike and he calculated that it was better to preserve as much energy as he could in case he needed it on the shore.

One hundred, two hundred — he mentally counted down until . . . He sprinted. The roar of the motorbike burst through the night. It was deafening. In a few seconds it would be on top of him. If he glanced back he'd be a dead man. He still might be, he thought, running hard, his feet striking the tarmac, his heart pounding, his blood pumping. To acknowledge the wound in his leg would be death. To think of anything other than reaching the shore, darkness and safety would be fatal. He had a second — maybe two if he was lucky. Two seconds between life and death. It wasn't much but it was all he had.

He swung into the road, running hard, past the empty units, his goal the small stretch of shingle shore where his tender and the Killbecks' fishing boat lay. He jumped down from the small ledge and rolled on to the ground as the rush of air brushed past him. The bike screeched to a halt. Marvik leapt up. Would the rider risk coming on to the stones? But no, the bike swung round, the rider revved up and was gone with a deep roar.

Marvik let out a long exhalation of breath. He'd thought the day had been full of blanks and getting nowhere. He'd been wrong.

CHAPTER FOUR

Sunday

He woke with a heavy head as though he had a hangover, but it was the combination of tension, lack of sleep and the legacy of his head injury sustained in combat — leaving the right-hand side of his face scarred — which was the cause. Coffee and painkillers would cure it, plus a blast of damp sea air.

He took his coffee up on deck, zipped open the canvas awning and breathed in deeply. He was alone except for the motor cruiser moored up to his left. He'd heard its tender return last night just after nine thirty. Two men had alighted from it and climbed on board. Marvik had watched their boat until the lights had gone out, then had remained tense and prepared in case he had a nocturnal visit from them or anyone else. But all was quiet except for the rain and the wind. The rain had stopped just after three a.m. The wind had also eased to leave a relatively calm, cold morning with only a slight ripple on the grey sea.

His thoughts returned to the motorbike which had tried to run him down, just as they had throughout the night. He acknowledged the professionalism of the rider and again considered who it might be. Matthew Killbeck would have told Adam about his visit, so Adam Killbeck was a possibility, despite the fact that Marvik had thought the motorbike rider had been leaner than the fisherman, and so far Adam was the only possibility, because apart from Irene Templeton and her impatient husband no one else knew he'd been asking after Bradley Pulford. And somehow he couldn't see either Irene or her husband on a motorbike trying to run him down or engaging someone with the skills to do so. Marvik didn't see Jensen having the skill to ride a powerful motorbike or the money to buy one either, and Matthew Killbeck was too old.

Marvik knew he hadn't been followed to Steepleridge or back. His phone might have been hacked, though, giving away his conversation with Strathen and his location, and that was a possibility he'd have to mention to Strathen.

He again cast his mind back to the people in the Italian restaurant, as he'd done throughout the night. There had been a couple in their thirties who seemed more interested in one another than him; two women in their late fifties who had spent their entire time looking at photographs on each other's mobile phones and gushing loudly in between shovelling lasagne into their mouths; a man in his mid-seventies and two men in their early forties, all of whom had come off boats judging by their clothes. There was no one who seemed intent on killing him, or at the least hospitalizing him. And none of them had followed him from the restaurant. In fact, no one had. But the motorbike rider could have seen him return to the bay earlier, before he'd headed back into town to the restaurant. Then all he had to do was wait for him to return.

He swallowed his coffee and called Strathen, knowing he'd be awake. He'd probably been working most of the night, delving into databases and hacking into systems to try and unearth some information on Pulford that could take them forward. He quickly brought Strathen up to speed on the attempt on his life and asked if it was possible that his phone could have been hacked and his location tracked from it even though he'd disabled the location application. The answer was as Marvik had expected.

'It's possible, especially if you've browsed the Internet.' He had, to look up the inscription on Bradley Pulford's grave.

'It would need someone with considerable expertise,' Strathen added when Marvik told him that.

'Then that rules out Adam Killbeck.'

'How do you know that?'

'I don't, you're right. For all I know he or Jensen could be a whiz at that sort of thing.'

'I don't suppose you got the registration number of the bike?'

'It wasn't top of my list as I was concentrating on staying alive,' Marvik replied caustically.

'Pity.'

Marvik smiled. 'I'll try to do better next time.' And he was certain there would be one, but whether the attack would come in the same manner he didn't know.

'Perhaps you should move the boat,' Strathen suggested.

'And disappoint Easy Rider?'

'There is that.'

'Any joy with the Seacombes?'

'Yes, or no, depending on the way you look at it. Alice died in 1953 and John in 1956, so unless they left some money and instructions in their wills for their adoptive son to be buried with an elaborate headstone, or it was paid for out of what Bradley Pulford left, it means someone else was fond enough of him to cough up for it.'

'I'll return to the church. Irene Templeton, the church warden, is bound to be there, it being Sunday. I'll see if I can get anything more from her about that inscription without her husband hassling her.'

'Then say a prayer for me.'

'I thought you were beyond saving.'

'Probably.'

'If I can't get anything further from Mrs Templeton, I'll ask the funeral directors on Monday for details of local stone masons. They might have kept records of who paid for Bradley's headstone.'

He rang off and was about to descend into the cabin when his attention was caught by the sight of a woman on the shore who was studying the Killbecks' fishing boat. She looked up and out to sea, running a hand through her long wavy hair and then glanced at her watch. Perhaps she had an assignation with Adam Killbeck. Maybe she just wanted to buy some fish or go fishing, or perhaps she was a tourist looking around, but there was something about her manner that made him curious, and if she was acquainted with the Killbecks then perhaps she could tell him more about them.

He grabbed his rucksack — which was always readily prepared with water, rations, Ordnance Survey map, compass and wet-weather leggings — locked up, climbed into the tender and headed for the shore. She looked up at the sound of his engine but made no attempt to leave. As he jumped out and pulled the small boat on to the shingle shore, she smiled a nervous greeting at him.

'Do you know if this fishing boat belongs to the Killbecks?' she asked a little hesitantly.

'I believe so. Why?' he enquired politely, thinking with a flash of disappointment that she couldn't know them while curious as to her reasons for asking.

'I've been told they take people out with them occasionally.'

'You want to go fishing?' he asked, startled.

Her fair skin flushed and her blue-grey eyes dropped for a second before coming back to rest on his face and away again. He could see she was uneasy. He was a stranger. He looked threatening because of his scars.

'I want to survey the coast beyond St Alban's Head,' she explained, 'and short of chartering a boat I thought this might be the next best thing.'

It was a lie. He saw that immediately and his interest deepened.

'Who told you about the Killbecks?' he asked casually.

She flushed again and said, 'The guest-house proprietor where I'm staying.' Another lie.

'Doesn't she know where they live?'

'No, she just mentioned it. I guess I could wait until they show up.'

'They might not, it being Sunday. They'd probably have been here by now.'

'Yes, I suppose they would,' she answered somewhat dejectedly.

'I'd offer to take you on my boat but I have to see a couple of people today.'

'No, that's fine,' she said hastily, confirming his thought that her reason for wanting to see the Killbecks was a lie. So what was the real reason? Only one way to find out.

'I'm Art Marvik,' he said, hoping she'd reciprocate with an introduction. She made to smile politely but it froze on her lips as she studied him with baffled interest.

'Marvik? Not any relation to Doctor Eerika Marvik and Professor Dan Coulter?' she asked doubtfully.

He was momentarily stunned. How did she know of his parents? But as quickly as he framed the question the answer came — she'd mentioned surveying the coast beyond St Alban's Head and there were a number of shipwrecks in that location, so she could either be a treasure-seeker or a marine archaeologist. He thought the latter. Did he deny it? He often did if he had the misfortune to meet someone in the same or similar profession as his parents. But admitting his parentage this time might be one way of gaining her confidence and extracting more from her about her interest in the Killbecks.

'I'm their son,' he said.

Her eyes widened. 'My God. But that's amazing. I never thought . . . How — why, I mean . . . why are you here?' she stammered. 'Is it anything to do with maritime archaeology?'

'No. But I'm guessing that must be your interest or profession.'

'The latter. I'm a marine archaeologist.'

As he'd thought. 'Is that why you want to survey the shore from the sea, because you're here to research a wreck?'

There was a fraction's pause. He could see she was deciding whether or not to continue the lie. It seemed she couldn't.

She looked sheepish for a moment. 'No. I'm sorry about that but I didn't know who you were.'

'And knowing that makes a difference?'

'Of course.' She beamed.

He thought her very trusting. How did she know that the son of Eerika Marvik and Dan Coulter wasn't a complete psychopath? Or that he was even telling the truth.

She said, 'I'm Sarah Redburn and I'm here because my father, Oscar, went missing from this area in 1979. I think he might have known a man called Bradley Pulford who was cremated here on Friday. I was hoping his relatives, the Killbecks, might be able to throw some light on what happened to my father.'

Marvik just about hid his astonishment. Crowder had made no mention of anyone called Redburn but that didn't mean he didn't know of her or her father, Oscar. Marvik didn't think Pulford's death had been publicly announced and neither had there been any press coverage on his identity being revealed or the link to the Killbecks. But perhaps Crowder had informed her or she'd discovered the information via another source — one he was very keen to learn about. He didn't usually speak about his parents but if it made her open up to him about her father's connection with Pulford then he'd sacrifice his feelings.

'Breakfast?' he suggested.

She looked pleased at the invitation. 'Only if you have time.' He had lots of it, now.

CHAPTER FIVE

They filled the short walk to the café with talk of the town and the weather, each aware that the sense of intimacy the café would provide would serve them better. Marvik ordered breakfast — coffee and a bacon sandwich for them both — and chose a table in the window affording him a good view of the wide sandy bay where a few boats were anchored. To his right he could see the pier arching out to the east, affording shelter for his boat and the other boat anchored there. They had the place to themselves.

She shrugged out of her sailing jacket to reveal a grey long-sleeved jumper with wide pink stripes across it. On closer scrutiny he could see the fatigue on her face and there was an air of innocence about her that bordered on vulnerability. Perhaps she spent too much time studying wrecks of the past and not enough time living and interacting with people of the day to be wise to them. Or perhaps he was mistaken and underneath that shy manner was a very shrewd and calculating woman.

'I'm sorry about your parents,' she said, pushing a slender hand through her long hair.

'It was a long time ago.'

'The length of time someone's been gone doesn't always make it easier.'

He eyed her keenly. That was said with feeling. Their coffee arrived, preventing him from asking her about her father, and once the waitress had left them with the parting shot that the bacon sandwiches were on their way, Sarah continued before he had a chance to speak.

'My area of research is similar to Doctor Marvik's,' she said a little timidly, as though afraid he would accuse her of being presumptuous for trespassing on such hallowed a reputation as his mother's. 'I'm particularly interested in the social implications of seafaring — for example how navigation, boat technology and the maritime environment have all affected the development of communities. How people living in coastal areas have been influenced by the sea both socially and commercially.' Her eyes darted towards the bay and back to rest on him. 'I've worked in the Solent, the Mediterranean and the Indian Ocean. And, of course, the brilliant partnership between your parents, with Professor Coulter being an expert in oceanography and ocean turbulence and Doctor Marvik in submerged landscapes, made their work so valuable.' She blushed. 'Sorry, I'm gushing. But they were amazing,' she continued earnestly, hugging her mug of coffee with both hands. He noted there were no rings on her fingers or signs that there had been any. Her nails were short and bitten.

Then she looked solemn and her brow furrowed. 'They were killed in the Strait of Malacca but nobody seems to know why they were there. Their death was a great loss to the profession. Oh, I'm sorry, that sounded callous. I didn't mean . . . Of course, it was a terrible tragedy for you.'

'Like I said, it was a long time ago.' But her words and her enthusiasm had conjured up memories of his parents. He'd been shocked when he'd been told by his headmaster of their death but not grief-stricken. How could he be when he had rarely seen them for six years and had felt a sense of abandonment? He'd tried to feel and, at least, show some signs of sorrow in the ensuing days — it was expected — but there had been only a sense of bitterness which he had channelled into action as soon as he could by joining the Marines.

He recalled their accident. An underwater earthquake had killed them while diving. They'd been below alone with only one dive operator on the boat — Frederick Davington — who had alerted the authorities. Their bodies had been recovered two days later. Davington had maintained they hadn't been engaged on any research project and there was no submerged wreck or notes to contradict that. Marvik had met up with Davington once after his parents' funeral, which had proved a futile meeting and had been at his instigation, perhaps looking for some glimmer of hope that his parents had spoken of him, only they hadn't. He'd had no idea what he had expected from it and even now only vaguely recalled Davington, who had looked drawn and ill and had died six weeks afterwards from a severe asthma attack. It had been years since Marvik had thought of the diving accident and years since he'd spoken of his parents except to the shrink, Langton, who he'd seen after his head injury, and then he'd said little. He'd had no need to discuss them with his colleagues in the Marines. No one would have been interested anyway. Occasionally he'd get correspondence from fans of his parents, academics and professionals like Sarah, but his solicitor was instructed to deal with those.

'Wasn't there anything in their papers about it?' she asked keenly.

'No.' It wasn't a lie because he didn't know. There might have been but he hadn't looked at them, not even after their death. He'd given instructions for all the paperwork on the boat and in their house to be packed up and despatched to the bank safe deposit in London, where they still languished. The rest of his parents' belongings had been sold or given away. He hadn't even overseen that but had left it to his parents' executor, their solicitor, Michael Colmead.

She was about to say something more but was prevented by the arrival of their bacon sandwiches. She tucked into hers with relish. Marvik glanced up as the café bell rang and a man in his mid-fifties wearing a sailing jacket entered with a newspaper tucked under his arm. He took a seat at the far table near the counter.

'Have you ever been back to where they died?' she asked him shyly.

Only to deter, apprehend and kill pirates, he felt like saying. In the Marines he, along with Strathen, had assisted the Singapore government on missions and on covert assignments targeting and bringing down pirates, many of whom were associated with organized criminal gangs. The region had been declared a high-risk war area. Things had improved recently but pirate attacks still occurred. They had probably done so in 1997 when his parents had dived there, but there had been no evidence pirates had bothered them and Davington hadn't reported any disturbances. Besides, seventeen years ago piracy hadn't been such a problem as now. A huge amount of world trade passed through the Straits. The thoughts of Singapore brought his mind back to Bradley Pulford.

He said, 'I don't follow in my parents' footsteps.'

She looked up with sympathy. 'It must be painful for you. At least you know what happened to yours,' she said sadly.

He liked her eyes and her soft, gentle manner. 'Tell me about your father?' he said, glad at last to get down to the real business of why he was here and to push thoughts of his parents to the back of his mind.

'He was reported missing in January 1979 when my mother was eleven weeks pregnant with me.'

That made her thirty-six. Could she be Pulford's child? A daughter he had left behind in 1979 before showing up in Swanage and charming his way into Stacey Killbeck's bed in 1989? Had Sarah come here in search of her stepbrother?

'That's tough,' he said.

'It was on my mother. She died seventeen years ago. My father's disappearance is the reason why I became so keen on marine archaeology. I used to walk this coast as a child with my mother who never gave up hope that he'd return. This is where she thought he had disappeared.'

Marvik's interested deepened.

'We'd stare at the sea and I'd imagine him coming out of it, and that led to a curiosity about what was under it and the lives it had claimed and whether the artefacts that had gone down with the people in the ships that had been wrecked could tell me something about them as individuals . . . certainly about their lives. It's like trying to piece together the puzzle of someone's life.'

'And you've tried to do that with your father's?'

'Yes, but it doesn't make any sense.' She chewed her sandwich. Marvik said nothing but ate. The smell of toast and bacon filled the air. The café was getting hot and a film of steam was beginning to form in the corners of the window. The café bell rang again and a dark-haired, stocky man in his mid-forties entered. He glanced at them. His face registered no reaction and he took a table in the centre of the café and withdrew his phone. Marvik swallowed his coffee, his eyes swept the bay. A few boats were anchored up. There didn't seem to be any activity on them. Nothing seemed out of order. A woman with a dog stopped to talk to a man in his seventies in a sailing jacket, who leaned down and ruffled the dog's fur, smiling; a jogger ran past them, and the seagulls swooped and dipped on to the sandy beach. Marvik turned his attention back to Sarah Redburn as she continued.

'The official report said that he'd come to the Jurassic Coast fossil hunting and must have got caught out by the tide and drowned. He told a friend, Gordon Freynsham, that it was where he was heading, but as far as my mother knew my father had never expressed any interest in fossils. It was Gordon Freynsham's passion, though. He was a geology student at the polytechnic in Southampton — it's now the Solent University. My father, Oscar, was president of the student union with a degree in history and politics; he was twenty-six when he went missing. Mr Freynsham's a renowned fossil dealer now. He trades off the coast of Lyme Regis but last year he fronted a television series on fossil hunting. You might have seen it if you're into that kind of thing.'

'I'm not.'

'Well, it was a hit. They're making another series with him presenting it.'

'The Jurassic Coast is a hell of a stretch to check — it covers ninety-five miles from East Devon to Dorset. What made your mother believe he came here?'

'They lived in Southampton, and Oscar was studying there so it would have been much easier and closer for him to get to this part of the coast rather than the Devon end of it. I've spoken to Gordon Freynsham but he says he has no idea where Oscar was going and I don't think the police really bothered to look. They thought that he'd left mum because she was pregnant, which of course is a possibility, but according to what she told me and what I've discovered about him from my own research, it doesn't sound right.'

'Why not?' he asked keenly.

'Because of the timing. He was very into politics and he disappeared in the middle of industrial action, something that I find difficult to believe, given how radical he was. He was always involved in demos and protests.'

'Against what?'

'You name it, he'd protest it: rising rents, racism, war, capitalism and anything that smacked of it, gay rights, not to mention the protests against the government. The usual stuff that was happening in the seventies: dock strikes, miners' strike, firefighters' strike. But it was during the Winter of Discontent in 1978 and 1979 under James Callaghan's Labour government when Oscar was on the picket line at Southampton docks waving banners in support of the dock strike that he went missing. And from what I've learned of him I don't think he'd have taken a day off to go fossil hunting.'

It didn't sound true to Marvik either. 'What was the strike over?'

'The Labour government had agreements with the Trade Union Congress to restrict pay rises in an attempt to control rising inflation but these agreements ended in July 1978. The government wanted to restrict pay rises to five per cent but the TUC wasn't having it. The government threatened to impose sanctions on government contractors who broke it. Ford motor car workers were the first to strike in October and the company conceded and awarded a seventeen per cent pay rise.'

'Which kick-started the others.'

'Yes. This included lorry drivers, who not only disrupted fuel supplies but also picketed major ports to prevent the import of goods. The dock workers came out in support. It escalated with more workers going on strike on the twenty-second of January, including nurses, ambulance drivers and refuse collectors. Grave diggers went on strike in Liverpool and Manchester for a fortnight. Liverpool City Council had to hire a warehouse to store the unburied corpses. Makes the mind boggle, doesn't it?' She smiled. He returned it and swallowed his coffee.

'The lorry drivers got a twenty per cent pay rise at the end of January and by then Oscar had gone missing. The last time anyone saw him was on the twenty-first of January. It was the day before national industrial action and also bitterly cold, so why did he take a day off from his protests?'

'Perhaps he'd got fed up with being cold.'

'Then he'd have stayed in or gone down the pub, not trekked out along the coast,' she said with vigour. She pushed away her empty plate and sat forward with an eager expression on her fair face.

'My mother firmly believed he'd had an accident and his body must have been washed out to sea. Every time a body was discovered on the shore along the south coast or on the Isle of Wight it was examined to see if it was Oscar, but there was no routine DNA testing in 1979, only dental records to compare and none of the bodies matched Oscar's. As time went on the police stopped comparing unknown remains with records of my father. It was too long ago for them to be his anyway. There wouldn't have been anything of him left.'

'But you have a new lead.'

She swallowed her coffee and studied him uncertainly. Perhaps she wasn't sure how much to tell him. After a moment though her expression cleared and she continued, 'On the twenty-fourth of January a man contacted me claiming to know something about Oscar's disappearance.'

'Did he give a name?' Marvik thought the timing fitted with it being Pulford, whose body had been discovered in Freshwater Bay on the twenty-eighth of January.

'No. He asked to meet me. I was sceptical, as you can imagine. He could be a complete nutcase. He contacted me on my mobile phone. My website gives details of the marine and heritage consultants I occasionally work for and he said he'd phoned them and they gave out my number. I asked them if they had, and they said nobody could remember doing so but they must have done. He said that he knew about Oscar being president of the students' union and told me that after obtaining his degree in history and politics he'd stayed on to do another degree in sociology, and that my mother's name was Linda — she was a nurse and that she had been pregnant with me when Oscar disappeared. He sounded genuine but just to be on the safe side I agreed to meet him in a public place. In a coffee shop in Southampton. He didn't show. I rang the number he'd called me on but there was no answer and no voicemail. I was disappointed and angry and tried to forget it but it nagged away at me. If it was a hoax it was a sick one and why bother? The more I thought of it the more I considered it to be genuine and either he'd got cold feet or he'd had an accident and had been unable to get a message to me. He could have died.'

Or been killed, Marvik added silently.

'I went to the police. They said it was probably a cruel joke. But I said the file was still open on Oscar's disappearance and this was new information so surely they should note it, although I realized there was little, if anything, they could do about it. I asked them to trace the telephone number. They said they would, but not very enthusiastically — after all, what is one missing person from 1979 when they have a whole load of recent crimes to handle? I didn't expect to hear from them again but they contacted me soon afterwards to say it had been made from a pay phone at Ocean Village, Southampton. That didn't get me any further forward. I was working on a project at Eastbourne, along the coast in East Sussex, but in my spare time I thought I'd do some checking.' She glanced down and stared into her almost empty coffee cup.

And being an archaeologist, Marvik thought she'd be good at research and digging out facts. She'd also have the patience for it.

He said, 'You thought this man could be your father.'

She looked up. 'It was possible. I decided to check out the men who had died in the period from the day he called me to a week later. I realized he could have had an accident and be seriously ill, unable to communicate, but I thought I'd start with the obvious assumption first. I didn't expect anything but it felt that at least I was trying to do something. I started with the premise that either this man was my father or he had known my father so he would be aged between say fifty and sixty. I researched the deaths of men in that age range for the period from the twenty-fourth to the thirty-first of January in or near Southampton. There weren't many so I rapidly managed to eliminate them. None had any connection with the Southampton Polytechnic of 1979 or the strikes, and none of their relatives claimed to know of an Oscar Redburn.'

Marvik thought she ought to meet Strathen. He'd be impressed by her methods.

'Then I came across reports in the newspaper archives of a man's body washed up on the Isle of Wight on the twenty-eighth of January who hadn't been identified. I got a copy of the coroner's report which said that he had been in the sea for three to four days and that he was aged approximately mid-to-late fifties. There was no record of his identity in the report so I asked the police if he could have been the man I had been due to meet. They told me his name was Bradley Pulford and his family had been traced. His cause of death remained undetermined but it was either an accident or suicide. His relatives lived in Swanage. They wouldn't give out the address. I arrived yesterday, too late for the undertakers or the crematorium office to be open so I contacted the local vicars and priests just in case there had been a funeral service, and I found the vicar who had held it on Friday. All he could tell me was that Bradley Pulford had worked as a fisherman with a family called Killbeck, and they weren't churchgoers. He didn't have an address for them. I looked them up in the phone directory but they're not listed and I couldn't find anything about them on the Internet, except for someone called Jensen Killbeck from Swanage on one of the social networks but no address for him. I asked the guest-house proprietor but she didn't know them, so I came down to the bay to find a fishing boat and hopefully the owners of it.'

He could tell her where Matthew Killbeck lived but he only had her word that what she was telling him was the truth. He needed Strathen to check her out first and to get some details on Oscar Redburn. He also needed to get to the church in Steepleridge to see if Irene Templeton could tell him more about the headstone of the Bradley Pulford buried there in 1959.

'What will you do now?' he asked.

'I'll stick around and see if they show up at the fishing boat or if anyone else does who might be able to tell me where I can find them. If they don't then tomorrow I'll call on the undertakers and get an address. I'm hoping to be able to speak to one or a couple of the family before I leave for Gibraltar in two days. I'm undertaking an exploration there. It would be good to know one way or another if Bradley Pulford had any connection with Oscar.'

Marvik wondered if the undertaker would tell her about his appearance at the funeral and his request for Matthew Killbeck's address, but by then he hoped to have told her himself and there would be no need for her to call on the undertakers. He'd be interested to see Matthew Killbeck's reaction to her.

'Have you any information on Bradley Pulford?' he asked.

'No. I haven't had time to do any research on him.'

And even if she had he wondered if she would have discovered what Strathen had.

The man reading his newspaper rose and paid his bill. Marvik's eyes swivelled to the bay. Everything looked fine. No sign of any mad motorbike rider. It was time he was moving and time he was telling Strathen all this. As though sensing he was ready to leave she plucked her jacket from the back of the chair, saying, 'I'd better go. They might be at the fishing boat.'

He paid the bill, ignoring her protest to contribute her share. Outside, she said slightly nervously, 'There's something else I'd like to talk to you about.'

He could see that it concerned his parents. 'I've got a couple of things to do but perhaps we can get together later. Where are you staying?'

Eagerly, she said, 'I'll give you my mobile number.'

They exchanged numbers. Marvik said he'd call her but he wasn't sure when. She looked pleased and relieved at his suggestion. She headed back in the direction of the lifeboat while he made for the town and the nearest taxi office, mentally replaying their conversation. There were several things that didn't add up, such as why hadn't she told the police she thought she might be Pulford's daughter and asked for her DNA to be compared with the body found on the Isle of Wight? Perhaps she had, only she wasn't ready to tell him that yet. She'd said that she'd discovered the newspaper article about Pulford's body being washed up on the beach — was that the truth? He wasn't certain. And why had she been reluctant to tell him where she was staying? Was she and her story for real or was she a plant primed to contact him to discover what he knew? All that stuff about being a marine archaeologist could be bullshit. All someone had to do was check out his name and trace it back to his parents and their profession and do some research. Or perhaps she'd been reticent to reveal where she was staying because she didn't completely trust him despite his parentage.

While waiting for a taxi to become available he called Strathen from outside the office and relayed what had happened.

'I'll get what I can on her and on Oscar Redburn,' Strathen said.

In the taxi on the way to Steepleridge, Marvik considered the fact that she was for real. What would happen if she located one of the Killbecks? He didn't much care for the thought because someone had tried to kill him after he'd been enquiring about Pulford and now she was doing the same. Was she in danger? Perhaps. And perhaps he should have stayed with her. He considered turning back but the traffic had ground to a halt. The driver radioed through to see what the problem was: an accident ahead just outside Corfe Castle. After consulting his Ordnance Survey map, Marvik paid off the driver. He'd walk the rest of the way. It was just under four miles across country from Corfe Castle and they were half a mile outside that village with its historic ruined castle perched on the knoll.

He set off at a brisk pace, feeling uneasy about leaving Sarah in Swanage. His only consolation was that she was unlikely to come across the Killbecks and even if she did no one was going to make an attempt on her life in daylight. But the latter wasn't much comfort: a road accident, a hit-and-run, could be arranged. The sooner he spoke to Irene Templeton again the sooner he could return and arrange to meet Sarah.

He turned his thoughts to what she had told him about her father. It sounded unlikely that Oscar Redburn had gone fossil hunting. He'd probably used it as an excuse to get away — not from the strike but from his pregnant wife. And maybe he'd got sick of being a student. He'd started a new life somewhere with a new woman and that could have been what both Joshua Nunton and Bradley Pulford had done in 1990. But perhaps the Bradley Pulford cremated at Swanage on Friday *had* been Oscar Redburn, which was why he knew so much about the past. He'd been returning home to tell his daughter why he'd abandoned her and her pregnant mother.

A fleeting idea crossed his mind that perhaps Nunton and Pulford had left together in 1990. He only had Matthew Killbeck's word that Nunton had left *after* Bradley. Perhaps they'd decided to seek adventure elsewhere together. Perhaps they had been in a relationship. Just because one of them, probably Pulford, had fathered a child — maybe two — it didn't mean he wasn't homosexual. And perhaps that was the reason why both Adam and Matthew were reluctant to talk about either Pulford or Nunton.

By the time he reached Steepleridge, Irene Templeton and the church congregation had gone. He was frustrated but not surprised. It had taken him much longer than he'd anticipated despite having marched and jogged much of the way over the hilly terrain. He hoped he'd find her address or contact number inside the church — her being a church warden — and was pleased to discover it on the back page of the parish magazine, copies of which were on a table along with postcards, leaflets and a visitor's book inside the church. He headed there only to meet with disappointment. There was no sign of anyone at the whitewashed, detached thatched cottage. Irritated that he'd had a wasted journey and increasingly worried about Sarah Redburn, he made for the coastal path back to Swanage. It was a ten-mile trek and the weather was growing increasingly overcast and windy. Neither bothered him. Thoughts of Sarah Redburn did. He recalled her gentle manner and her earnest expression. Surely she was genuine.

There had been no call from Strathen and when Marvik tried his number a couple of times on the route back he found he couldn't get a signal. He'd wait until he was on board to call him. The motor cruiser that had been anchored up close to him had left. He was alone on this side of the pier, although there were still a handful of boats anchored in the wide bay on the other side.

He told Strathen he'd had no luck finding Irene Templeton, but he knew where she lived and would try again.

Strathen said, 'I can't get anything on Oscar Redburn but Sarah Redburn checks out. She has a website but I assumed that could be fake so I dug deeper. She is who she claims to be, a marine archaeologist if it's the Sarah Redburn you met, aged thirty-six, nice figure, long, wavy light-brown hair.'

'Sounds like her — you got a picture?'

'I'll send it over. She's got a BA (Hons) in Archaeology at the University of Southampton and an MA in Maritime Archaeology. She's worked as a maritime archaeologist for English Heritage and for a couple of consultancies in the UK.'

Marvik found himself looking at a smiling Sarah Redburn, tanned, relaxed but still with that edge of shyness about her.

'That's her. Anything more?'

'Not yet. I'll keep looking.'

Marvik called her number the instant he came off the line but there was no answer. He should have pressed for her address. Maybe she was avoiding him because she couldn't see how he could help her and she didn't like him. But a marine archaeologist keen on his parents? He doubted it. She'd maintain contact with him even if she couldn't stand the sight of him. Perhaps she'd found the Killbecks and after speaking to them had decided to go home, wherever that was. She hadn't said and Strathen hadn't given him an address, perhaps because he didn't have one for her.

He showered, changed and made something to eat, after which he again tried her number. She still didn't answer and he didn't leave a message. He considered calling on Matthew Killbeck to see if Sarah had found him, then decided against it. He didn't want to alert him if she hadn't been there. So why wasn't she answering? Was she safe? He hadn't read of any accidents. Maybe he should ring the hospitals and check? Maybe he was just being paranoid.

He spent another restless night, thinking about Sarah and alert in case he was targeted. He'd already checked over the boat. No one had boarded it or broken into it and if someone was intent on destroying it and him on board then they'd had ample time to do so. But no one seemed interested in him anymore. Why? Because they were more interested in Sarah? Or because, despite her credentials, she had been sent to get information from him to pass on? But what the hell had he said? Nothing.

Where was she? Certainly still not answering her phone when he tried it just after sunrise. And she wasn't on the shore waiting for the Killbecks to arrive. Feeling restless and uneasy he flicked on the radio and reached for the kettle to make a coffee but his hand froze as the newscaster's voice announced that a woman's body had been found on the beach not far from Ballard's Point, Swanage. Every muscle in his body tensed. He grabbed the pay-as-you-go phone that Crowder had issued to him for use during his missions and, with his mind racing, he punched in a number. It was answered on the third ring. Quickly he relayed what he'd heard, adding, 'I need to know who she is. I think it could be Sarah Redburn; she's been here asking questions about Bradley Pulford. I had breakfast with her yesterday morning. She thinks Pulford might have been connected with her father, Oscar Redburn, who went missing in 1979.'

There was a fractional pause. 'I'll call you back.'

Marvik went up on deck. His heart was pumping fast, his mind swimming with thoughts. He kept his eyes peeled to the shore, willing her to show, but deep inside he knew she wouldn't. He felt a coldness inside him that had nothing to do with the chill of the March morning. The seconds ticked by agonizingly slowly. It seemed as though he was in limbo for hours yet it was only a matter of minutes before his phone rang.

Solemnly, Crowder announced, 'A credit card found on the body is in the name of Sarah Redburn, and there's a railcard displaying her photograph. There doesn't seem to be any doubt.'

Marvik's body stiffened. His fists clenched. A tight ball of fury knotted his gut and along with it a self-loathing. He'd caused her death. 'How did she die?' he asked, his voice taut with emotion, trying to shut out the image of the smiling, apologetic, shy woman across the café table yesterday.

'The initial report says she was strangled. There's no mobile phone or bag with her, just the purse in her sailing jacket. No sign of sexual interference. That's all I can get for you for now. You'll look into a possible connection between Oscar Redburn's disappearance and Bradley Pulford?'

You bet I bloody will. And he knew exactly where he'd start.

CHAPTER SIX

Monday

'You're not responsible,' Strathen said when Marvik broke the news to him. 'But telling you that doesn't make it easier or better.'

'No, but I'll get the bastard who did it.'

'*We'll* get the bastard,' Strathen corrected.

Marvik took a breath. He stared ahead at the grey, turbulent sea as he headed west out of Swanage Bay. There wasn't another boat in sight. He'd let an innocent woman die. It was pointless going through the 'if onlys' — he'd already done that, but still they tormented his troubled mind. If only he'd insisted on knowing where she was staying. If he'd stayed in Swanage and said he'd help her. If he'd told her that he'd been at the funeral and what he knew of Pulford would she still be alive? He didn't know. And neither did he know why she had been killed, but he was convinced it wasn't a random killing — it was linked to this mission. She could have been killed because of her association with him as a warning for him to lay off asking questions or because she was getting too curious about Bradley Pulford.

He voiced these thoughts to Strathen, adding, 'Crowder claims he knew nothing of Sarah Redburn or her father and I didn't stick around to find out if Sarah managed to track down the Killbecks. I can deal with that later. See if you can find out where she lives, Shaun. Crowder said he might be able to get it but that he'd already gone out on a limb to get the information about her murder.'

'The police will apply for her phone records.'

'Yes, and they'll see that I called her several times yesterday and this morning. They'll come asking questions, but it will take them a while before they get access to the records and locate me. I'm on my way to see Gordon Freynsham at Lyme Regis. He was the last person to see Oscar Redburn and Sarah said she'd visited him recently. I've got a fair bit of information on him from his website. He's got a degree in geology and a Masters in palaeontology. The first from the then Southampton Polytechnic where Sarah told me he studied with Oscar, the second from Durham University. He's worked overseas as a geologist and is now a fossil trader, a business he set up in 1989.'

'The year Pulford returned.'

'Yes. Maybe it's a coincidence.'

'Yeah,' said Strathen dubiously.

'He sells online and through a shop in Lyme Regis. I'm just hoping he's there. His website says he's often at fossil shows around the UK, Europe and America and he also gives guided fossil-hunting trips along the Jurassic Coast of Devon and Dorset. I don't want to have to trek around the entire coast trying to locate him. He's in the process of fronting a new television series of *Jurassic Coast* though so the likelihood is he's staying local.'

Marvik had considered calling the number given on the website but had decided against it. He wanted to catch Freynsham unaware to see his reaction when he put questions to him about Oscar Redburn. And although Marvik had no reason to suspect that Freynsham would lie, or that he had anything to do with Pulford or Sarah's deaths, Marvik wasn't going to take that chance. Much better to have the edge of surprise. The website boasted that the shop was open seven days a week. Marvik hoped to find the owner on site or, failing that, close by.

Strathen said he'd also see what he could get on the dock strike of 1979 as well as on Oscar Redburn.

It was mid-morning when Marvik moored up on one of the few visitors' berths in the lee of the harbour. It gave him some protection from the prevailing westerly wind. He located the shop with ease. It had a prominent position on the waterfront and seemed to be doing a brisk trade. He introduced himself to the middle-aged, faded woman behind the counter as a journalist who would like a quote from Mr Freynsham. She disappeared into the back of the shop saying she would see if her husband was free to speak to him. Marvik breathed a silent sigh of relief, glad he had located Freynsham. This would save time. A couple of minutes later she waved him through to a small room crowded with wooden sample cabinets, like those in old-fashioned pharmacies. There were also a couple of modern grey filing cabinets, a large oak desk, littered with papers, books and fossils, and a chair in front of the desk. The room was cold and smelt of dirt and decay. Behind the desk sat a slender man in his mid-fifties with collar-length light-brown hair swept back off a narrow face with a crumpled, lived-in look and an air of superiority in the light-brown eyes behind the heavy rimmed, fashionable spectacles. He waved a hand in a feminine gesture at the seat and smiled. It vanished the instant Marvik said he'd like to ask him some questions about Oscar Redburn. The skin paled beneath his tan and his eyes registered dread as he shifted uneasily.

'Who?' he asked, feigning a baffled expression.

Marvik said nothing, just continued to stare at him.

Freynsham squirmed under the icy gaze. He removed his glasses and licked his lips. 'Why do you want to know about Oscar? He disappeared years ago.'

'That's exactly *why* I want to know about him.'

‘I don’t know anything about it,’ he said, replacing his glasses and avoiding Marvik’s eye contact. ‘I don’t remember him.’

Marvik sat forward and in a low, harsh tone said, ‘Then let me refresh your memory. You were at Southampton Polytechnic together and you were the last person to speak to Oscar Redburn before he vanished. You also told the police that Redburn was coming to the Jurassic Coast fossil hunting — a strange thing for him to do when it wasn’t his field of interest or expertise.’

Freynsham’s eyes darted to the door where Marvik could hear voices coming from the shop. ‘Who are you? Why are you asking about Oscar?’

Marvik remained silent.

‘Are you family?’

‘No.’

‘Police?

‘No. I’m not a journalist either but the media might be very keen to know about your connection with Oscar Redburn, especially given the fact that his daughter was found dead this morning not far from here.’

Freynsham’s face went ashen. ‘Dead! You mean . . .’

‘Murdered. Yes. And I know for a fact that she contacted you about her father.’ Marvik could see he’d struck gold. He could smell Freynsham’s fear. ‘So why don’t you tell me what really happened in 1979 and why Redburn disappeared or do I have to go to the tabloids with the story? It would make very salacious reading, you being a television personality. Sarah Redburn murdered and your connection with her father. And the police would certainly be very interested.’

That did the trick. ‘I can’t talk here.’ Freynsham sprang up, grabbing his waterproof jacket from the back of his chair.

Marvik felt a stab of victory but it was short-lived when he recalled it was too late to tell Sarah, and his resolve hardened as he followed Freynsham into the shop, which was crowded with tourists.

'Just popping out for a while,' Freynsham said tersely to his wife.

She looked set to protest as more people tumbled into the shop but a glance at Marvik silenced her. As Freynsham headed for the door he was halted by a man in his forties who proceeded to tell him how much he enjoyed the fossil-hunting programmes on the television and that he was looking forward to the new series. Freynsham muttered all the right things but he was clearly agitated and keen to get away. That went for Marvik too.

He followed Freynsham out, wondering what he had to hide. Marvik's interest deepened as Freynsham seemed very keen to put as much distance as he could between them and the people in the streets. He was heading for the Cobb, the long sea wall that curved far out to sea and provided no protection from the elements. It was a risky place to be in wild weather. The gaudy yellow notices warned pedestrians that it could be hazardous, especially in high winds, and the wind was rising. Freynsham ignored the warnings and strode on. The waves were slapping against the concrete structure, whipping up flicks of spray over the edge. They had the place to themselves. Perhaps Freynsham thought he could push him off the far end of the wall when they reached it. Was he a killer? He didn't look like one but driven by desperation to cover up something from his past which Sarah had ignited might have made him one. Lyme Regis was fifty-five miles from Swanage, about eighty minutes by car. Freynsham could have arranged to meet Sarah on the beach or in a secluded place above the bay and killed her.

Freynsham, deep in thought, a frown on his narrow forehead, the salt from the sea spray coating his spectacles, made no attempt to talk; it was as if he was somewhere else, and perhaps he was, in 1979. Could Redburn actually have gone missing from here? wondered Marvik. Had Freynsham and Redburn argued and had Freynsham pushed him over the edge? Was that why he wanted to come here to confess to the murder, where there would be no witnesses and where he thought he might do the same to Marvik? But surely the man wouldn't be such a fool to think he could get the better of him?

Freynsham marched on until they were on the furthermost exposed part of the Cobb. Here there was no protection, just a drop into the sea. The cliffs and hills stretched out behind them and to their right and left, the chill wind barrelled off the sea and the spray cascaded up at them. It only then occurred to Marvik that perhaps Freynsham, finally faced with someone who had come in search of the truth and who wasn't going to be fobbed off with lies, was going to throw himself in. Marvik steeled himself in case he had to dive in to save the man. In this type of sea and at this time of year it would be a close-run thing.

Taking a breath, Freynsham turned to face Marvik. 'I can't tell you anything that can help shed any light on why he disappeared. Just like I told his daughter. I'm sorry she's dead.'

'Did you kill her?' Marvik asked sharply.

'No!'

Marvik eyed him disbelievingly. 'Then why come all the way out here just to say that? You could have told me that in the shop.'

'You wouldn't have believed me and you'd have made a fuss, maybe even wrecked the shop.' His voice was taut with an edge of fear. 'Here no one can see or hear us. I can't afford any bad publicity. I have a reputation to consider — you saw that. I'm very well known.'

And an arsehole, thought Marvik, eyeing him steadily. He didn't have time to piss about and he wasn't in the mood. He didn't know what game Freynsham was playing but it wasn't one he was going to join in.

Swiftly he grabbed Freynsham, spun him round and wrenched his arms behind his back in a tight grip. Freynsham squealed in pain. Marvik leaned close to his ear and in a threatening tone said, 'OK, so we're alone, in the middle of fucking nowhere, no one can hear us and no one can see us, and if they do I'll say I was trying to persuade you not to jump. Is this what you did to Redburn? Did you push him off here or off a cliff and hope his body would never be recovered? Did you?' Marvik bellowed the last two words, making Freynsham start.

'You've got it wrong.'

'Have I? Then stop pissing me about — you're not on television now.'

'All right, all right. Just let go of me.'

Not bloody likely. Marvik tightened his grip.

'Stop. Please, I'll tell you.'

'Then do it quickly before I shove your scrawny carcass off this wall and tell the world you were so fucked off with fossil hunting and the TV that you decided to end it all.'

'You wouldn't.'

'You want to take that risk?' Marvik put his foot out in front of Freynsham. 'One shove and you trip over my boot and into the sea.'

'OK. I was in love with the bastard.'

Marvik eased his vice-like grip on Freynsham's arms but still held on to him. 'Go on.'

'Not that there was ever anything physical between us,' Freynsham hastily added. 'Oscar was all man and I have never had a homosexual affair. But I was infatuated with him. He was charismatic, clever and fun. He was also evil, vindictive and highly manipulative. He could get people to do exactly what he wanted, when he wanted. Everyone worshipped him. He had only to click his fingers or say the word and people fell over themselves to please him, especially women. Linda wasn't his only girlfriend. She probably wasn't the only one he got pregnant either. But he married her. She was a nurse and willing to continue working even after the baby was born. That suited Oscar fine. He could live off her wages.'

Marvik released his hold.

Freynsham rubbed his arms and turned to face Marvik. 'I didn't kill him and I didn't kill his daughter.'

'Not sure I believe that, Gordon. Is this where you arranged to meet him and when he laughed at you for declaring your undying love you pushed him into the sea?'

'No!'

Marvik made to step forward. Freynsham hastily continued, 'Yes, we came here but I didn't kill him. I had a car. I was the only student with my own transport. It had been my dad's and he passed it on to me when he was given a new one. He'd got a promotion and a company car, a Ford. It was a big deal in those days and probably why Oscar latched on to me,' he added with sourness. 'I used to ferry him around.'

'And you thought a day in the West Country would make Oscar putty in your hands,' sneered Marvik.

Freynsham flushed. 'He told me I was nuts and depraved and walked off. I was shocked and hurt. I nearly threw myself in.'

'What stopped you?'

Freynsham remained silent. Marvik continued, 'You thought of a way to get even with him for hurting you.'

'No. I returned to the car expecting Oscar to be waiting there for me with that cocky mocking expression on his face but he wasn't. I looked for him. I couldn't find him so I drove back to Southampton and tried to forget about my humiliation. I wasn't sure that I could face Oscar the next day. I was on the verge of chucking in my degree when Linda came to me to say that Oscar hadn't been home and did I know where he was. I said I had no idea, which was the truth — no one knew we'd been together at Lyme Regis. I asked around at the Poly but no one had seen or heard from him. I went round to the house Oscar and Linda were renting. I couldn't say that I had seen him only the day before and where because, just as you have done, people might think I'd pushed him in.'

'Did anyone know about your feelings for Oscar?'

'No. I made sure never to tell anyone. You won't go to the press, will you? Think of what it would do to my wife and son.'

'Go on.'

'I'm telling you the truth in exchange for your silence.'

'You told the police he'd gone fossil hunting. You could have just said you had no idea where he was.'

'I know. I should have done but I panicked and said the first thing that came into my head.'

And Freynsham was the panicking kind. Still, Marvik knew there was more but was this in any way connected with Pulford? How could it be except for Sarah, and Sarah was dead. Was that because she had contacted this man or because she'd been seen with him? Or was it both? Or even neither.

'Why would Oscar go missing in the middle of industrial action when he thrived on protests?'

'You know about that? Because he was bored. It wasn't giving him the attention and kudos he wanted.'

'But to miss the big day of action when many workers were going to come out on strike doesn't seem to be in character.'

'It does if you had known him. Oscar wanted to be a big fish in a big pool, not a little one in a little pool, and with the nurses and ambulance drivers joining in the protest Oscar's small part and ours at the docks was nothing. Hospitals are much bigger news: how the workers are putting patients' lives at risk and all that kind of stuff. The media would lap that up and they did. When Oscar didn't show up, I just thought he'd gone off with some tart for a few days but I couldn't tell Linda that, and I didn't tell his daughter either.'

'What did you tell her?'

'That I had no idea where Oscar had gone, which is the truth. And I had to stick to my original statement.'

'When did you tell her this?'

'Months ago.'

It was a lie. Marvik clenched his fist and stepped forward.

'Early February,' Freynsham hastily corrected. 'It was the first time I'd met her and no, she had never been in touch before. She asked me if I had a photograph of Oscar because she didn't have any and she couldn't find any of him in the university or newspaper archives.'

Marvik wondered if that was true. Sarah hadn't told him that. If Oscar Redburn had liked the limelight so much then surely the local newspaper photographer would have covered the protest and taken pictures which had included Oscar.

And there would have been pictures of him as president of the students' union.

'I said I couldn't help her.'

Marvik didn't believe that. 'OK, so let's go and get that photograph.'

'But I haven't—'

'Now.'

Freynsham nodded. 'My car's at the back of the shop.'

They set off down the Cobb; the waves were breaking over the top, spraying them as they hurried, the wind pushing them along. Freynsham drove in silence to the northern outskirts of the town and turned off just before the signpost to the village of Uplyme. Judging by the style and size of the detached house, Freynsham had done well for himself. It was set back from the road, screened by hedges and approached via a broken wooden five-bar gate and weed-strewn gravel drive. He pulled up in front of the porch and, unlocking the front door, disabled the alarm. Marvik stepped into an untidy and grubby hall piled with books and boxes. Freynsham left Marvik in the hall while he ran upstairs. Marvik could hear him in a room at the back of the house rummaging around. He reappeared a few minutes later, his face flushed and hair awry, carrying a photograph which he handed to Marvik.

'It's the only one I have,' he said.

Marvik wasn't sure if he believed that, but recording the minutiae of life hadn't been the trend in 1979 like it was now.

'The colour tone's gone off,' Freynsham said, handing it over. 'That's Oscar.' He pointed at the orange-tinted picture of two men. Marvik found himself studying a man with long, wavy light-brown hair, a narrow face, moustache and lively, laughing dark eyes. Sarah didn't look like her father and neither did her personality match his, if what Freynsham had told him was true. Perhaps she took after her mother. Freynsham was on the left of Redburn.

'Why didn't you want Sarah to have this? You could have scanned it and emailed it to her.'

'I didn't want it all raked up again. I thought she might give it to the newspapers or the police or both and try to get the case on Oscar's disappearance re-investigated.'

'You didn't show the police this?'

'They didn't ask. Linda probably gave them a photograph.'

Then why hadn't Sarah a copy of that? Perhaps she did have, on her computer or mobile phone, neither of which had been found with the body according to Crowder, but they could be in the room in her bed and breakfast accommodation. Marvik tucked the picture into his jacket pocket. Freynsham opened his mouth to protest then closed it again.

'I'll return it.'

'No need,' Freynsham promptly replied, obviously in the hope of getting Marvik out of his life for good. Marvik wasn't certain he could do that. He asked to be dropped off on the seafront but made no attempt to alight. Instead he asked Freynsham if he knew a man called Bradley Pulford.

'No.'

Marvik scrutinized him carefully. His bewilderment seemed genuine. 'How about Joshua Nunton?'

Freynsham shook his head. Anxiously, he said, 'Will you be back?'

'Depends on what I find.'

'You think Oscar is still alive?'

Marvik paused for a moment. 'No.'

'Then why—?'

'I'll be in touch.'

Marvik watched Freynsham drive away before heading for his boat. What was it about Oscar Redburn that Freynsham hadn't told him? Had Redburn re-surfaced in 1989 as Bradley Pulford? But why? Marvik had no evidence to support that, except that Sarah's murder must mean something. And although he was reluctant to return to Swanage in case he was questioned by the police, he knew he had to because he needed to know if Oscar Redburn had reincarnated himself as Bradley Pulford, and that meant talking to the Killbecks.

CHAPTER SEVEN

'Matthew's not here,' a plump, friendly woman in her late sixties announced. She introduced herself as Abigail and explained that she lived next door and once a week looked after Mary to give Matthew a bit of a break. 'He usually goes out walking along the coast, often all the way to Lulworth Cove, but sometimes he only goes as far as the lost village of Tyneham. Do you know it?' She didn't give Marvik the chance to answer before chatting on. 'But today he's had to go out on the boat with Adam. Jensen's sick, says he's got flu, but if you ask me it's a hangover and bone idleness.'

Marvik thought they were late getting back. It would be dark soon. He hadn't seen the fishing boat in the bay because he'd changed his mind about mooring up in Swanage. Instead he'd headed farther along the coast to Poole marina and taken a taxi from there for the twenty-mile journey back to Swanage. No point in making it easier for the police to find him, he'd told Strathen on the phone earlier.

'Matthew?' a querulous voice came from behind Abigail.

She glanced over her shoulder then back at Marvik. 'Poor soul. She doesn't know where she is or who she is half the time.' Turning back, she called out, 'No, Mary, it's a friend of Matthew's.'

'Has the devil got him?'

'You'd better come in for a moment. She won't be convinced until she sees you.'

Marvik once again stepped over the threshold into the narrow hall of the small house. He wondered if it was worth showing Mary Killbeck the photograph Freynsham had given him. Confused she might be but perhaps her long-term memory wasn't too bad.

The room was as suffocatingly hot as it had been the last time and Mary was in the same seat to the right of the electric fire. Although thin and frail there was still a trace of prettiness about her troubled features. This time, though, instead of eyeing him in a puzzled but friendly way she shrank back, afraid, as though he was going to hit her. He tried a reassuring smile but it had no effect.

'Where's Matthew? What have you done with him?' she wailed at Marvik.

'Matthew's safe — he's gone fishing with Adam,' Abigail tried to reassure her.

'No. He's taken Matthew,' and she pointed at Marvik.

Abigail threw him an apologetic glance before addressing Mary gently. 'No one's done anything with Matthew, my love. He'll be back soon. Mr Marvik is a friend of Matthew's.'

But Mary was shaking her head and looked on the verge of tears. Abigail sighed and rose from her crouching position. 'I'm sorry.'

'No need to apologize. I'll go down to the boat.' There was no point in showing Mary the photograph.

Abigail followed him out with Mary's cries ringing after them. 'She means no harm. It's just the dementia.'

Marvik said he hoped he hadn't unsettled her too much. He asked Abigail if either Adam or Jensen owned a motorbike. She said neither of them did. Perhaps he'd been mistaken in thinking Adam had been trying to run him down. Or perhaps he kept his bike out of sight of Matthew's neighbours.

He made for the bay, hoping that he wouldn't miss them as they drove back in the pick-up, and was relieved when he saw them unloading the boat. He'd heard nothing more from Crowder and there had been no further news about Sarah's murder on the radio. Both men eyed him suspiciously and with a degree of hostility. There had also been a flicker of surprise in Adam's eyes. He'd have noticed his boat had left the bay and would have assumed they'd seen the last of him.

Marvik thrust the photograph of Oscar Redburn and Gordon Freynsham in front of Adam and without preamble asked if he recognized either man.

'No,' he grunted, barely glancing at it. But that wasn't surprising. Marvik hadn't expected him to recognize a man he'd known in 1989 when he had been twenty-three from a photograph that had been taken when Adam was only twelve. Matthew was different, though.

'And you, Matthew?' Marvik said.

'Neither of them are Bradley, if that's what you're thinking.'

'Not even this man,' Marvik pointed at Oscar Redburn, 'without the moustache and long hair?'

'Even if you put him in a blonde wig and painted him pink he'd still not be Bradley.'

Marvik held their aggressive stares and thought they were telling the truth.

'We've never seen either of them before,' Matthew added.

'Do you know or have you heard of an Oscar Redburn or Gordon Freynsham?'

'No.'

'What about you, Adam?'

'No. Now sod off and leave us be.'

'Afraid I can't do that,' Marvik grimly replied, tucking the picture in the inside pocket of his waterproof jacket. 'Sarah Redburn.' He watched their reaction carefully. There was only puzzlement mingled with antagonism. 'Do either of you know her?'

Matthew answered, 'No.'

Marvik swivelled his gaze to Adam.

'No.'

Were they lying? Had Sarah tracked them down yesterday or early this morning? He didn't know the time of her death. Perhaps they were late back from fishing because they'd started out late this morning, anxiously waiting to hear the news of when her body would be found and making sure they had covered their tracks. But why should they murder Sarah?

He watched the truck pull away before turning back to the town. He wondered if the police had traced Sarah's next of kin and who that might be. Had they found anything among her personal belongings in the guest house that could tell them who her killer was?

As a taxi took him back to Poole he thought over what he'd learned during the day. It didn't amount to much, just a photograph and a brief biography of a man who had spurned the declaration of love from another. Could he believe Freynsham? Had Oscar Redburn really been the way Freynsham had described or was that just his jaded view? Could Freynsham have killed Oscar? Could he also have killed Sarah to prevent her from stirring up the past? A TV star being questioned by the police didn't go down well with the public, who would probably come to their own conclusions as to whether or not he was guilty of a crime and more often than not would reach the former verdict based on editorial coverage and social media comments.

Marvik's contemplations took him to the marina where, after paying off the taxi, he looked up, surprised and pleased to see Strathen waiting for him. He was in need of company and Strathen would have known that. They'd been on too many missions together not to sense how the other was feeling and thinking. Poole was only an hour's drive from where Strathen lived, just outside the village of Hamble to the east.

Strathen climbed out of his Volvo. 'Fancy a drink?'

'A crate load. On board. I've got beer.'

'And food?'

'Yes.'

'Good, I'm famished. You've no idea how hungry research makes you.'

Marvik laughed and climbed on his boat, leaving Strathen to follow. Even with the limitations of his prosthetic leg, he did so with agility and speed.

'Any joy with the Killbecks?' Strathen asked, following Marvik into the main cabin.

'They claim Oscar Redburn is not Bradley Pulford.' Marvik reached into the fridge and handed Strathen a beer. He took one for himself, opened it and handed the bottle opener to Strathen before sitting down at the galley table. 'What did you get on Redburn?'

'Remarkably little given that he was supposed to have been such a well-known agitator and president of the students' union, but that could be explained by the fact that the files for 1975 to 1980 were destroyed in a fire when the new wing to the now university was being built in 2000. There weren't any pictures of him in the local newspapers either, and only a couple of casual references.'

'Which was why Sarah asked Freynsham if he had a photograph and the lying git said he hadn't.' Marvik took a swig of beer.

'But there was considerable coverage on the dockers' strike.' Strathen eased himself on to the seat opposite Marvik. Outside the wind was whistling through the masts. The boat rocked gently.

Strathen continued, 'The lorry drivers had refused to deliver to the docks and those that defied the strike were blocked by the pickets, who, as Sarah told you, were joined by students and others who came out in support of them, including public sector workers. The editorial coverage of the day was scathing of the dockers, labelling them as skivers and greedy communists who wanted to bring the country to its knees. It wasn't much more favourable to the Labour Callaghan government. The local press singled out one man in particular for more derision than others: Jack Darrow, the shop steward, who had a record of violence. There was a photograph of him at the dock gates but as I said no photograph of Redburn or the other pickets, and there was no mention of Redburn's disappearance. But what is interesting is that Jack Darrow was found dead in the hold of a cargo ship on the twenty-third of January.'

Marvik raised his eyebrows. 'Two days after Oscar Redburn went AWOL. Did the police make any connection between the two?'

'If they did the newspapers didn't cover it.'

'And Sarah didn't mention it; neither did Freynsham.'

'Maybe he didn't think anything of it. The newspaper report was very sketchy — just said Darrow had been found dead in a cargo hold and union funds had gone missing, leaving readers to draw their own conclusions: i.e. Darrow had his hand in the till and had been discovered. Faced with his union reputation in tatters, he'd thrown himself into the hold. There were two paragraphs on the inquest. Immediate cause of death was severe trauma to the brain and multiple fractures. The coroner brought in an open verdict.'

Marvik said, 'Could Redburn have killed Darrow and then taken off scared?'

'Maybe. It didn't say how long Darrow had been lying in that cargo hold.'

'Perhaps that was what Freynsham was so worried about when I started asking him questions. He knew Redburn had killed Darrow — perhaps he'd even witnessed it or helped him do it — but why should they kill him?'

Strathen shrugged. His penetrating grey eyes in his rugged face looked thoughtful for a moment.

Marvik continued, 'Time to report to Crowder. I want to know what the police have got on Sarah's murder. I'll ask him for a meeting. And no fobbing off,' he added grittily.

He made the call while Strathen inspected what they had on board to eat. A couple of minutes later, Marvik came off the phone. 'He's on his way, by boat — should be with us within ninety minutes.' Marvik hadn't asked where Crowder was coming from but given the timing it sounded as though it might be Portsmouth, to the east of Poole.

They ate mainly in silence, making no reference to their mission but concentrating on the meal that Strathen had cooked while Marvik had showered and changed. His thoughts had constantly turned to the shy, apologetic woman he'd had breakfast with yesterday and her death, and yet he could make no sense of it or of what they had learned so far. He hoped Crowder would change that.

'Sounds like Crowder arriving now,' Marvik said as he caught the deep throb of a powerful engine above the howl of the wind. He heard the boat come alongside on the pontoon. Neither of them went out to assist. They knew that Crowder could handle a boat alone and Marvik guessed he would be by himself, just as he always was for a meeting with them.

The boat dipped and swayed as Crowder climbed on board. He nodded a greeting at them, his round, weather-worn face serious and his deep brown eyes solemn. Marvik offered him a beer but he declined. Marvik knew nothing about the fit, dark-haired man in his early fifties who slid on to the bench seat beside Strathen. He had no idea if he was married or had kids — grandkids, even. That wasn't Marvik's concern. He had no need to know. All he knew was that Crowder was intelligent, determined, could handle a boat and had an inner strength that showed in his calm, unperturbed manner.

He pulled off the expensive sailing jacket to reveal a navy jumper over a pale blue polo shirt. In his quiet, steady voice, he said, 'So far there is no trace of Sarah having been booked into a hotel or guest house in the area. If she was staying with a friend, he or she hasn't come forward. Enquiries are progressing. The initial time of death has been put between nine p.m. and midnight on Sunday.'

'I rang her at six and again at eight. She didn't answer.'

'It's possible she could have been held against her will and her phone monitored.'

Marvik felt a chill run through him at the thought of Sarah afraid and hurt. He tensed and said, 'The killer would know I had called her.'

'So will the police once they have access to her phone records.'

'And they could leap to the conclusion that I'm the killer. I don't have an alibi.'

Crowder said, 'We can deal with that later if we have to. She was strangled with some kind of a cord and that's all I have on the method of her death.'

Marvik tried to blot out the picture of a ligature thrown around her neck and the cruel, painful death.

'Have they found her next of kin?' he asked.

'Not that I'm aware of yet.'

'What about her address? And don't tell me you don't know it because I won't believe you.'

'Her last registered address is a rented furnished flat in Eastbourne. She moved out a week ago. No one knows to where yet. She doesn't have a car but she does have a driving licence. The police are checking if she hired a car or van to move her belongings, and they're talking to her neighbours. The landlord has no mail for her so it's probable she used a forwarding address or a PO Box number. She's registered as self-employed so they've got no company personnel records to check but they'll contact a previous employer who might be able to give them a next of kin.'

'Freynsham told me that Sarah contacted him in early February to ask him what he knew about her father's disappearance. He told her he knew nothing and apart from him telling me he had been with Redburn at Lyme Regis just before he disappeared he told me precious little too, but he was very scared that his contact with Redburn might be made known to the media. Perhaps he called her or sent her a text to say he had new information and arranged to meet her, then killed her. He might have told her to bring her research with her so he could destroy it after killing her. I'd like to know what he was doing Sunday night and if he has an alibi.' Marvik placed the photograph that Freynsham had given him on the table. 'That's Oscar Redburn.'

'Is it?' Crowder asked quietly.

Marvik eyed him sharply. 'You know what he looks like?'

'I didn't say that but you only have Freynsham's word it's Oscar.'

'He didn't look as though he was lying.'

Strathen, peering at the photograph, said, 'Maybe all those appearances on TV have turned him into a damn good actor.'

They had a point. Marvik addressed Crowder. 'What do you know of Jack Darrow?'

'Nothing. Who is he?'

Strathen enlightened him, adding that perhaps Oscar Redburn killed Darrow and Freynsham helped him to leave the country. 'Freynsham could have spun you a line, Art. He could have driven Redburn to Weymouth where he caught the ferry to Cherbourg. Redburn stays abroad for years but returns in 1989, reinventing himself as Bradley Pulford.'

'But why the devil as Pulford? Does any of this make any sense to you?' Marvik demanded of Crowder.

'Not yet. But it seems that someone doesn't want you asking questions about Redburn or Pulford.'

'So we keep asking,' Marvik said grimly.

Crowder returned to his boat and they heard it leaving a few minutes later.

Strathen rose. 'I'll return to Hamble and see if I can get you anything by the morning.'

Marvik hoped he would. And he was determined to get more out of Freynsham tomorrow, even if he had to threaten to throw him off the Cobb again.

He tried to blot out thoughts of Sarah and the manner of her death but both intruded on his sleep and disturbed him more than the rising wind and the rain ricocheting off the boat. He wasn't sorry when the trilling of his phone woke him. It was six a.m. and Strathen.

'I've found a relative of Jack Darrow's.'

'How?' Marvik asked, swinging out of his bunk.

'By spending a long, hard night trawling the Net.'

And only now would Strathen grab a few hours' sleep before setting off for the National Archives Office at Kew.

'I found a reference to Darrow's death on the Stevedores' Union website archives. He left a widow, Audrey Darrow, now deceased, and a son, Nigel Darrow, living in Hartlepool. It's amazing what information social networks can give you about people. I found Bryony Darrow, whose home town is Southampton. The electoral roll for Southampton in 2004 shows her as being an occupant in a house belonging to a Nigel Darrow. She's no longer there but her social networking profile gave me the area where she lives, and as it is such a small place, it wasn't difficult to track her down. Eel Pie Island.'

'Where the devil is that?'

'It's a very small private island on the Thames at Twickenham with a fluctuating population of about a hundred, generally famous for its artistic community. The island was also famous for its jazz and blues concerts in the sixties. Bryony Darrow is an actress, aged twenty-eight. She's had various minor roles in TV soaps. She's also done some regional theatre work and has some good reviews but then she'd hardly post crummy ones on her website. She was born in Southampton and studied at the University of Surrey, Guildford School of Acting. Looks as though she's still waiting for the big break. She's very active on the social networks and there are a number of pictures of her on the Internet. She's a looker: oval face, short blonde hair, blue eyes, nice figure. The electoral roll confirms her address as Tidal Cottage, Eel Pie Island. It doesn't say what her current acting role is so it's my guess she's resting, as they say in the business, or working as a waitress in a cocktail bar to coin a lyric from The Human League number one UK Christmas hit in 1981 and US hit in the summer of 1982.'

'Before my time — well, almost.'

'I don't remember gurgling it as a baby either. But Bryony Darrow might be working in that cocktail bar today or she might be at home.'

'And she might know nothing about her grandfather's death; it was before she was born.'

'You mean all my hard work has been for nothing!' Strathen said with mock hurt. 'I could call in on my way back from Kew. I know she'll be around at some stage because she's posted on social media that she's got an audition today. She doesn't say what for or the time — just that it's a key part.'

Marvik hesitated. 'No. I'll see her. And not because you say she's a looker.' He half joked but his mind flicked to Sarah. She'd been a looker too.

Strathen followed his train of thought because in a more serious tone, he said, 'Let me know what you get and I'll call you if I pick up anything useful on Bradley Pulford's death from the Registry of Shipping and Seamen at the National Archives.'

'I'll head back to the Isle of Wight and fetch my car.' Freynsham could wait.

CHAPTER EIGHT

Tuesday

It took Marvik much longer than he had anticipated to reach his cottage at Newtown Harbour on the Isle of Wight because the high winds and heavy rain that had swept in during the night refused to abate during the early morning. He was a skilled sailor, with a sturdy craft, and prepared to take risks but he wasn't foolhardy or in so much of a hurry as to risk his life and possibly those of others who might need to rescue him. The storm would ease. The forecast was for it to blow itself out by mid-morning, and it did. The wind was still strong but not gale force and the rain had stopped. More rain was predicted for later in the day but by then Marvik hoped to be talking to Bryony Darrow.

The boat bucked and rolled in the long, high waves as he traversed slowly across the Solent to the island. Eventually, just on two, he eased the craft into the relatively quiet waters of Newtown Harbour and moored up on the pontoon close to his rented cottage. He hurried towards his Land Rover Defender, hoping it would start. He hadn't used it since Crowder had summoned him to Hamble on Friday morning. It seemed longer than that. He didn't stop to enter the cottage. Everything looked OK from the outside. He had no neighbours, which was the way he preferred it. He'd chosen to rent it for its isolation and peace, affording him the chance to re-evaluate his life after that first failed maritime mission in Civvy Street. He'd wanted time to reflect on his future. And now? What did he want? He wasn't sure and the present was not the time to consider such matters.

He climbed into his car and headed towards Fishbourne and the car ferry to Portsmouth. He caught the three o'clock sailing and estimated that by the time he got to Portsmouth, through the city traffic and to Eel Pie Island it would be about five thirty p.m. if the A3 to London wasn't too busy. Again he considered, as he'd done several times throughout the day, if he was wasting his time, not only because Bryony Darrow might have nothing to tell him about Oscar Redburn's connection with her grandfather but she might not even return home. For all he knew, that audition might lead her to being immediately summoned to Hollywood. Strathen said it hadn't when Marvik called him on the ferry.

'It would be all over social media if she had,' Strathen announced. 'I'm still at Kew but I've managed to get more on Bradley Pulford's death in 1959.'

Marvik listened eagerly in the quiet corner he'd found on the ferry away from other travellers. There weren't many.

'Pulford was working on board the merchant cargo ship the *Leonora* on 14 August 1959 while it was docked at Singapore. He started his cargo watch at six a.m. along with three other men. All the crew were British, as was normal in those days, instead of a mixture of foreign nationals. Pulford was keeping watch that the cargo was being loaded correctly into hold number one. Another man, Sandlings, was on hold number two and there was a man on watch at the gangway — Hampson. They were all out of sight of one another, the boat being huge, although not as gigantic as they are these days.'

Marvik could see one heading towards the ferry — it was packed so high with dark red and blue containers that the bridge was hardly visible.

'The third officer was in the ship's office when, at six fifteen, Sandlings radioed up to say that the cargo was loaded into hold number two. He was told to radio Pulford and tell him to get some breakfast. When he got no response he assumed Pulford had switched off his radio or turned the volume down. Sandlings went off to breakfast and Hampson joined him fifteen minutes later. At seven twenty, when Pulford still hadn't shown for breakfast, Hampson began to ask if anyone had seen him. No one had. He alerted the third officer and they began a search for him. They found him lying eighty-five feet below in the bottom of cargo hold one, bay sixteen. The third officer immediately alerted the Master, a Jim Albany, who radioed the quayside to call an ambulance. It was too late, though. When the crew reached Pulford it was obvious he was dead. The post-mortem found Pulford died of multiple fractures. Tests showed there was no alcohol or drugs in his system. Neither had he suffered a heart attack, aneurism or stroke. He was found lying face down. It was customary for the crew to walk across hatch covers above partly open holds and it was concluded that this was what Pulford had done and had slipped.'

'Or was pushed,' Marvik said. 'By a crew member, perhaps? This guy, Hampson. He showed up late for breakfast.'

'Someone could have got on board from the dock. There was no one on the gangway after Hampson went down for breakfast. And although we don't know the exact details of Jack Darrow's death twenty years later, it sounds remarkably similar.'

'If Darrow was killed by the same person who killed Pulford then it certainly wasn't Oscar Redburn — he was only two years old in 1959. But, *if* Pulford was killed, what did he know or do to make him dangerous enough to be taken out?'

'It might have been an internal squabble with another crew member, or perhaps it *was* just an accident.'

'You don't believe that any more than I do. Why would someone take his name thirty years later?'

'Could still be a coincidence and the Pulford of 1989 just happened to be walking past that graveyard.'

'Then he'd have been taking a detour around it because that grave was at the rear.'

'Maybe he just liked visiting old churches.'

'Yeah, and maybe I can walk on water,' Marvik said, eyeing the container ship as it drew closer. Car alarms were sounding on the ferry as it rolled in the swollen waves. 'What happened to Pulford's personal effects?' he asked.

'They must have been shipped home along with his body.'

'And someone must have paid for the burial and that headstone.' He hadn't forgotten that he had intended to check out the stone masons, only tragic events had overtaken that. Anyway, he thought, the stone masons of 1959 might no longer be in existence.

Strathen said, 'The shipping company might have coughed up for it or the Seamen's Charitable Association. I'll see if I can find out.'

Strathen rang off. Marvik spent the remainder of the ferry crossing thinking over Pulford's death in 1959. It didn't get him much further so he postponed it as he negotiated the motorway out of Portsmouth and headed towards London. The traffic was heavy and he got caught in the tailback on the Hog's Back at Guildford caused by an earlier accident. Eventually, though, he arrived at the Embankment at Twickenham and parked the Land Rover in a residential area just beyond the pay-and-display car park. No cars were permitted on the tiny island, a fact he'd checked out that morning while kicking his heels in Poole waiting for the storm to subside.

He made his way across the footbridge over the River Thames — it was the only access to the Island — and turned right along the lane until he found the small, detached redbricked cottage at the end of it. Ahead was a copse. The house was squeezed between a large detached one on its left and a chalet style one on its right, the last in the lane. There was no sign of life in either property and neither had there been in the handful of houses he'd passed on the way. Most were obviously used as weekend retreats or holiday homes. There was also, disappointingly, no answer to his knock on Bryony Darrow's door. So perhaps she was working in that cocktail bar that Strathen had mentioned, or still kicking her heels at that audition.

He surveyed the tiny brick-built cottage with only one window on the ground floor to the left of the door and another window above it, but even such small properties like this cost a fortune to buy here and he didn't think Bryony Darrow was the type of actress who could afford it. But then, for all he knew she could be shacked up with a rich boyfriend, or perhaps a sugar daddy paid for it. Whatever the case it didn't matter — what did was talking to her and Marvik felt restless and irritable at the delay and increasingly frustrated that he'd come here probably for nothing when he might have got more out of Freynsham. Sometimes, though, following your instinct got results. And he, like Strathen, knew they had to follow this line. He just hoped they were right. There was nothing for it but to wait for as long as it took, until midnight if necessary — maybe all night if she was at a party celebrating the fact she'd got the part. Or she could have decided to stay with a lover for the night. If there was no sign of her by midnight he'd drive back to the West Country and shake something out of Freynsham, which was probably what he should have done in the first place, given that he could be Sarah's killer.

The house backed on to the River Thames. Opposite it was a long line of hedges and trees. There were no streetlights. It had started raining again, but this time a thin, irritable drizzle. The light was fading fast. He could hear the drone of the traffic from the urban sprawl of Twickenham behind him. Across the river lay another urban sprawl punctuated by fields and Richmond Park.

He headed for the copse and found a vantage point where he could see anyone approaching the cottage and where he could shelter from the worst of the rain even though the trees weren't in leaf. As the minutes ticked by he became increasingly convinced that she wouldn't show. Maybe she'd gone straight from that audition to a job in a cocktail bar, or a coffee shop or retail outlet. If that was the case he hoped she didn't work long hours.

It was just before seven when he saw a woman approaching and from Strathen's description Marvik knew it was Bryony Darrow. She was wearing a red coat, knee-high black boots with a low heel and a frown on her attractive face. Her phone was in her hand and her eyes glued to it while her fingers slid over the screen. She barely looked where she was going but pushed open the iron gate as though on autopilot and marched up the path, only lifting her eyes from her phone to unlock the weatherworn door. Marvik saw the hall light flick on and was about to follow her when he froze. Two coppers were heading towards him, and to the house at the end of the lane.

He shrank back and watched as they knocked on the cottage door. Bryony Darrow opened it; she had removed her coat to reveal a short, woollen, sleeveless black dress that clung in all the right places on her slender yet shapely figure. It had zipped pockets on either side of her hips and they were nice hips. Marvik couldn't hear what was being said. He watched the surprised reaction on her fair face and then a troubled expression crossed it as she stepped back to let them in. Perhaps there'd been a burglary in the area. Or perhaps she'd committed a crime and they were questioning her about it. But it disturbed him that the police had arrived now. Their timing was interesting, to say the least.

They weren't inside for long. Within ten minutes she was letting them out. As the door closed on them, and they headed back down the garden path, the younger male cop talked into his radio. They turned and made for the Embankment. As soon as they were out of sight Marvik walked up the path, lifted the brass knocker and rapped loudly. The door was flung open and Marvik found himself facing a clearly upset Bryony Darrow. He wondered if the police had come to break bad news to her about a family member — if so, now would not be a good time to ask her about her grandfather's death. She started visibly at the sight of him — his scars probably alarmed her. Fear flashed into her blue eyes. The door closed a fraction.

Hastily, he apologized for disturbing her, adding, 'I'd like to talk to you for a moment. My name's Art Marvik. It's about—'

'Marvik?' Her eyes widened. 'You've come about Sarah?'

'You know her?' he asked, amazed.

'She moved in last week, that is her things are here but she had to go straight out on a marine expedition.'

Marvik thought rapidly. Of course. The police had traced Sarah's address to here and had just told Bryony about Sarah's death. But had they asked about him? No, it was too soon for them to have discovered his identity from phone records. But Bryony Darrow had recognized his name, which meant Sarah must have spoken of him after their meeting.

'Can I come in?' He didn't give her a chance to refuse but entered, forcing her to step back. Her eyes flicked over his face, resting briefly on the scars and away again as though embarrassed.

He wondered how the police had managed to trace Sarah here given that Crowder had said her previous landlord didn't have a forwarding address. Perhaps she'd hired a car or van to move her belongings and the police had obtained the address from them. Or maybe she'd mentioned where she was going to live to a neighbour. However they had obtained it, it was strange she had decided to move here, miles from the sea. OK, so she was surrounded by a powerful river that led to the sea but it was hardly what he would have expected of a marine archaeologist. He'd have thought a coastal location more to Sarah's taste, such as the one she'd vacated at Eastbourne. But then what the hell did he know about her tastes? All he knew was that she'd had a lovely smile, shy, kind eyes, an apologetic manner and had been passionate about her subject and about her missing father, and that was why she had come here — she had teamed up with the granddaughter of a man who had known her father.

'My parents were marine archaeologists. That's how I know Sarah,' he explained.

'She told me.'

'When? On Sunday?'

'Yes. She was very excited about meeting you.'

'Did you tell the police this?'

'No. Why should I?' she said, puzzled and eyeing him uncertainly.

'You know about Sarah's death and that she was murdered.'

She nodded. 'The police have just told me. I can't believe it. Why would anyone kill her?' But she was studying him as though she was coming to the conclusion that he might have done so.

'Sarah said she'd been researching my parent's expeditions,' he bluffed. 'I wondered if there was something in her belongings about them. I don't want the police to get hold of anything. It's private. Where are her things? Upstairs?' He saw by her expression that they were and before she could protest he was heading down the narrow hall towards the stairs.

Searching for papers about his parents was the last thing on his mind: he was keen to check if there was anything in Sarah's belongings about her research into her father's disappearance. He'd ask Bryony about that in a moment, but first he wanted to see what there was. And his timing had been good because the police hadn't searched through her belongings yet. Those two coppers hadn't been inside the house long enough for that, and nothing had been taken away by them. But then they wouldn't know that her father's disappearance could have anything to do with her death — it still might not have — but he didn't believe that for one second.

Bryony Darrow hurried after him but halted on the stairs as her phone pinged. On the landing Marvik paused for a second. There were two bedrooms, one at the front of the house and one at the rear next to the bathroom which he could see through the open door. It must have been converted from a bedroom because in the days when this house had been built, around the turn of the twentieth century, there had been no bathrooms — just a tin bath in front of a coal fire and a toilet in the backyard.

He entered the front bedroom and crossed to the window without putting on the light. Scanning the road he couldn't see anyone loitering and there was no police presence. Bryony entered and switched on the light. Marvik hurriedly pulled across the curtain and turned to survey the neat, small room. There were three large cardboard boxes on the floor. The bed was made up but there were no personal items such as make-up and jewellery on the dressing table or the chest of drawers. He turned his attention to the boxes, which were sealed. Withdrawing his penknife, he slit open the one marked 'books and files', silently grateful that Sarah had been methodical.

'Did the police ask you about her things?' he said, taking out the items and placing them on the bed after briefly studying them.

'Yes. I told them they were here but they didn't come upstairs. Look, I'm not sure you should be doing that?' she added anxiously, her nail-varnished fingers playing with her phone.

Ignoring her, he briskly checked the contents of the box with growing disappointment. There was nothing that looked as though it was remotely connected to Sarah's father. That information could be on her computer. And that was missing, same as his parents' computer had been, he suddenly thought, *if* they'd had one. He didn't know, but the reason it had flashed into his mind was because he was staring at his father's name. His heart constricted. His lie to Bryony had become a reality. On the notebook he was holding was written 'Professor Dan Coulter' in Sarah's handwriting. But before he could register the full impact of what he was seeing he caught the sound of movement outside; it could have been the wind in the trees or an animal but he didn't think so. He stuffed the notebook into the inside pocket of his jacket.

'You can't take that, it's Sarah's,' she cried.

'She doesn't need it now.' His prints would be all over the room but that hardly mattered as Bryony Darrow would tell the police he had been here anyway.

'I think you'd better leave.'

He did, too, because his finely tuned senses had caught the sound of movement from outside. Speedily he crossed the room, switched out the light and returned to the window, where he drew the curtain back a couple of inches. Yes, there it was: a darkly clad figure at the front of the house. And it was no police officer.

He turned and grabbed her hand.

'What are you doing?' she cried, pulling back from him.

'Be quiet,' he commanded.

'Let me go,' she cried, struggling to release herself but his grip was too strong. She winced and applied her other hand to prise his fingers from her wrist but she could only let herself be pulled along with him on to the landing.

'There's someone trying to break into the house,' he said.

'Then I'll call the police.'

He caught the sound of the letterbox being pushed open and the unmistakable smell of petrol. 'Too late for that. By the time they get here we'll be nothing but charred remains.' They couldn't go downstairs. The only option was the rear which backed on to the river. He pulled her into the bathroom.

'Please let me go,' she pleaded.

In order for them to escape he had to release her but he couldn't let her do anything foolish such as rush downstairs. That way they'd both be killed.

'You have to trust me, Bryony,' he said earnestly, turning to study her terror-stricken features. 'Sarah was killed because of something she had discovered about her father and that makes you vulnerable because the killer might believe you know what that is.'

'But I—'

'It's to do with your grandfather's death.'

She looked at him as though he was mad.

'There isn't time to explain now. We've got to get out of here. I have to let go of you to open this window and we have to climb out on to the kitchen roof and down into the garden. It's our only chance.' He could see she wasn't convinced. 'If you want to live and carry on with your acting career then I suggest you do as I say,' he added sharply.

She nodded. He released her hand but the moment he did she turned and fled on to the landing. He cursed and raced after her, but as she reached the landing there was a great crash and a roaring sound. The searing heat leapt up the stairs. She cried out and turned, petrified, towards him.

Marvik grabbed her and pushed her into the bathroom. 'Shove some wet towels under the door. Do it,' he bawled and she sprang to action. He examined the window. It was double-glazed and locked.

'Where's the key?' he shouted.

'I don't know,' she stammered, running towels under the cold tap in the bath and transporting them dripping to the door.

The smell of the fire reached in under the cracks in the door and floorboards. Bryony coughed. 'The top window is always open.'

That was no bloody good — only a child could get through it. He'd have to force the lock on the large window beneath it. Exerting all his strength, he pressed the handle down, noting that it was loose. Good. He did it again. He didn't have time to arse around with it; he pushed the might of his shoulders against the window jamb as he wrenched the handle. He could hear the fire crackling below. A neighbour or someone on the opposite bank would see the flames and call the fire brigade, but by the time they reached here it would be too late. He gave the handle another wrench and pushed at the window — this time it budged. He threw it wide open, thankful it was one very large window and hadn't been split into two. He reached behind him and grabbed Bryony. He could feel the heat of the fire on the soles of his shoes and smoke was drifting in through the cracks of the door.

'Climb out and sit on the window ledge,' he commanded.

She stared at him incredulously and made no move to obey. There wasn't time for a debate. In one fluid movement he reached out, lifted her off her feet and placed her on the window ledge. She cried out and gripped the underside of the ledge with both hands. He climbed out beside her. The fire hadn't reached the kitchen extension below. It was flat roofed but there was still a drop to it and from that to the ground of about eight feet. The roof was strong enough to walk on. There was no time to lose.

He jumped on to it, landing expertly, and reached his hands up to her. 'Jump towards me. I'll catch you.' She looked dubious. 'You have to, Bryony. It's your only chance. Do it. Now!' he barked.

She launched herself off and crashed into him. He staggered back but immediately steadied himself. He pulled her along to the edge of the extension.

'Stay there.'

She nodded, frozen, as he jumped down on to the ground, landing nimbly on both feet before rolling over and springing up. He knew she wouldn't be able to do the same but he'd already seen a garden table which he ran to and placed under the side of the extension.

'Climb down onto that. It's only a short drop from there.'

'It might be short to you but it looks like a bloody giant leap for mankind to me.'

He smiled despite the horror of the situation. She was still afraid but making a valiant attempt to overcome it. 'Imagine you're in a film,' he encouraged her.

She managed a terrified grin. 'Wish I'd given this part to the stand-in.'

She hesitated. As she did there was a great crash of exploding glass and she was on her belly lying on the flat roof, easing her way down with her hands clasping the roof, glancing behind her as she slid down towards the table. Marvik, already standing on the table, reached out, grabbed her, steadied her and then, jumping down on to the ground, urged her to do the same. Taking her hand, he shouted, 'Run!'

'Where to?' she gasped as she tried to keep up with him. 'There's only the river.'

They reached the bank. Marvik looked back at the blazing house.

Breathing heavily, Bryony said, 'Surely we're safe now.'

But they weren't. Or rather, he wasn't going to take a chance on that.

'We can't get across the river.'

'We can by boat.'

'I don't have a boat.'

'Your neighbour does,' Marvik said, glancing at the powerful modern motor cruiser moored up at the end of the neighbour's garden to his left.

'You can't just take it.'

Watch me. 'Climb over,' he commanded, nodding at the low fence.

When she hesitated he lifted her off her feet and plonked her down the other side. Then, vaulting over the fence, he turned to the boat, praying it had enough fuel to get them away. If it didn't there was a rowboat farther along the bank. He didn't fancy rowing on the Thames in the dark and the rain but he would if he had to. There wouldn't be a key in the boat but that wouldn't stop him. Bryony looked as though she was about to head back towards the house but, grabbing her, he pushed her towards the boat. 'Do you want to end up like Sarah?' he threatened.

Her eyes widened in horror. He couldn't take a chance on letting her go for fear she'd run round to the road in front of the houses. Marvik knew the arsonist would be waiting for her.

Keeping a firm grip on her, he unzipped part of the canvas awning and pushed her on board. Still holding her he promptly inspected the helm, then with his free hand extracted the multipurpose penknife from the pocket of his trousers. She had stopped resisting him and was staring around in stupefaction, shivering and hugging her arms across her chest; the shock was just hitting her. He'd have to risk letting go. He sat her on the seat at the helm next to the pilot and inserted a slim metal device into the key at the helm; turning it, he prayed it would start. The engine spluttered into life and with relief he saw that the tank was half full.

He could see the fire devouring the house and heard the distant sound of fire engines. Within seconds he cast off and, as he jumped back on board, in the light of the burning house, he saw a tall, lean figure in the garden of the neighbouring house. Would he come after them? No. The figure turned away and Marvik breathed a silent sigh of relief. He opened the throttle, headed out into the river and made for the centre of London.

CHAPTER NINE

The river was quiet. It was only as they drew closer to London that they passed a couple of working barges. The Thames Clipper and river cruisers had ceased to run for the day but Marvik kept his eyes skinned for the Metropolitan Police Marine Unit. He didn't think the boat they were on would be reported stolen for some time — it could be days before the owner visited his property and noticed it missing — but being on the river on a dark wet March night might be enough for the police to pull them over or note the name of the craft.

The city lights blazed either side of them and the squeal of brakes, the rumble of traffic and car horns grew louder and more persistent as they headed deeper into the city. Bryony remained silent, huddled in his waterproof jacket, sitting beside him at the helm. The drizzling rain was sweeping in behind them but they were protected from the worst of it by the canvas awning and the helm, and yet still it seeped into his bones and wrapped its depressing damp tentacles around him. Bryony's hair had gone curly with the damp and her face was drawn, blotchy and streaked with the black traces of smoke from the fire, as his must be. She dashed terrified glances at him as though at any moment she expected him to throw her overboard. She was understandably in a state of shock. He needed to get her shelter, warmth and a hot drink. For now he handed her his rucksack and said, 'There's a bottle of water in there.'

She hesitated but took it, and after a moment drank thirstily from the bottle and handed it back.

'You might want to use some to clean up your face. Here.' He found a tissue, soaked it and handed it to her.

'All my clothes and make-up were in that house,' she wailed, wiping her face.

'They can be replaced.' Marvik swallowed some water and then, pouring some in his hands, rubbed them over his face. 'Is there anyone you can stay with in London?'

'Why would anyone want to set fire to it? Why would they kill Sarah?'

'If there's no one you can stay with I'll book you into the services club or a hotel.'

She pulled herself together. 'No, I can stay with Liam. He has a flat near Earls Court. I'll have to tell him what happened.' She eyed Marvik with apprehension. Clearly she still didn't trust him even though he'd saved her life. He wondered, though, if he'd put her at risk by going there in the first place, just as his speaking to Sarah had led to her death. Had he been followed or tracked?

It seemed so.

'What did the police tell you about Sarah's death?' he asked.

'Not much, just that her body had been found on the beach at Swanage and they were treating it as suspicious. They asked if she had any boyfriends or had agreed to meet someone she'd been corresponding with online.'

'And you said?'

'I don't know. Sarah split up with someone five months ago.'

'Did you mention me to the police?'

'No.'

But she was looking at him as though she wished she had.

'How did they know Sarah was intending to live with you?'

'I don't know — they didn't say.'

He thought it was the truth. Perhaps Sarah had arranged to have her mail forwarded to the house on Eel Pie Island. 'Who else knows that you and Sarah were going to share a house?'

'No one. I haven't told anyone. I didn't see any need to. Besides, we only decided to a fortnight ago.'

'Why did you decide that? How did you meet?'

'Look, what is this, the third degree?'

He held her gaze before putting his eyes back on the river.

After a moment, she said, 'Sarah contacted me at the beginning of February through my website. She said that her father had known my grandfather and that she'd like to talk to me. She told me her father had disappeared while he was on the picket line with my grandfather in 1979 and she was trying to find out what had happened to him. We met here, in London, for coffee and got on really well. We emailed each other and met up a couple more times. She said she was giving up her flat in Eastbourne because she was going to Gibraltar on a marine expedition and was going to put her things in storage. I said why not leave them with me and stay with me until she went abroad. Now it's all burnt to cinders and she's dead.'

Marvik left a short pause before saying, 'What did you tell her about your grandfather's death?'

'Nothing, because I don't know anything!' she cried with exasperation. Then, more evenly, she continued, 'He was killed in an accident at the docks years ago, that's all I know. Dad never spoke about it.'

'And what did Sarah tell you about it?'

'The same. She didn't know any more.'

But Marvik wondered if that was the truth. 'Who helped her to move?'

'I did. I borrowed a friend's car. Can I call Liam?' He nodded.

She rose and headed out into the cockpit, unzipping one of the pockets in her dress and reaching for her phone. He heard her talking softly and reached for his phone. He found the contact details for Chelsea Harbour marina, called up the harbour master's office and said he was dropping someone off and would require a berth for a couple of hours, maybe less. Within fifteen minutes he was edging into the marina and Bryony had said that Liam was happy for her to stay with him.

'I'll have to tell the police about the fire,' she said, eyeing him nervously.

'Of course.' She'd mention him but by then he would be long gone from here and he hoped that by the time the London police connected it with the Dorset force's investigation into Sarah's murder, he and Strathen would have more answers as to why Sarah had been killed and by whom.

The lights from the exclusive riverside apartments blinked down at them through the rain on to the sleek, expensive motor cruisers moored up in the marina, making the craft they were on board look like an old tugboat. Marvik silenced the engine and tied off.

Bryony climbed off and handed him his jacket. 'I'll hail a cab.'

'I'll come with you.'

'No need,' she said hastily.

'I want to make sure you're safe and I don't expect you have any money on you?'

'I hadn't thought of that. My bag was in the house,' she said despondently.

But not her phone. That obviously never left her side.

'Here, take this.' He thrust some notes into her hand as they walked towards Lots Road. She stared at the money and then at him. He also gave her back his jacket, which she reluctantly took and put around her shoulders.

Marvik hailed a taxi. It didn't take long to reach Kempsford Gardens — it was just over a mile. He would have walked but he didn't think Bryony would have agreed to that.

He made to pay off the taxi but she had the cab door open.

'There's no need to see me in,' she said hurriedly. 'I'll be fine.'

'I'm sorry, Bryony.'

She paused and viewed him with a bewildered air. 'Yeah, well, I expect the experience will come in handy when I'm cast in the next James Bond movie.'

He smiled. 'I'll look forward to seeing it. Good luck.'

'You're not meant to say that to an actor. But I think it's you who needs the luck.'

He held her gaze for a moment and saw a flicker of something behind the blue eyes that he couldn't quite interpret. Perhaps it was guilt or regret, or maybe even sadness. He took back his jacket and watched her climb the stone steps to the door. She turned and waited for him to leave. He gave instructions for the driver to drive on and turn right just before the main Warwick Road, where he told him to stop. 'Wait for me,' he commanded, climbing out. He wasn't sure he would. It was a chance he had to take. 'Keep the meter running.'

'You bet I will, but will you be back to pay me?'

'Yes.'

Marvik ran back towards Kempsford Gardens, where he saw Bryony walking briskly in his direction. He returned to the taxi, told the driver to turn around and head towards Warwick Road. He was in time to see her climbing into a taxi. He gave instructions for his driver to follow it.

'Got another man, has she? Your girlfriend?'

Marvik made no comment. The driver shrugged and fell silent. They travelled east across London, over Waterloo Bridge, and were soon in the backstreets around Waterloo station. Bryony's taxi pulled up outside a five-storey Victorian house that had been converted into flats. It had seen better days.

Marvik paid off the driver and watched Bryony from the shadows of a property on the opposite side of the street. She didn't glance around but pressed the third buzzer in the row on the intercom and was admitted.

Marvik crossed the road and hurried to the house. He examined the card by the side of the door but the name had become illegible with age and weather. He didn't want to press the buzzer Bryony had tried, knowing that she wouldn't admit him and even if he gave a false name she might be suspicious. He wanted the element of surprise and to know who she was with. Liam, possibly, but why the elaborate charade with the Earls Court flat? Perhaps it was simply because she didn't trust him and was afraid of him. He pushed the first buzzer. No answer. He tried the second. A crackly, laconic voice sounding half asleep asked him what he wanted.

'I'm trying to get hold of the tenant in flat three. I've got a delivery. I can leave it outside his door.'

The door buzzed open without further questioning, even though it was very late for a delivery, but then maybe the owner of that flat didn't care or was used to packages being dropped off at unusual times. Marvik took the stairs two at a time. The house smelt of stale fat, curry and drains. The carpet was worn and stained, and the flaking paint on the walls was so caked with grime and grease that it was difficult to see what the original colour had been. Marvik wondered who Bryony could know living in such a dump — surely not a boyfriend or fellow actor or actress. He knew the acting profession was tough, but this tough?

On the landing he stepped around the litter of paper and cans. There was a pile of rags in the corner. He didn't dare to think what might be under them. What would Bryony have done if he hadn't given her money for the taxi fare? Marvik didn't think the occupant of this flat would have been able to have paid it. He doubted if he or she even had the price of a cup of tea! The place smacked of drug addicts.

Flat three was on the second floor. It faced the front of the house. Beside it was another door to flat four and behind Marvik, a corridor that led down to three further doors — two on the right and one at the far end facing the rear. Marvik rapped loudly and with force on the scuffed paint of the crumbling door on the left. He could bust it open in seconds but he waited, imagining a startled silence inside the room. No one came and no one looked out of flat four to see what the commotion was about. He rapped again, this time louder with his fist, and didn't stop until footsteps approached and the door eased open a crack. The pale, spotty face of a man in his early twenties peered at him with wary, bloodshot eyes.

'Bryony left something in the cab,' Marvik said, thrusting open the door and barging inside. The skinny young man sprang back with a cry of alarm, running a hand through his fair, dishevelled hair. His thin, dirty grey T-shirt hung off his skeletal frame and his tattered jeans off his waist, revealing the band of his underpants. The high-ceilinged bed-sitting room reeked of sweat and unwashed clothes. The furniture was shabby and dirty, the bed unmade and the sheets grubby. Clothes, cans of lager and takeaway foil trays littered the floor.

'Hey, you can't come barging in here.'

'Shut up.'

'I'll call the police.'

Marvik would have thought they were the last people this man would want sniffing around. He spun round, grabbed the boy's arm and twisted it up his back. He screamed in agony. Ignoring his cries, Marvik raised his voice. 'Bryony, are you coming out or do I have to break your boyfriend's arm?'

She stepped out of the small kitchenette, her face transfixed with rage. 'Let him go, you bastard.'

'With pleasure.' Marvik thrust the man away from him so that he fell sprawling on the unmade, soiled bed. 'Now shall I call the police?' Marvik reached for his mobile phone.

'No!'

'OK, so tell me who he is and why you tricked me.'

'He's my brother. Ben, are you OK?' She crossed to him. He nodded and rubbed his arm. Angrily, she rounded on

Marvik. 'Why the hell should I tell you anything? You killed Sarah.'

'If I did then why didn't I kill you?'

'Because you sent an accomplice to torch the house, only he didn't realize you were inside,' she snapped back.

'If I'm a killer why did I give you money and make sure you were supposedly safe with a friend? Why didn't I just throw you in the river and run over you with the boat?'

'Because . . .' But her words trailed off. She couldn't find an answer.

Marvik's brain was racing. There had been no Liam and maybe there had been no telephone call on the boat — Bryony had just pretended to call this mythical Liam when instead she'd intended heading here all the time, but why? Because she believed him to be a killer? That much he could understand and maybe her brother was all she had left in the world, except he would have expected her to go running to a lover if she had one and if not a girlfriend. In her profession there would have been many associates she could have called on to help her. So why here? Was she afraid for Ben?

He took in the scruffy, filthy flat, his eyes narrowing as they rested briefly on the crooked fire alarm close to the kitchenette. He crossed to the window, keeping his back to it and his eyes on Ben and Bryony while his mind teemed with thoughts and his ears picked up the sounds in the street. There was a motorbike cruising slowly. It stopped but the engine kept running. He glanced out. Yes, there it was — a few houses down on the right. Not a powerful Hondo but a Triumph, and a rider clad in black. He was about the same height as the man who had tried to run him down but bulkier. Maybe he lived here? Perhaps he was lost or delivering something, or perhaps he was waiting for someone. Him or Bryony?

Marvik stepped away from the window. 'Now that you're safe in your brother's hands, I'll leave you in peace.' He made no effort to move, though.

She marched to the door and threw it open. After a moment he swiftly crossed the room but when he reached her, he grabbed her arm, pulled her outside and yanked the door shut behind him. Putting his hand over her mouth to prevent her from screaming, he pulled her a little way along the corridor and hissed in her ear, 'I'm not a killer but there is one on your trail. He tried once at the cottage and he's going to try again. You and Ben have to leave here at once. You're not safe. The flat is bugged and there's a video camera behind the smoke alarm.' Her eyes widened. 'I'm not kidding. If you don't believe me then take a very careful look out of the window when you go back and you'll see a motorbike rider in black who is watching this flat. I can lead him away but I've no guarantee that he won't come back and deal with you and your brother. Sarah was killed because of her father and he's the link between you and her. Sarah began to ask questions about his disappearance in 1979 and came to you. She's dead because of it and you will be too. Your grandfather could have been murdered.' Marvik saw that he'd struck a familiar chord. Maybe it was what Sarah had believed. 'I'll let you go. You can scream if you like or call the police but they won't protect you. I hope I can.' He released her. She said nothing but stared at him, confused and afraid. He said, 'You need to leave now and make sure Ben comes with you.'

'How do I know you're not luring us to our deaths?'

'You don't, but if you want to hang around and be killed, fine. That arsonist could have set fire to the house any time after Sarah's death but he didn't. He was waiting for you to arrive home. But the police turned up and then me. The arsonist didn't want those coppers' deaths on his hands — it wasn't part of his plan — but he wasn't worried about me.'

'This can't be real!' But there was doubt in her eyes and her voice.

'We haven't got much time. Tell Ben that you need a drink after everything that's happened and you need company — his. Promise him a drink, drugs — whatever you need to in order to get him to leave with you. I'm going now; otherwise our motorbike rider will wonder what we're doing. Tell Ben I made a pass at you. We got chatting and you thought that maybe you might take me up on my offer of a drink. Think of something — you're an actress so act the part.'

She gave a tired smile.

'Make for Waterloo East station as though you're going to the bar next door. You know it?'

'Of course.'

'Turn into the station. I'll be there waiting for you.'

She nodded.

'Switch off your phones.' He didn't want anyone picking up their location on that.

He left, hoping and praying that she'd do as he asked. He didn't turn to look at the motorbike but he could hear the engine running. It didn't follow him, which bore out his theory. At the end of the street he turned right and then left and was soon heading towards the entrance to Waterloo East. Inside he bought three tickets for Charing Cross, and then called Strathen on his pay-as-you-go phone. He gave quick instructions without explanation.

As he waited by the entrance he listened for the sound of that motorbike, trying to pick it out from others he could hear roaring past on the Waterloo Road along with the squeal of brakes and rumble of the buses. Music from the nearby bar and the voices and laughter of smokers outside mingled with that of the screeching and clanking of the trains on the lines behind and above him.

Then they entered, Ben looking dazed, Bryony frowning with concern. She hurried towards Marvik, pulling her brother along with her. She was wearing a baggy old green jumper of her brother's over her black dress.

'He followed us,' she said breathlessly.

'Hey, I thought you said we were going for a drink,' Ben protested.

'We are but not here,' Marvik answered, urging them along to the platform as a train was coming in. 'Get on.'

They did and within seconds the doors shut and the train was pulling away. There was no sign of the man who had been on the motorbike. Within three minutes they'd be at Charing Cross. Would the motorbike rider know that was where the train was heading? Would he get there before them or before Marvik could get a taxi? He hoped not.

Marvik instructed Ben to remove his shabby jacket, which he did with a resigned shrug. Marvik expertly searched it and the hem with Bryony eyeing him with disbelief. None of the other six people in the carriage took a blind bit of notice. He handed it back to Ben as they pulled into the station. It was free of a tracking or listening device.

He hurried them through the station and climbed into a waiting taxi, giving the driver instructions to make for Chelsea Harbour marina, just over four miles away. There was no sign of the motorbike rider or anyone following them. At the marina he led them down to the boat.

Worried, Bryony said, 'We're not going back to Eel Pie Island, are we?'

'No. I'll take you to safety.'

'And where's that?'

But Marvik didn't answer. He broke open the hatch that led to the cabins below.

'There might be warm clothes or bedding in there.'

Bryony climbed down and Ben followed her.

Marvik cast off. He fuelled up, paid the marina manager for the fuel and the use of the berth, and headed up the Thames towards the sea.

CHAPTER TEN

Wednesday

It was dawn when he finally moored up at Sovereign Harbour Marina, Eastbourne, on the south coast where Strathen was waiting for him on his boat. They were sixty-seven nautical miles east of the Hamble where Strathen said he had set off from at midnight. Both Bryony and Ben were asleep in the cabin below.

Marvik had made good time and no one had stopped them. The boat probably still hadn't been reported missing. He'd stalled Bryony's questions. She didn't put up much resistance. The shock and drama of the evening coming on top of the news of Sarah's death had numbed her for the time being. She had been exhausted. Ben had said very little but Marvik had noticed how he was constantly fidgeting, sniffing and sweating. It looked as though he'd need a fix and pretty soon. Marvik would have to get him to a doctor but that might not be easy because Ben would have to give details of the medical practice he was registered with in London and admit to being a drug addict. He might already be listed as an addict, and although that information was confidential Marvik couldn't take the risk that the people intent on stopping them didn't have access to medical databases, especially the one that listed registered addicts. Whoever had bugged Ben's bedsit knew that he was hooked on heroin. They might even have been supplying him in order to get information from him. But what kind of information Marvik didn't know — he intended to find out.

'I'll wake them,' Marvik said to Strathen, who had climbed on board. 'We'll transfer to your boat.'

'I've got food, drink and warm clothing on board.'

'No methadone?' Marvik said, tongue in cheek.

'Like that, is it? Which one?'

'The boy.'

Strathen raised his eyebrows, forcing Marvik to add, 'Yeah, I know, by the time we were his age we'd already been on several missions and seen more of life than he'll ever see in his lifetime, and judging by the way he's going I doubt if he'll make old bones.'

Marvik went below and nudged Bryony who was asleep next to her brother. She had managed to find a blanket to cover them. She started violently and sat bolt upright, fear on her pallid face. Registering him, her expression relaxed. Rubbing her eyes and running a hand through her hair, she swung her legs over the side of the bunk and dashed a concerned look at her brother before asking where they were.

'Eastbourne. We're swapping boats. Wake your brother and come up on deck. And hurry.'

She reached out and gave Ben a push; he groaned and stirred. Marvik left her to it. He was keen to get moving. They'd eat and drink on the move. He still needed explanations from Bryony, and the police were bound to be looking for her, but Strathen said he hadn't picked up any news on the fire yet.

'Did you find anything in the house?' Strathen asked.

'Only a notebook with my father's name on it.'

Strathen's eyebrows rose. Marvik would have said nothing except for the fact that Bryony might let it slip and he didn't want Strathen to think that if he had held out on that he might be holding back on other information.

Murmured conversation came from below. Marvik heard Bryony's sharp tone ordering her brother to do as he was told. She appeared on deck and started at the sight of Strathen, not because he had a prosthetic leg, which didn't even show beneath his casual trousers, but because she hadn't expected company. Her surprise gave way to a dubious expression and Marvik said that he and Shaun had worked together in the Marines.

'But you're not working for the Marines now,' she said, still bewildered. 'Just who do you work for?'

'Ourselves,' Marvik answered shortly. 'Let's get moving.' He indicated the boat moored up next to them. Bryony gave it the quick once-over and then nodded. She obviously approved. And why shouldn't she? thought Marvik. It was larger, more powerful and far more modern than the one they had been travelling on. Ben didn't seem to take much notice of it. With his shoulders hunched and his hands in his pockets, he shuffled on to Strathen's boat sniffing, shivering and twitching.

Strathen told Bryony she'd find a couple of warm jumpers and jackets below in the forward cabin. 'They'll be far too big for you but they'll do the trick. There are also two buoyancy aids — you'd better put them on.'

'We're not planning on abandoning ship, are we?' she said half-jokingly.

'Just a precaution. And if you're hungry there's bread, eggs, bacon, tomatoes and sausages. And coffee and tea.'

She went below as Marvik cast off and Strathen manoeuvred the boat out of the marina and into the English Channel. To Marvik, he said quietly, 'The weather forecast isn't good.'

The early morning sky was heavily overcast. There had been a respite in the rain for a few hours overnight but as Strathen had said it looked set to return and the wind was already picking up.

Bryony called up. 'Do you want something to eat?'

'Bacon sandwich would be nice,' Strathen shouted back.

'Make that two.' Marvik had forgotten when he'd last eaten. 'Any progress at your end?'

'I couldn't find anything more on Bradley Pulford — the real one, that is — but then how do we know that the real one is buried in that grave at Steepleridge?'

Marvik eyed Strathen, troubled. 'But his body was identified by the crew and the captain.'

'You're right. I just threw that in as a possibility. I don't think they would all have lied or colluded in saying he was dead when someone else was lying in the bottom of that cargo hold.'

Marvik could hear the clattering of plates and the welcome smell of bacon wafted up to them. 'Her brother's bedsit is bugged and there's a small video camera behind a crooked smoke alarm.' Strathen cocked an eyebrow. Marvik continued, 'A motorbike pulled up outside and followed them to the station. It wasn't the same one that tried to run me down.'

Before Strathen could comment, Bryony called out, 'Do you want to eat up there?'

Marvik went below.

'It's getting a bit choppy,' she said warily. Ben was looking paler.

Marvik took over cooking the breakfast and in a few minutes, he was carrying two plates and two mugs of coffee up to the helm on the aft deck. Bryony followed with a plate of toast and a mug of tea for herself. Her body swayed and staggered with the roll of the waves and her eyes narrowed with concern at the grey swirling mass of sea ahead.

Strathen put the boat on autopilot and flipped the seating round from the helm to face Marvik and Bryony across the table. The deep coving around the seating and the canvas awning protected them from the elements.

'Ben's not hungry,' she said. 'I'm not sure I am.' But she bit into her toast. Marvik could see that she was lost in thought. Her make-up had worn off and she looked younger and prettier.

'I wonder if I would have got the part?' she said after a moment. 'I was auditioning for *Eastenders* yesterday. It went well. They called me back for today. They'll give it to someone else now. Might have been a breakthrough for me.'

'There'll be others.'

'I bloody well hope so.' She rounded on him, suddenly angry. 'If you hadn't arrived, I'd have been in with a chance. Instead, I'm on this damn boat in the middle of a shitty sea heading God knows where. Why?'

'You know why,' Marvik answered solemnly, picking up his mug of coffee.

'You can't seriously think this has anything to do with my dead grandfather, Jack Darrow?'

'What do you know about him? And this time the truth, Bryony. Please.'

She looked about to repeat she knew nothing, then exhaled. 'It's not much and it doesn't explain why Sarah was killed,' she began belligerently. She sipped her tea and continued, 'Sarah's father, Oscar, was friendly with Jack — they were on the picket line at the docks during a strike in 1979. Oscar disappeared and Jack was found dead at the bottom of a cargo hold. I didn't know about Oscar Redburn's disappearance until Sarah told me. I looked up the details of my grandfather's death in the press once. It said he'd probably committed suicide after filching money from the union. I asked my dad if that was true. He said how the hell did he know and not to rake it all up and upset my grandmother, so I didn't.'

'Until Sarah contacted you.'

'Yes.' She took another swallow of tea and stared across the cabin with a troubled expression at the rising swell of the sea beyond. 'We're not going to capsize, are we?'

Strathen answered, 'No, we'll be fine.' He took the boat off autopilot and slowed down.

'Go on,' Marvik encouraged Bryony.

'Sarah asked me if I had any of my grandfather's papers but I haven't and when I asked my dad he said he'd ditched everything after my grandmother died when he cleared out their council house, and besides there was nothing except pictures of their wedding and family outings, which he'd also thrown away. He said he had nothing relating to Jack and he didn't want it. It was as though he was ashamed because he believed the suicide theory and that Jack was a thief. But Sarah said that a lot of dirty tricks were employed during the strikes by the press trying to rubbish the strikers. I thought there must be an official report on the accident somewhere but I'm hopeless at research so Sarah took it up and she found it incredibly difficult to unearth the information. Apparently ports are very casual about reporting accidents and were even more so in 1979. She couldn't find any official report into the accident; even the shipping company didn't have a record of it.'

Marvik addressed Strathen. 'Shouldn't they have lodged it somewhere?' he asked, thinking that Pulford's accident in Singapore had been recorded.

'I can check but if the accident was on British soil and on a British ship then it wouldn't be in the Registry of Shipping and Seamen — that only contains deaths at sea and in overseas ports.'

Bryony continued, 'I requested a copy of the death certificate which told us nothing. Sarah helped me apply to the coroner's office for a copy of the inquest and that gave us slightly more. There was no cargo being loaded or unloaded because of the strike but there was still cargo on board the ships that had come in before the strike was called and it was to one of these that Jack had gone. The cargo was stacked up and there was a gap between each tower. The men used to walk across the top of the cargo stacks. Either Jack misjudged the gap and fell to his death or he deliberately threw himself down into the hold, unable to face the shame of what he'd done.'

A striking similarity to Pulford's death, and Marvik knew that Strathen was thinking the same.

Strathen said, 'Was any of the union money found on his person or in his house or bank account?'

'Not as far as I know.' She shivered inside the jacket Strathen had given her. It was too big and almost reached the top of her boots but that was an advantage in this weather even though they were under cover. 'It was years ago. And it was only a strike. People don't kill because of that.'

Grimly, Strathen answered, 'Don't you believe it. There was a lot at stake, especially then. The seventies was a decade of political turmoil with a succession of incompetent governments, ending in an election in 1979 that heralded eighteen years of a Conservative government and even more political unrest under Margaret Thatcher.'

'Yes, but whatever happened then can't have any bearing on things now,' she protested.

'It can if someone wants the truth to remain buried.'

'But what truth?' she cried, exasperated.

Strathen didn't answer and Marvik remained silent for a moment. They didn't know but whatever it was, it was explosive.

'Did you discuss any of this with your brother?'

'Yes, but he's not interested.'

Someone else was, though, and had listened in. Marvik wondered if the house in Eel Pie Island had also been bugged.

'What else did Sarah tell you?'

'Nothing. That was it,' she wearily replied. She bit into a piece of toast and then put it back on the plate, looking nervously at the heavy waves.

Marvik said, 'Did Sarah mention anyone else?'

'A man called Gordon Freynsham who was the last person to see her father. She'd been to see him but he said he couldn't help her. She'd hoped to get some pictures of her father but he said he didn't have any and neither did the university but I had one — have one.'

Marvik threw Strathen a look before his heart sank. 'Don't tell me it was in the house?'

'The original, yes, but I scanned it to my phone and to Sarah's. Do you want to see it?'

Marvik wished Sarah had shown it to him but he'd only met her once — why should she trust him? He nodded.

'It's on my phone. I'll fetch it.'

Marvik addressed Strathen. 'Will it be OK if she puts her phone on?'

'If the location tracker is deactivated possibly, but someone might still be hacking into her phone and the moment it's switched on it will send out an alert. We need to be quick.'

'I'll get her to send the picture to my phone.'

'Yours might also have been hacked.'

'The pay-as-you-go phone that Crowder gave me, then.'

Strathen nodded.

Marvik peered down into the cabin as Ben staggered up. 'I feel sick.'

He looked it. His face was grey, his eyes wild and staring, he was sweating profusely and trembling. Marvik quickly unhooked the rear of the canvas and steered Ben to a seat where he sat with his head over the side, retching.

Bryony followed her brother up on deck, looking very disturbed. She had her phone in her hand.

'Have you switched it on?' Marvik asked.

'Not yet.'

'We need to be quick.'

'Why?' Her eyes darted to Ben.

Strathen caught her meaning immediately. 'Where's Ben's phone?'

'On the table.'

Strathen rushed down and retrieved it. Climbing back on deck, he said, 'How long has he had it on?'

'No idea.'

And Ben didn't look in any fit state to answer. He was being violently sick. They'd have to get him to land and medical assistance as soon as possible. Marvik didn't want to run the risk of him dehydrating, which, given his seasickness and drug addiction, looked highly possible. His skinny frame was shaking uncontrollably as he leaned over the aft of the boat and he hadn't put the buoyancy aid on. The sea state was getting worse and the swell was increasing.

Stuffing his phone in the pocket of his trousers, Marvik crossed to Ben while addressing Bryony. 'Get me that buoyancy aid.'

She staggered below while Marvik tied a line to Ben's waist and clipped him on. He took the buoyancy aid from Bryony, who looked agitated, and managed to pull it over Ben's head without getting covered in spew. His face was deathly white, his eyes rolling and sunk in their sockets, and he couldn't stop retching. Bryony looked at him, horrified. Marvik gave her a line and clipped her on as she sat beside her brother with her arm around his shoulders, the boat rising and falling alarmingly.

Marvik took her phone from her, sent the picture to his and then switched hers off and handed it back to her. Fetching a bottle of water from the cabin, he said, 'We need to get Ben to hospital. Get him to drink some of this if you can; if not put some on his lips.'

She nodded, looking anxious. Marvik picked up the plates and cups and nodded at Strathen, who radioed up the coastguard.

Marvik put the dirty dishes in the galley sink and reached for his pay-as-you-go phone. He found himself studying five men — two were holding up a large banner brandishing the slogan 'A Fair Wage For Work'. The oldest of the men had to be Jack Darrow, a well-built, muscular man, good looking with fair hair and penetrating blue eyes in a square-jawed, rugged face. At the other end of the banner was a younger man, stocky, with a round face, a troubled frown, discontented mouth and deep-set eyes. He was of a similar age to the other three men in the photograph — early twenties — who were sitting cross-legged on the ground. On the left was unmistakably Gordon Freynsham with his narrow face and slightly feminine features, looking ill at ease, while beside him was a smiling and clearly confident Oscar Redburn with his long, light-brown hair framing a keen face. Marvik didn't know who the dark-haired, solemn man the other side of Redburn was but he looked sullen. Marvik got the impression that only Darrow and Redburn were comfortable with the photograph being taken. He wondered who had taken it and why Strathen hadn't found it in the newspaper archives.

Maybe it had been taken by a press photographer and then simply never used, but that didn't explain how Bryony had got hold of it. He climbed on deck.

Strathen said, 'The coastguard helicopter's on its way.'

They'd airlift Ben to hospital. They might even take Bryony with them. Would they be safe, though? He crossed to her. Ben was still retching violently.

'Bryony, where did you get this picture?'

'Ben gave it to me. Yeah, I was surprised he had it,' she added, interpreting Marvik's look. 'When I told Ben that Sarah and I were looking into granddad's past he said he'd found the picture years ago stuffed at the back of a drawer in grandma's house. He liked it because it showed what a rebel Jack was. Ben's a bit of an anarchist.'

Marvik doubted that. Ben didn't care about anything except where and when his next fix would come from. One of Darrow's colleagues must have taken it and given him a copy.

'Who's the man with your grandfather, at the other end of the banner?'

'No idea.' Her eyes flicked from her brother to the grey sky. 'Where's that helicopter?' Ben was groaning and Marvik could see he was on the verge of unconsciousness. Just then he caught the distant throb of a helicopter.

'He wouldn't be sick if you'd left us alone,' Bryony snapped. 'I don't want anything to do with those men and what happened back then. I wish I'd never answered Sarah's email. I wish I'd never asked her to share with me. I don't care what happened to Jack Darrow — all I care about is Ben.'

'He'll be OK,' Marvik reassured her, sincerely hoping that was the case. As the sound of the helicopter grew louder he unclipped more of the awning, leaving a small part of it covering Strathen at the helm, who had put the throttle into neutral. It had started to rain, that and the spray from the sea soaked them. Marvik had one more question to ask her. Holding his phone towards her he shouted above the wind, rain and the noise of the helicopter, 'Do you know who the other men with your grandfather are?'

'No.'

'Sarah must have pointed out her father to you.'

'Yes, of course she did.'

Crowder's words flashed before Marvik when he'd put the photograph that Freynsham had given him on the table: *You only have Freynsham's word it's Oscar.*

'Which one of them is Oscar Redburn?'

'What?' she cried tetchily, her eyes swivelling between the sky and her brother.

'Please, Bryony. It's important,' he shouted above the throb of the helicopter now hovering overhead. Strathen was on the radio to the helicopter pilot. 'Which one is Oscar Redburn?' Marvik insisted.

She glared at him, then back at the picture. 'Him, of course. That's Sarah's father.' She stabbed a finger at the picture.

'Are you sure?'

'Of course I am. That's what Sarah told me.' And that meant Freynsham had lied.

CHAPTER ELEVEN

Strathen dropped Marvik off on the pontoon at Gunwharf Quays, Portsmouth, where he quickly made his way through the waterside shopping complex and along to the nearby railway station. Strathen would continue his journey to the Hamble and his apartment where he'd resume his research into Jack Darrow and the union's past in the hope of identifying the man beside Darrow. Ben and Bryony had been airlifted from the boat and transported to St Richard's Hospital at Chichester. She'd wrenched off the jacket Strathen had given her, declaring she wanted nothing more to do with either of them. Marvik had asked her where she would stay now that she had nowhere to live. 'I've got friends. I'll call one of them,' she'd said coldly. Clearly she had no intention of telling him where that was. He urged her not to call them from her mobile phone but she'd eyed him with contempt. She blamed him for everything that had happened to her and her brother.

Consulting the departures board at the station, Marvik saw that he had twenty minutes before the train to Southampton. From there he'd catch the interconnecting train to Wareham and then a taxi to Kimmeridge Bay, where Freynsham's wife had told him on the phone he'd find her husband. He was filming there for most of the day. Marvik rang Crowder on the pay-as-you-go phone at the harbour railway station. Swiftly he brought him up to speed with events and the fact he was going to pay another visit to Freynsham and why.

'Bryony Darrow and her brother will need protection.'

'You know I can't authorize or arrange that,' Crowder replied.

Marvik did, but he'd asked anyway. It would have meant revealing that Crowder's department, the National Intelligence Marine Squad, were involved and that meant jeopardizing the mission.

Crowder added, 'Perhaps the local police will provide it once they connect her with Sarah Redburn and the fire at Eel Pie Island.'

And they would make the connection. The coastguard now had her details and they'd relay that to the police. Bryony would tell the coastguard officers and the hospital staff how she and her brother had come to be on board the boat and that meant the police would come knocking on Strathen's door. They'd ask for Marvik's whereabouts because his name was cropping up too frequently for the police to ignore — he'd had breakfast with Sarah, he'd called her mobile several times, he'd stolen a boat and he'd escaped a fire that could have killed the woman Sarah had befriended and where she had left her personal belongings. He wondered if the police might actually suspect him of setting the fire and then kidnapping Bryony and her brother. The latter didn't stack up, though, because he'd hardly have alerted the coastguard if that was the case.

Hitching up his rucksack containing some provisions and the notebook he'd taken from Bryony's house, which he still hadn't looked at, Marvik made for the coffee shop at the Wightlink ferry terminal where he bought a large coffee and returned to the platform to wait for his train. It was on time and, boarding it, he wondered if the police would search Ben's bedsit when Bryony told them the story, and if they'd find the listening device and surveillance equipment or if that would have conveniently vanished by the time they got there.

He swallowed his coffee, gazing out of the window as the densely urbanised streets of Portsmouth sped past him. As the train crossed the creek that made Portsmouth an island and swung west, Marvik's thoughts turned to the notebook in his jacket pocket. He had time to peruse it now but he didn't. He recalled that Sarah had said there was something else she had wanted to discuss with him — had it been the notebook?

He closed his eyes, just as he'd closed his mind to his parents and their fate for years. He'd been too busy to consider the past and often in too much danger to analyse why he'd shut them out. Langton, the psychiatrist, who had treated him after his head injury, said it was because they'd shut him out when he'd reached the age of eleven and he was trying psychologically to pay them back for that, and to deny the pain they'd inflicted on him because of it. Marvik thought that a load of old bollocks.

He was exhausted and needed sleep; he'd make do with forty minutes to Southampton and another hour from there to Wareham. Time enough after that to consider how he was going to play things with Freynsham. The train was scheduled to arrive at Wareham just after twelve thirty. He switched off all thoughts of the past and the mission and fell asleep almost instantly, conditioning his mind to wake within thirty minutes. It was a trick of mental discipline he'd developed during his years in the Marines. He woke as the train slid into Southampton station.

He climbed on to the train to Wareham and repeated the process, waking just before the train stopped an hour and ten minutes later at the country town situated close to the Jurassic Coast. He gave the taxi driver instructions for the small hamlet of Kimmeridge. It was about ten miles away. Marvik asked if there were any pubs or cafés close to the bay.

'There's Clavell's Café in the village of Kimmeridge,' the driver answered. 'It's run by a farming family and highly recommended.'

But Marvik wasn't interested in food. He thought that he might just find Freynsham and his television crew at lunch there. He couldn't envisage them sitting in the bay eating sandwiches, especially as it was cold and windy, but the heavy rain they'd had on the boat earlier that morning had already passed through the West Country, leaving an overcast sky and a dampness in the air that promised more to come. It wasn't ideal weather for filming.

Marvik hoped they hadn't abandoned it and that Freynsham hadn't returned to Lyme Regis because it would take him a while to reach there. But as the taxi rounded the bend in the country lane, Marvik spotted Freynsham's car in the café car park and asked the taxi driver to pull in.

There were five other vehicles parked. No one was sitting outside in the café courtyard and there was no one in the quiet and peaceful country lane. In the summer season it would be different. The area attracted a lot of visitors who flocked down to the rugged, spectacular bay, and as he made for the café entrance he saw opposite a sign adjoining some waste ground claiming that a Jurassic marine centre museum and exhibition gallery was to be built there. It made him think of Oscar Redburn and his last fossil-hunting trip, according to Freynsham, but Marvik didn't believe Oscar had ever come here or anywhere else along the coast, fossil hunting.

He pushed open the door and saw Freynsham sitting at a table in the corner along with two men and a woman. Freynsham looked up, started visibly and then frowned as Marvik crossed to him.

'A word,' Marvik said abruptly. Freynsham's colleagues' eyes swivelled to him, reflecting intrigue. Marvik wasn't in the mood for being polite.

'I don't think I have anything to say to you,' Freynsham said haughtily.

'In that case I'll sit down and say it.' Marvik made to draw a chair from a neighbouring table. 'Perhaps your colleagues will want to know all about your involvement with Os—'

Freynsham sprang up. 'We'll talk outside.'

'Pity. It's beginning to rain.'

Freynsham marched off, then paused and turned with a nervous countenance when he saw that Marvik wasn't following him. Marvik thought he detected amusement in the curious gaze of the film crew before he followed Freynsham. He had the feeling that Freynsham wasn't well-liked, only tolerated, and then barely.

Outside, Freynsham rounded on Marvik. 'What right have you to come here harassing me?'

'Think that was harassment? I haven't even started yet,' Marvik sneered. He grabbed Freynsham's arm tightly and forcibly marched him away from the café in the direction of a low building to its right. Freynsham tossed an anxious glance behind him.

'Worried they're filming this?' Marvik snarled. 'Perhaps it'll appear on an outtake. Oh, I'm not bothered about being identified. I haven't got a reputation to protect but you're a public figure. And when I let it slip that you killed a man—'

'That's a lie and you know it,' Freynsham protested, trying to free himself from Marvik's grip but it was too strong.

Marvik dragged Freynsham to the rear of the building out of sight of the road and prying eyes, not that there was anyone about and barely a car had passed them in either direction. If he needed to get rough there would be no witnesses but Marvik didn't think he'd have to go that far. The threat of violence would be enough to make Freynsham talk.

'Oscar Redburn vanished and now his daughter's dead. She came to you shortly before she was murdered. And the next words out of your lying little mouth had better be the truth or I'll beat them from you.' Marvik thrust Freynsham from him so violently that he staggered, lost his foothold and fell heavily back on to the muddy, leaf-strewn earth. Marvik loomed menacingly over the terrified man.

'I met her in February as I told you and that's all. It's the truth,' Freynsham gabbled.

'And you told her what?'

'That I had no idea what happened to Oscar.'

'And?'

'And nothing.'

Marvik grabbed the neck of Freynsham's sweatshirt and pulled him off the ground. 'Wrong answer.' He balled his fist as though to smash it in Freynsham's face.

Freynsham cowered back and held up his hands. 'I told her that her father was a manipulative bastard who cared sod all for the working man's revolution, or anything else. He was only interested in himself,' he cried, the sweat pouring off his brow.

'Now why would you tell her that?' Marvik didn't release his hold or lessen it.

'Because it's the truth.'

'Since when have you ever told the truth?' Marvik sneered.

'I did then and I am now.'

Marvik looked hard into his frightened face.

Freynsham hastily continued, 'I didn't want her to carry on looking for him, asking questions. I thought she might find out about the fossil.'

'What fossil?' Marvik said sharply.

Freynsham swallowed. 'The one I . . . he found.'

'Go on.'

'We used to go fossil hunting along the coast.'

'Not Oscar's scene, I would have thought,' Marvik said caustically.

'No, well, he only came with me twice and he struck lucky. All the years I'd been doing it and only minor finds, then he comes along and on the second trip discovers something amazing and very rare,' Freynsham said with bitter indignation. 'It was in a piece of rock from the Triassic period that dates back two hundred to two hundred and fifty million years.'

'And worth a lot of money?'

Freynsham nodded.

'And you killed him and stole it from him? Which was why you drove him to Lyme Regis the day he disappeared.' Was he right? Did that mean this had nothing to do with

Darrow's death or with Pulford — were he and Strathen just chasing shadows? If so, then why the fire at Bryony's house?

'I didn't kill him. He thought it was worthless.'

'Because you told him that.'

Freynsham swallowed and nodded.

'Did he believe you?'

'I don't know.'

Marvik was beginning to read between the lines. He still had hold of Freynsham. A drizzling rain that brought with it the feel and smell of the sea was driving into them. 'And when Oscar disappeared you helped yourself to it.'

'I went round to Linda's and there it was just lying in the kitchen among a load of junk. She had no idea that it was part of a rare fish that used to grind food with its mouth. I put it in my pocket. And the first thing that came into my head when she asked me where Oscar had gone was fossil hunting, and once I'd said it to her I had to say it to the police. It's why I didn't sell it for years. I thought it might look suspicious. It wasn't until I came back to the UK after working as a geologist abroad that I said I'd found it and I sold it to help establish the business.'

'And your reputation. And you never thought of giving any of the proceeds to Linda and Sarah,' Marvik said scathingly.

Freynsham coloured. 'That would have meant admitting Oscar had something to do with finding it.'

Marvik released his hold and pushed Freynsham away with disgust. He fell back but quickly scrambled up with a relieved expression that instantly changed to terror as Marvik reached into his jacket pocket. Clearly expecting a weapon, he let out a sob of relief when he saw Marvik withdraw his phone. Marvik found the photograph that he'd copied across from Bryony's phone and held it in front of Freynsham.

'Where did you get that?' Freynsham said, taken aback.

'Which one is Oscar Redburn?'

'You know. I gave you the other photograph. That's him in the middle squatting on the ground,' Freynsham said, puzzled.

That wasn't what Bryony had said. 'Who's this?' Marvik indicated the man on the end on the right, the one Bryony had told him was Oscar.

'Donald Brampton. He was studying politics and economics but he wasn't really interested in the downtrodden working man, and he's proved that.'

'How?'

'You've never heard of him?'

'Should I have done?' Marvik asked, trying to recall the name.

'Maybe not, unless you're into politics or economics. He's chief executive and owner of Front Line Economics. It's an international economic think tank that advises the government, business and the public sector. He's always popping up on TV and radio and he's frequently in the newspapers commenting on government policy, business matters, social and economic affairs. Getting involved in left-wing politics doesn't seem to have hampered his career,' Freynsham added acidly. 'But then he changed sides during the Thatcher years. After he got his Master's degree from the London School of Economics, where he went when he left Southampton Poly, he worked for the Adam Smith Institute, one of Margaret Thatcher's favourite think tanks. He obviously said and did all the right things because he's done very well for himself. He probably used that strike as a case study. I lost contact with him about fifteen years ago.'

Marvik wasn't sure that was the truth but he let it go. 'And the two men behind you?' Marvik knew who one was.

'The older man is Jack Darrow and beside him is Joseph Cotleigh. He worked with Darrow at the docks. Darrow was shop steward and Cotleigh was on the local trade union committee. If I remember correctly they were part of the National Amalgamated Stevedores' and Dockers' Union.'

'Where is he now?'

'No idea.'

'And Darrow?' Marvik asked, watching Freynsham closely.

'He died in an accident in the docks. Must have been just after that photograph was taken. I remember Oscar thinking that picture would make the newspapers or at least the local one, because a photographer from the local newspaper had turned up and taken some, but nothing appeared and Oscar was very pissed off about it. It was two days after that was taken that we drove out to Lyme Regis. Oscar had got bored with the whole protest thing. And I thought . . . well, you know what I thought.'

'When did you hear that Darrow was dead?'

'I can't remember. I was more concerned about Oscar being missing.'

'How did he and Darrow get on?'

Freynsham squirmed. 'Darrow was pretty scathing of us. He didn't rate students highly. And Oscar could wind people up. He'd come over as cocky and sometimes he'd take the piss out of things which to Darrow and Cotleigh were deadly serious. It was their livelihood they were fighting for but Oscar saw it as an opportunity to get himself in the limelight.'

'And you went along with it to be by your boyfriend's side,' sneered Marvik, and saw Freynsham flinch. 'What did Brampton get out of it?'

'Like I said, he just wanted first-hand experience of a dispute to help advance his political studies.'

'How did he react to Oscar's disappearance?'

'He said that Oscar had probably gone off to find a new cause which was more attractive, one with big tits and a nice arse. His words not mine,' Freynsham added with a sour note. 'He said Oscar wasn't interested in old fossils but tender young things.'

'You told him about the fossil?' Marvik asked, surprised.

'No, but Brampton knew I went fossil hunting.' Freynsham shifted and ran a hand through his wet, lank hair. 'Oscar couldn't have known the value of that fossil he found because I tried not to let on to him about it. I was furious he'd discovered it and he was mocking me so I said it was probably a woodlouse. He laughed and pocketed it. But now that I come to think about it maybe he did know, or suspect. He said he could read people like a book but I always thought he was too interested in himself to think about others. He did say something to me the last time we were together, though.'

'On the Cobb at Lyme Regis?'

'Yes. He said he was going on a treasure hunt.'

'You didn't mention that before,' Marvik said sharply.

'I've just remembered it.'

'Or made it up.'

'No. After I told him . . . well, you know . . . He laughed at me, said I was perverted and walked off. I called after him. I said, "Where are you going?" and he said, "Treasure hunting". I thought it was a snide dig at me and that he was going home to get the fossil and sell it.'

'Why didn't you run after him?'

Freynsham looked down. 'Because I felt ashamed and humiliated, then angry.'

'How did he get back to Southampton?'

'I don't know. Maybe he hitched a lift.'

'But he did return home?'

'Must have done because the fossil was there. Linda hadn't seen him, though. She was on night duty and when she arrived home late the following morning he wasn't there. She thought he must have gone out early.'

Or the previous night, thought Marvik.

'She was tired and went to bed. When he still hadn't returned the next day she phoned my lodgings and that's when I went round.'

Marvik left a brief pause before saying, 'What do you know of Joseph Cotleigh?'

Freynsham glanced nervously back in the direction of the café. 'Nothing. We didn't speak.'

'Bollocks. You were on the picket line with him, standing there freezing your balls off, waiting for the world's press and a few lorry drivers to turn up. You must have talked about something.'

'Please. I have to go.'

But Marvik loomed large over him.

'Oscar used to do most of the talking — bullshit I now know. Brampton was quiet but then he never said very much. Darrow was serious. He seemed a good man, well-liked and respected by his colleagues from what I could see. I got the impression that Cotleigh was his protégé. A rising star in the union but a bit hot-headed. Darrow was often trying to calm Cotleigh and Oscar down. They wanted to take more direct action but Darrow argued against it, said it would only backfire on them and make them unsympathetic with the public.'

'What happened to Joseph Cotleigh?'

'No idea.'

'You didn't ask him if he knew where Oscar had gone?'

'Why should I? I'd had enough of both Oscar and protesting. I knuckled down to my studies. You won't say anything about the fossil, will you?'

'Not unless I find you're lying or holding something back.'

'I'm not,' he cried earnestly.

'Did Sarah ask you about the people in this photograph?'

'No. I didn't know she had it. Where did you get it?'

Marvik pushed his phone back in his pocket and picked up the rucksack.

'Can I go?' Freynsham asked nervously.

Marvik held his stare a moment, then nodded. Freynsham scurried away in the direction of the café. Marvik followed and saw Freynsham hurriedly cross to the television crew who were standing by their car. They greeted him with curious stares and by their gestures were commenting on his dishevelled and mud-spattered appearance. Marvik wondered what he was telling them. Was there more he could have extracted from Freynsham? Possibly, but until he and Strathen had more information he didn't know what questions to ask. They climbed into their car and, Freynsham, with a nervous glance at Marvik, clambered into his. Maybe he should have asked Freynsham for a lift back to Wareham.

So, who had lied about the identity of Oscar Redburn? Freynsham or Bryony? Or perhaps Sarah had lied to Bryony when she'd pointed out her father in the photograph. He needed another opinion and he knew where he might get it. Retrieving his mobile phone, hoping he could access the Internet, he punched in Front Line Economics and was soon reading that their head office was in London. He rang the company and asked to speak to Donald Brampton. He was dutifully asked for his name.

'I'm an old friend,' he answered evasively, and was put through to Brampton's secretary.

'Doctor Brampton is at a conference,' came her reply when he asked to speak to him. 'Can I ask who's calling?'

'When will he be back?' Marvik asked.

'Not this afternoon. The conference finishes at five thirty and then there are drinks.'

'Fine, I'll catch up with him at the hotel. It's the Sheraton on Park Lane, isn't it?' Marvik named the first prestigious London hotel that sprang to mind.

'No, the London Marriott, County Hall.'

Marvik knew it. In fact, he'd motored past it last night on the boat with Bryony. It overlooked the Thames and wasn't far from the London Eye. It was also conveniently close to Waterloo station. He rang off. Two o'clock. He had four hours to get to London.

CHAPTER TWELVE

Marvik stepped inside the plush interior of the Marriot Hotel just off the South Bank and viewed the conference and meetings board in the lobby. He'd called Strathen at Wareham while waiting for the train to take him to Southampton and then on to London. He'd explained where he was heading and why and asked him to see what he could find on Joseph Cotleigh.

'How's Ben?' Marvik had asked.

'In a coma,' Strathen had replied. 'And Bryony's with him. The police haven't shown up here but they could have gone knocking on your door on the Isle of Wight.'

They'd be disappointed then, thought Marvik. He still had to collect his car from where he'd parked it last night at Twickenham. He wondered if the police had noted the cars in the area and matched them with local occupants, or run them through the vehicle licensing database. He doubted they'd had time.

There was only one conference flagged up on the board and it was the one that interested him: Economics and the Future of the Free Market. It was being held in the King George V room and he'd find that simply by heading towards the sound of voices coming from his right.

He marched briskly along the thickly carpeted, wood-panelled corridor, past the toilets on his right, noting that the whole area was dedicated to meeting rooms and there didn't seem to be anyone about. The voices grew louder and even before he reached the T-junction of corridors he could see, through the open door, a crowd gathered inside the conference room. The noise level was almost deafening, and he wondered if he'd ever locate Brampton in among such a crowd of predominantly dark-suited men.

Given his casual clothes he stood out a mile but he didn't care about that. He stood at the entrance and surveyed the packed room. There were only about five women in among what must be over a hundred men. Economics was obviously still a male preserve. A slight man with spectacles dressed smartly in a navy-blue blazer hurried towards Marvik.

'Can I help you, sir?' he asked politely, while eyeing him a little warily, not because of his clothes, thought Marvik, but perhaps because of his scars and build. The man's name badge said he was the event organizer.

'I'm looking for Doctor Brampton.'

The man scoured the room, then pointing to his right, said, 'He's over there talking to the woman in the red jacket. I'll fetch him for you.'

'No need.' And Marvik dived into the throng before the slight man could prevent him. Not that he would have done. As Marvik headed towards Brampton, his first impression was of a confident man who took pride in his appearance. His suit was good quality and clearly made to measure. He was stocky but Marvik thought that might easily turn to fat in a few years' time. His short, light-brown hair was peppered with grey, giving him an air of distinction rather than ageing him, but as Marvik drew closer he noted a puffiness about Brampton's cheeks that made him think of a hamster. And there was a smugness about his expression and appearance that said he was a man used to being listened to and having his own way. His face was less lined than usual for a man in his late fifties. He'd worn well, certainly better than Freynsham. Brampton could have passed for early fifties.

'Doctor Brampton, I'd like a word. It won't take long.'

Brampton's keen eyes rapidly weighed up Marvik while the woman beside him scrutinized him with interest.

'It's important. It concerns Oscar Redburn.'

That did the trick. Marvik saw a flicker of annoyance behind Brampton's eyes but his voice was silky smooth and showed no trace of anxiety or irritation as he addressed the woman in front of him. 'Will you excuse me?' Marvik almost expected him to add, 'my dear'. He wasn't sure what the dusky-skinned woman beside him would have answered to that — she simply raised her perfectly shaped eyebrows at Marvik and gave him a look that held promise and mischief.

He followed Brampton as he weaved his way through the crowd towards the door. No one stopped Brampton but a few of the delegates nodded at him and tossed Marvik a curious stare.

Brampton placed his half-full wine glass on the table by the door. It was clear he wasn't going to ask Marvik to join him in a drink. There was no reason why he should. Besides, Marvik would have refused it. He needed his wits about him and fatigue and alcohol did not mix.

He followed Brampton back down the carpeted corridor towards the small lobby directly opposite the entrance to the hotel. It was deserted. Marvik could see the uniformed doorman standing outside the glass doors, shuffling his feet in the brisk March wind. Obviously Brampton wasn't keen on being overhead by his contemporaries, although given the noise level of the crowded room Marvik doubted they would have been heard anyway.

There were easy armchairs placed in the lobby but Brampton didn't sit. It was his way of saying that he expected Marvik to leave as soon as possible and that he had little to say. As if to reinforce this, he began, 'I can only spare you a few minutes, Mr . . . ?'

'Marvik.' The name didn't appear to mean anything to Brampton. The grey eyes scrutinizing him were slightly puzzled. Marvik continued, 'I want to ask you about Oscar Redburn and the dockers' strike in 1979.'

'That was a very long time ago. What's your interest?'

It was said lightly but Marvik detected the edge of unease behind the smooth, educated tone. Brampton didn't exhibit as much surprise as Marvik would have expected. Was that because Sarah Redburn had approached him? But how could she have done? Freynsham hadn't given her Brampton's name and neither had Bryony because she had thought this man was Oscar Redburn. Why should she think that, though? Why had Sarah told her that? Or perhaps she hadn't and Bryony had simply got it wrong. She had been worried about her brother and hadn't been thinking straight when Marvik had asked her. No, if Brampton wasn't alarmed to see him then either Freynsham had forewarned him or Brampton was involved in Sarah's death and the fire at Eel Pie Island.

'Sarah Redburn,' Marvik said abruptly.

Brampton looked puzzled. 'I don't know her.'

'She's Oscar Redburn's daughter and she's dead.' Marvik watched him closely.

Brampton smoothed his tie with his right hand; the amber ring on his third finger matched the stone in his tie pin and his cufflinks. 'I'm sorry to hear that, but as I said, I don't know her.'

Marvik continued, 'Her body was discovered on Monday morning.'

'Tragic,' he uttered, looking sorrowful and glancing at his expensive watch. 'But I don't see what her death has to do with me.'

'She was strangled.'

He raised his greying eyebrows. 'Do the police know who did it?'

'No idea. I'm not a police officer and they haven't taken me into their confidence.'

Brampton continued to look bewildered. 'But you think her death has something to do with her father's disappearance?'

'Why should I think that?'

'You wouldn't be here otherwise,' Brampton snapped, dropping the mister smooth act. 'And you said you wanted to talk about Oscar. But I can't see how his daughter's death could be connected. Oscar disappeared years ago and I've no idea where he went or what happened to him.'

'But you were friendly with him. When did you last see him?'

'I can't remember exactly.'

'Then this might help you.'

Marvik removed his phone from his jacket pocket and showed Brampton the photograph. 'This was taken shortly before Oscar disappeared.'

Brampton scowled at it then up at Marvik. He looked very irritated. 'Where did you get that?'

'Did Oscar tell you where he was going?'

'No.'

Marvik caught the annoyance behind the word and the flash of concern in Brampton's eyes. 'Where do you think he went?'

'I have no idea except it was probably connected with a woman. He was married but only because he got the girl pregnant and she made him do the decent thing. That was the way it was back then. But Oscar hated being tied down.' Brampton cast an impatient glance over his shoulder towards the corridor, as though he was keen to get back to his après conference drinks.

'And?' prompted Marvik.

'And what? That's all I know, except that Gordon Freynsham thought Oscar had gone to the coast in search of fossils, but that's as likely as someone in the Russian mafia collecting seashells. Oscar used to laugh at Freynsham's fascination for old relics. He couldn't see the point of grubbing around for them.'

But maybe Redburn had changed his mind after he'd discovered that one such fossil he'd inadvertently stumbled on was worth sixty thousand pounds. Marvik had checked on the Internet on the train and found that piece of news tucked away on Freynsham's website. But had Oscar Redburn really gone on a fossil-hunting expedition with Freynsham? Or was that a lie? Maybe Freynsham had discovered the rare fossil and told Redburn about it to impress him. Redburn had stolen it and Freynsham had killed him and dumped his body in the sea before taking the fossil back. Sixty thousand pounds was a powerful enough motive for murder. But none of that explained why someone had shown up in Swanage in 1989 bearing the name of a man who had died in 1959 in Singapore.

Brampton continued, 'Oscar used to take the piss out of Freynsham. He knew Freynsham was in love with him. He thought it a huge joke. Who'd have thought Freynsham would end up on television with a big following, many of them women? Oscar would have been sickeningly jealous. He was the one the women flocked to. He was charming, clever and very ambitious. He'd have hated both Gordon's success and mine.'

'In what way, ambitious?'

'He *said* politically.'

'But that was a lie?' probed Marvik at the sneer in Brampton's voice.

'He was more interested in being in the limelight than serving the common man. Not that that doesn't apply to some politicians.'

'And I guess you'd know about that.' It was Marvik's turn to sneer.

'What do you mean by that?' Brampton sharply rejoined.

Marvik thought he'd hit a nerve there. 'You've rubbed shoulders with quite a few of them if the information on your website is to be believed. And you've changed your spots since these days,' Marvik indicated the picture. 'Not such the hot-headed activist now.'

'We all do foolish things when we're young. Now, I must be—'

'Who are the other men in the picture — the two behind you?' Marvik knew who they were but he wanted to check that Freynsham hadn't lied to him about the man beside Darrow being Joseph Cotleigh.

With an exaggerated sigh and an impatient glance at his watch, he said, 'I don't remember.'

'Try,' Marvik said, threateningly moving closer.

'It was a long time ago. I forget.'

'Then let me help you.' Marvik stepped even closer, forcing Brampton to take a step back. His eyes darted to the door but the doorman was looking outwards and no one was approaching.

'This man is Jack Darrow.' Marvik pointed to the younger of the two men. 'Or maybe not, given your reaction.'

Brampton shifted uneasily and his face flushed.

Marvik pressed on, keeping his voice low and threatening, 'He died soon after this picture was taken.'

'Why can this be of any interest to you?' Brampton cried in exasperation. 'As you said, Darrow is dead. They're both dead.'

'Both?' Marvik narrowed his eyes but held his stance.

Brampton exhaled. 'The other man is Joseph Cotleigh. Darrow fell, or threw himself, into a cargo hold on one of the ships in the docks that was waiting to be unloaded, and Cotleigh threw himself into the sea. Not a very glorious end for either of them.' There were beads of perspiration on Brampton's forehead but he resisted the temptation to brush them away. Only just though, thought Marvik, noticing his hand twitch.

'How do you know that about Cotleigh?' demanded Marvik.

'Because I was there when they both died. No, let me re-phrase that, I was still at Southampton Polytechnic. Jack Darrow died just before the end of the strike, probably about a day or two after that picture was taken, and Joseph Cotleigh's body was found on a beach in early February.'

'Where?' Marvik's antenna was twitching.

'On the south coast somewhere. Suicide. He'd helped himself to union funds.'

'I thought that was what Jack Darrow was supposed to have done.'

'They probably split it between them.'

'Did Cotleigh have any relatives?'

'I've no idea. Now I have to get back.' He stared at Marvik as though expecting him to leave but Marvik made no effort to move. Again he held out the photograph.

'Which one is Redburn?'

'Him, of course — the man between me and Gordon.'

So Freynsham had been telling the truth on that score. But he'd withheld information about Cotleigh being dead. He must have known that. Or perhaps he really had got down to his studies after Oscar had vanished as he'd claimed and blotted out everything else.

'That's all I can tell you,' Brampton snapped.

Marvik left a short pause, then nodded. Brampton faltered for a moment before brushing past Marvik and walking briskly along the corridor. Marvik watched him go. When Brampton reached the large conference room he turned. Marvik saw his worried stare before he swung back and almost bumped into the woman in the red jacket. They exchanged brief words, which to Marvik didn't look that cordial, before Brampton entered the conference room and the woman headed towards Marvik.

'Fancy a drink?' she asked, smiling at him.

'Not really.'

'Pity. You look far more interesting than those stuffed shirts.' She retraced her steps and pushed open the door to the ladies' cloakroom.

Any other time he might have accepted. She was mid-thirties, dark-haired with deep brown eyes and a very good figure. But his thoughts were preoccupied with Sarah. Besides, he needed to stay here to see what Brampton did next because it was clear he'd been unnerved by Marvik's visit.

He took a seat at the rear left-hand side of the lobby where he had a clear view of the entrance. Brampton had given him some interesting additional information. How much of it had Sarah discovered? Had she traced Brampton? He didn't think so. Was this connected with Pulford showing up in Swanage in 1989? Marvik hadn't asked Brampton if he recognized the name — maybe he should have done. And he hadn't forgotten the fact that Joshua Nunton had been reported missing shortly after Pulford. But did they have anything to do with Oscar Redburn and Jack Darrow or had he and Strathen stumbled on another crime that had no connection with the Killbecks, Bradley Pulford and the body that had been washed up on the Isle of Wight in January?

His head was spinning with it all and thudding with fatigue, the pain exasperated by his injury sustained in conflict. He massaged his temples, blinking several times, and then focused his eyes and reached for a strip of tablets in his jacket pocket. He'd swallowed two of the strong painkillers when, suddenly alert, he saw Brampton emerge from the corridor and exit the hotel. He didn't even bother to look at the lobby.

Marvik rose and followed but at a safe enough distance not to be spotted. Brampton headed across the concourse and out into Westminster Bridge Road where after a few paces he turned right down on to the South Bank. It was busy with commuters and tourists and Marvik weaved his way through them keeping Brampton, dressed in a black overcoat and carrying a black leather computer case, in his sights. It had stopped raining and the early evening lights were coming on in buildings that lined the Thames. Brampton was heading for the Royal Festival Hall. Marvik suspected he could be making for Waterloo station and home, wherever that was, but if he was then he had left the conference drinks party early, certainly before anyone else. Perhaps he had another engagement or was under orders to get home for an early dinner. Perhaps he'd grown bored with his fellow delegates. But Marvik's instinct told him there was something not right about Brampton and that his rapid exit from the drinks party had been prompted by his visit.

Brampton halted in front of Foyles bookshop and retrieved his phone. It must have rung. Marvik hung back. He expected Brampton to walk on with the phone pressed to his ear but instead he crossed to the river. Marvik watched a bulky man in his forties wearing dark clothes and a baseball cap rammed low on his face rise from one of the seats facing the river and cross to Brampton's side. Brampton still had his phone to his ear and now his lips were moving but Marvik didn't think he was taking any call. His conversation was directed at the bulky man beside him who didn't look at Brampton but stared out across the river. Marvik saw the bulky man's lips move. Marvik retrieved his pay-as-you-go phone and took a couple of photographs, then watched Brampton replace his phone in his coat pocket and head on towards the National Theatre.

The bulky man turned in the same direction and Marvik set off after him. He saw Brampton turn up alongside the National Theatre in the direction of Waterloo station but the other man continued onwards. Strathen would be able to discover where Brampton lived, if Crowder wouldn't tell them, and Marvik was very curious to know who this man was — the one that Brampton didn't want to be seen with.

Suddenly the man swung left and with surprise Marvik saw him entering Festival Pier. Marvik hurried along the Embankment where he halted and looked back over the river to see him climb into a waiting motor launch. The man at the helm was leaner and slightly taller — about mid-thirties, wearing a black waterproof jacket under a buoyancy aid. He also had a black baseball cap rammed on his head. Marvik made like a tourist and took a couple of photographs. There was no name on the side of the motor launch, and as it swung out into the Thames and headed towards Blackfriars Bridge, no name on the rear of it either.

Turning back, Marvik caught a glimpse of a woman in a red jacket hurrying away from him. Troubled, he made his way to Waterloo station. There was no sign of Brampton on the crowded platform. Perhaps he'd already got on board a train or he might be in one of the shops or cafés. Marvik wasn't going to look. He caught the first train to Twickenham and found his Land Rover Defender where he'd parked it. Scanning the area, he couldn't see anything suspicious, but he checked under the vehicle to be on the safe side and then under the wheel arches to make sure there was no tracking device on it. It looked clean. He'd have to chance it. He headed for Hamble.

CHAPTER THIRTEEN

'OK, so we've got a number of questions,' Strathen said as they sat in what he called the operations room of the ground-floor apartment in the Grade II-listed whitewashed house that bordered Southampton Water. It was a stone's throw from Hamble marina and situated at the end of a property-free, tree-lined road surrounded by landscaped gardens. Marvik remembered the last time he and Strathen had sat here discussing one of Crowder's missions. It had only been a month ago and his thoughts returned to the woman who had been with them — Helen with her purple hair. But it was the scarred tissue on her wrists that he now remembered rather than the colour of her hair and her forthright manner. Behind the latter had been a vulnerability like Sarah's. They'd both had a tough time, Helen with her sister's murder and Sarah with her father's disappearance. He'd let Sarah down and perhaps by leaving Helen to go off alone he'd also let her down. He told himself the mission had been accomplished, they'd found who had killed Helen's sister and that was all that mattered. Helen wasn't his responsibility. But he'd like to know where she was and what she was doing. He hoped she was OK.

He returned his thoughts to the present. He'd parked his car next to Strathen's Volvo in the private car park at the rear of the grounds. No one had followed him from Twickenham and there had been no one watching the house. Strathen had cooked a curry while Marvik had showered and changed into some of Strathen's clothes, which were a good fit. The steaming hot jet of water had done something to invigorate him but he knew that fatigue would finally catch up with him and the hot food and warmth of the flat would speed it up.

Strathen said, 'I've found five references to Cotleigh's death. His body was discovered washed up on the beach at Chale Bay on the Isle of Wight on the second of February 1979. Yeah, not far from where Bradley Pulford's body was found at Freshwater Bay in January. A case of history repeating itself?' Strathen took another fork of curry and continued. 'Cotleigh was reported missing by his landlady on the twenty-sixth of January, three days after Jack Darrow's body was found in that cargo hold, but Cotleigh could have been missing before then and no one noticed. His body was discovered by a walker eight days after his landlady had reported him missing, so you can imagine the state of it.'

Marvik could. He'd seen many corpses after the sea had claimed them.

Strathen continued, 'Decomposition and the sea life must have made good inroads into it. Death by drowning is about all I can gather from the press reports. No relative was quoted so perhaps there wasn't anyone but the coroner's report will give me more. I've applied for access to it. Crowder could get it quicker than me but I don't expect he'd ask for it.'

Marvik didn't either. 'So Cotleigh must have been identified by dental records.'

'Probably. DNA testing wasn't comprehensive then and I shouldn't think there'd have been enough left to get fingerprints. Brampton was right when he told you about union funds going missing. The press story was that both men had conspired to cream off money given to the union by the Trades Union Council. One of the press articles suggested that Cotleigh had killed Darrow and then tried to abscond to France with all the money and had met his death accidentally. A pang of conscience wasn't mentioned. Both he and Darrow were painted as evil scheming bastards.'

'Which they might have been.'

Strathen nodded acquiescence. Then, after a moment, added, 'On the other hand, they might have been squeaky clean and murdered, their deaths made to look like suicide and an accident.'

'Oscar Redburn was in Lyme Regis with Freynsham on the twenty-first of January, or so Freynsham says. The next day Freynsham discovered from Linda that Oscar hadn't returned.'

'And she waited another day before reporting him missing.' Strathen scowled up at the board where he had enlarged the picture of the five men in the photograph that Bryony had given them. 'One of them goes AWOL and two end up dead.'

'Was Redburn the killer? Did *he* run off with the funds?'

'Maybe. And maybe, despite what the Killbecks say, he returned in 1989 as Bradley Pulford.'

'But why as Pulford?' Marvik said, puzzled, polishing off his curry.

Strathen shrugged. 'There has to be a reason why he assumed that name, but I'm blowed if I can find it. Yet . . .' he added feelingly.

Strathen saw it as a challenge and so did Marvik. He said, 'I wonder if the police have found where Sarah was staying and any further leads on her murder. What did she do for the rest of the day after we had breakfast together? I mentioned her to Adam and Matthew Killbeck and they seemed genuinely not to know of her. I don't think she traced them. Was she followed back to her guest house? Or did she arrange to meet her killer? Maybe she knew him.'

'Freynsham or Brampton?'

'My money would be on Brampton. He's smooth, successful and confident, and he has contacts judging by what I saw on the Embankment. One of those contacts might have taken her out if Brampton has something to hide about his involvement in that dock strike of 1979 and Darrow and Cotleigh's deaths.' Marvik had already relayed what Brampton had told him and given Strathen the photographs he'd taken on the South Bank. Strathen had enlarged them, printed them off and pinned them on the board alongside a circle with 'Brampton' written in it. Marvik could see the right-hand profile of the bulky man's face and the narrow features of the man at the helm on the motor launch. He didn't recognize them but he would if he saw them again despite the fact that they'd kept their hats low and neither had any distinguishing features. 'Any ideas on who they might be?' he asked.

'Police? Intelligence? Or maybe a couple of crooks Brampton's locked in with.'

'The surveillance of Ben's bedsit smacks of a professional organization. But not the torching of the house. That was your basic Molotov cocktail.'

'You're thinking there is more than one party involved?'

'Aren't you?'

Strathen nodded. But they still had no idea why.

'Any more news on Ben?' Marvik asked, taking a swig at his beer.

'Not since I spoke to you earlier. I'll check again later.'

Marvik returned his thoughts to Pulford. 'Where does the real Bradley Pulford fit into all this?' Strathen also had his name on the whiteboard in a circle, along with the year of his birth, 1939 and his death, 1959, and the manner of it — Singapore, accident on board the *Leonora*, with a question mark.

'There were two coroners' courts in Singapore then,' Strathen said. 'Prior to the early sixties the coroners were retired senior police inspectors who conducted the inquests. Even if I could get hold of the report though I don't think it will tell us much more than the information I got from the Registry of Seamen and Shipping. The inquest was probably a formality. It looked like an accident. Maybe it was. But that doesn't explain why *a* Bradley Pulford shacked up with the Killbecks in 1989, or why he ended up on the Isle of Wight beach, dead, in January this year. Perhaps we've been side-tracked by those five men from 1979 and they have nothing to do with this.'

It was an idea that had already occurred to Marvik. 'I might think that if Sarah Redburn hadn't been killed and Bryony Darrow hadn't almost been fried alive,' Marvik said wearily. He was too tired to think straight.

'Let's turn in, Art. We'll come at it fresh in the morning.'

Marvik drained his beer and stashed the dishwasher while Strathen rang the hospital.

'No change,' he announced, coming off the phone. 'Bryony's still there with Ben.'

Marvik retired to Strathen's spare bedroom, the one Helen had slept in. He wondered why his thoughts kept returning to her. Perhaps it was the association that she too had been in danger like Sarah, except he hadn't realized Sarah was in peril. If he had then he'd have made damn sure to protect her. And what about Bryony Darrow? Was he going to let her be killed? Not if he could help it, but aside from forcibly holding her he didn't see what he and Strathen could do.

He switched off thoughts of the mission and mentally willed himself to sleep and to wake when ready, with no inner alarm clock to alert him from slumber this time. He'd let nature take its course, except someone had another idea. It felt as though he'd only been sleeping for a few minutes when Strathen was shaking him.

'We need to leave,' Strathen said urgently.

Marvik was up and out of bed in an instant, the result of years of training. As he threw on his clothes, Strathen, already dressed, said, 'There are two men about to enter the grounds from the front and another one, probably two, coming in from the dinghy park to the south.'

Marvik grabbed his rucksack and followed Strathen into the operations room where he had already wiped clean the board. He picked up a bulky folder and his laptop and stuffed them into a bag. There was a rucksack at his feet which Marvik knew had already been packed in case of emergencies. The training never left you.

'I've got sensors on the entrance and on the vulnerable points to the house — that is the dinghy park and behind the car park. No one's entered by the latter yet. If there were three of them I reckon we could see them off but with four the odds are shortened, especially with this leg, and there could be another couple in a car farther down the road.'

As he spoke Marvik followed him into the hall. 'Could it be police?'

'It's possible but they don't usually come at three in the morning unless it's a drugs bust, and I don't think we should stop to find out.'

Marvik didn't either. 'Where's our exit route?'

'Below.' Locking the door to his apartment, Strathen turned and jerked his head at the door to the right of the stairs, which clearly led to the basement. He unlocked it and then re-locked it from the inside and shot a bolt across. He took a small pencil torch from his pocket and Marvik did the same. They didn't want to switch on the light and alert their intruders of their location by the betrayal of a beam of light under the door.

Silently and swiftly, Marvik followed Strathen down the stairs. Strathen tackled them awkwardly but expertly and rapidly. Marvik knew that Strathen would have several exit routes worked out. He'd hoped he'd never need them but this was the second time in just over a month they'd had to duck out and on both occasions because of a mission for Crowder and his National Intelligence Marine Squad. Maybe Strathen needed to move apartments, thought Marvik. He'd bought this one and established himself as a private intelligence security consultant after his discharge from the Marines. He could always sell up or let it, not that he needed the money and neither did Marvik. Both of them had inherited substantial amounts, but where to relocate? Marvik didn't know where he wanted to be and maybe Shaun was happy to stay here.

The basement had been kitted out as a fitness centre. Marvik wondered if Strathen had organized that, and maybe he was the only occupant who used it.

Strathen said, 'Fortunately this building was occupied by the US Marines in the Second World War and, knowing them as we do, Art, they'd make an escape route in case of bombing or invasion. All I had to do was locate it.'

He turned right into a labyrinth of corridors and then ahead was a gentle slope which led up to a hatch. It was unlocked. Reading Marvik's thoughts, Strathen gave a wry grin. 'I unlocked it from the outside a couple of days ago in case of emergencies. It's fitted with an electronic sensor linked to my phone and computer — it hasn't been tampered with but we go careful in case these guys really are smart aleck buggers and have managed to disarm it without my knowledge.'

Unlikely, thought Marvik, knowing Strathen's high level of expertise. Strathen insisted on going first. He'd already taken the precaution of switching off his phone so that it wouldn't sound an alert and warn whoever was after them. Marvik had also switched off both his mobile phones.

Strathen pushed open the hatch and scoured the horizon before climbing out. Marvik followed. They were at the rear of the house but had come up just behind an outhouse. It was pitch black with no moon or stars to guide them but that suited them fine. It meant it was not so easy for anyone to spot them. But it also meant it would be difficult for them to spot the intruders if they were lying in wait for them.

Strathen gestured ahead. Marvik nodded and, keeping low, they ran past the tennis courts to a dense patch of shrubs and some trees. Beyond the trees was a solid-looking fence, but Strathen expertly removed a panel and indicated to Marvik to squeeze through it. He did and then took Strathen's computer case and rucksack and waited while he did the same and replaced the panel.

They were in a densely populated copse but there was a rough path through it. Strathen led the way, obviously having previously carried out a reconnaissance of the area, probably after their last encounter with intruders and their appointment to Crowder's team. After about half a mile they came to a small clearing, in front of which was another dinghy park, much further along than the one that adjoined Strathen's house. Beyond it was the dark ripple of Southampton Water.

Strathen pressed on and Marvik followed until they had come to a public slipway. The area was deserted and there was no sign of their intruders behind them, but still they didn't speak. Strathen nodded at one of the rowing boats and Marvik dropped his rucksack into it. Strathen did the same with his belongings. Together they carried the boat down the short concrete pier and climbed in. The owner had thoughtfully left the oars in the boat, or had that been Strathen's doing?

The tide had turned and was on the rise. That would help, thought Marvik as Strathen began rowing, and the wind was behind them. Pity there wasn't a second set of oars or an outboard engine, but if Strathen got tired Marvik would relieve him, though he knew Strathen wouldn't. He had good upper body strength made even more powerful by his physical training since the loss of his leg.

'Thought I'd get in some practice for the next Paralympics or Invictus Games if they introduce para-rowing,' he said wryly.

Was it a joke? Perhaps not.

Marvik knew they couldn't risk going to Strathen's boat because whoever had found the apartment probably knew of his boat in the marina at Hamble. They were heading for Southampton — a distance of about seven nautical miles. It would take them about an hour to reach there, probably longer given that it was night, but Marvik had every confidence in Strathen and at least at this time of night they'd avoid container ships and cruise liners coming out of Southampton docks, which reminded him of Jack Darrow and their mission. Who were the men who had come for them? There were two possibilities.

'Only two?' Strathen said cynically when Marvik voiced this to him.

'Two likely ones,' Marvik amended. 'I gave my name to Brampton and he passed it on to his contact who, accessing the vehicle licensing database, got my car registration number and managed to track the vehicle to your address. So they come in mob-handed. To do what, though? Tell us to lay off?'

'I don't think they'd have gone about it politely.'

Neither did Marvik. 'MI5?'

Strathen shrugged. 'They don't usually come in groups.'

'Perhaps they thought it necessary given our backgrounds. We could easily have overpowered one operative, two and even three, but more would be tougher.'

'Maybe,' Strathen acquiesced, pulling rhythmically on the oars. 'You said there were two possibilities.'

'Someone was tracking Bryony or Ben Darrow or both of them. Ben had his phone switched on while he was on board and the coastguard had details of your boat. It'd be easy enough to get your address from that, and whoever is behind this waited until they saw me arrive at your house. Someone was watching the house from outside, or they'd rigged up surveillance equipment linked to a monitor.'

'So we're back to the intelligence services or someone who has a private army of heavies and sophisticated surveillance equipment, and that brings us back to the fact that whoever it is he doesn't want us asking questions either about Bradley Pulford or about what happened in 1979 to Darrow, Cotleigh and Redburn.'

'Would they have got details of my boat?' Marvik wondered aloud.

'Probably.' Strathen showed no signs of fatigue as they skirted past one of the lighted docks on their left, hugging the shore. 'Which means we need another mode of transport. I can't row around the south coast for ever.'

'And there's me thinking you were superhuman.'

'I wish.' Strathen continued, 'We'll get another boat.'

'Where?'

'Ocean Village Marina. I know someone who will lend us his. Giles Ebdon.'

They fell silent and it wasn't until they were approaching the marina that Marvik spoke. 'Do you ever think of Helen?' he asked.

'Sometimes. You?'

'Yes. Do you know where she is?'

'No. You?'

'No. Could you find her?'

'If I wanted to.'

'And you don't?'

'It's not up to me to find her, or you, Art.'

'I know.'

Marvik wondered what Shaun's thoughts of Helen were — perhaps as confused as his. Had they helped her by turning all her beliefs about her sister's murder on their head? Perhaps she was wishing they and Crowder had left well alone, or maybe she had picked up the pieces of her life and was OK. Perhaps she'd returned to work in what she had called that crap call centre where she took crap phone calls from irate customers. But he hoped not.

He postponed his thoughts of her as Strathen pulled into Ocean Village Marina and negotiated the boat in the lights of the pontoons to where Marvik could tie up. The security cameras might pick up their arrival. Two men entering the marina by rowboat could only mean one thing: they were out to steal equipment or a boat. But no alarm sounded and no one came to see what they were doing. Marvik was pleased to see that both he and Strathen knew the duty manager in the marina office, Alex Russell. They were greeted warmly despite the unusual hour of their arrival. Strathen said they were going to pick up another motor cruiser as soon as the hour was decent. Alex accepted that without question.

'It's too early to call Giles,' Strathen explained to Marvik outside the marina office. It was only just on four thirty. 'There's a new twenty-four-hour café in the High Street. We can get something to drink and eat there.' They headed north into the city for a short distance.

Marvik was surprised to find the café busy. There were a few young people who looked as though they might be students and some who looked as though they were late-night revellers who hadn't yet returned home. They weren't drunk, though. Then there were a couple of older people in their sixties who were there for their own reasons, huddled over laptops and their phones. He also noted there were three computers. It was run along the lines of a cybercafé.

They ordered a full English breakfast and two large Americanos and found a seat close to the window. Marvik had a good view south towards the Town Quay while Strathen could see up the street towards the city centre. How long would it take for the intruders to work out where they were, Marvik wondered, and where they'd go next? That depended on who had informed on them. But they couldn't know this was where they had come, or that they'd escaped by boat.

Strathen said, 'The most likely scenario is that Brampton is the leak and summoned up the heavies after you scared him with that photograph and made him tell you about Cotleigh. Now he's got to make sure that you don't live long enough to follow it up. And that means there is something about Cotleigh's death to follow up. So we keep on it.'

'And the heavies will report back that they failed. So Brampton will have to second-guess what we'll do.'

'Freynsham will be watched and possibly warned off. He might even be killed.'

'He's survived so far so maybe he doesn't know anything other than what he's told me.'

'Brampton might not want to take that risk.'

'He will for now if he thinks I'll show at Freynsham's.' But Marvik thought he might wrong foot them and, although he could scare the shit out of Freynsham, he didn't think he'd have anything more to tell him. He said as much, adding, 'It's the Bradley Pulford of 1959 we need to know more about. There's still that inscription on his headstone and the fact that he was brought home to be buried despite not having any living relatives. I could talk to Irene Templeton again and see if she can give me the name of someone who might know more about Bradley Pulford. If I get nothing there then I'll head for London and tackle Brampton again.'

'Brampton's got some powerful friends and that ties in with Crowder appointing us to this mission. Whatever happened in 1979, someone doesn't want it exposed, and perhaps that someone is who Crowder is after. I can get as much as I can on Cotleigh but if he's the link then my betting is I won't get much — the records will have been conveniently lost. I'll probably discover there was a fire, like the one at the university that destroyed the student union files.'

'But Brampton doesn't know that I know about the phoney Pulford of 1989,' Marvik said, pleased now he hadn't asked Brampton if he knew or had heard of a Bradley Pulford.

'Unless he's had the Killbecks watched.'

Marvik considered this, then said, 'The motorbike that followed me after the funeral service and the one which tried to run me down the night before I met Sarah for breakfast could both have been the guy on the motor launch.'

'Which means there is a lead to follow and Pulford, phoney or real, means something. Give me a few minutes.' Strathen rose as their coffees arrived, delivered by a tall, skinny man in his mid-twenties who looked tired. Marvik sipped his while Strathen took up position at one of the café's computers. He returned to the table at the same time their breakfast arrived.

'The inquest into Sarah's death is this afternoon at two p.m. at Bournemouth Coroner's Court. It will probably be opened and then almost immediately adjourned but it could give us more background about her death and I'd like to see who shows up for it. I'll attend while you talk to Irene Templeton. We'll moor up at Poole marina and use taxis from there.'

'You're sure we can get this boat? Giles might be away on it,' asked Marvik, eating.

'He's not. I saw it in the marina. And Giles Ebdon was a friend of my father. He'll happily loan it to me.'

Strathen's father had been in the diplomatic service and had died in China when Shaun had been five. More than that Marvik didn't know except that Shaun had been raised by his aunt and both his aunt and his late father had left him considerable fortunes which Strathen seemed to have eschewed, apart from buying his boat and his apartment.

He said, 'I'll buy a couple of cheap phones in Bournemouth so that we can keep in touch — ones we can ditch when we no longer need them. And we use public phones and computers as much as we can. And cash, of course, talking of which—'

'I've got plenty on me.'

'Me too. I thought we might need it.'

After they finished breakfast Strathen returned to the computer terminal. There was still an hour to go before they could decently call Giles Ebdon at seven a.m. and Marvik was impatient to get moving. The street was quiet with only the occasional early morning commuter heading for work. He took out his pay-as-you-go phone and made to switch it on to view the photograph but knew that was a mistake. Despite Crowder telling him it was secure, he wondered if it was. Did he suspect Crowder? No. But Crowder's system and phone could have been hacked into, especially if they were dealing with intelligence. And they could be because the assignments that Crowder gave them were ones that involved corruption, deceit and murder at the highest level. It was why he and Strathen had been hired: to take risks, to play outside the rules. Only it had resulted in death — Sarah's — and he wasn't sure that he wanted to be a party to that if it meant the innocent had to die as well as the guilty. But then hadn't that been the way of his life since joining the Marines? Sometimes, and quite often to protect the innocent, others who were also innocent died. He crossed to Strathen.

'Nothing on Cotleigh, as I expected.' Strathen logged off and hauled himself up. 'Right, let's ask if we can use the marina office phone.'

He called Giles Ebdon who said he'd meet them at the marina in fifteen minutes. Ebdon, a fit, distinguished-looking man in his late sixties and with a military bearing, handed over his boat keys without a quibble and told Strathen to keep hold of the boat for as long as he liked.

'Does he know what you do?' Marvik asked as they made the sleek, modern motor cruiser ready.

'Only that I run an intelligence security company.'

'He didn't ask why you wanted the boat.'

'Giles was trained not to ask questions. Or rather, not those sorts of questions.'

Marvik raised his eyebrows but made no further comment. As they made for Poole he thought of his forthcoming trip to Steepleridge, hoping that Irene Templeton might be able to give him something or someone who could tell him why Bradley Pulford had died in Singapore in 1959. Whether that would help them discover why Sarah Redburn had been killed on Sunday night though was an entirely different matter.

CHAPTER FOURTEEN

Thursday

'I'm sorry I can't help you,' Irene Templeton said after Marvik had apologized for disturbing her and explained why he was there. He'd been economical with the truth, saying he was assisting a friend in trying to trace what happened to her father who had gone missing years ago and thought he might have known Bradley Pulford. She must have seen his disappointment because she quickly added, 'But my father might be able to.'

'He knew Bradley Pulford?' Marvik hardly dared to hope.

'Oh, yes, quite well. Would you like to speak to him?'

Marvik said he would very much and asked where he could find him.

She stepped back. 'Here. Come in, Mr Marvik.'

He tried not to get his hopes up too high. This could be nothing. Or perhaps it could be the break they were seeking. Curbing his excitement, he followed her into the hall, saying, 'Call me Art.' He was impressed she'd remembered his surname but maybe they didn't get many strangers in Steepleridge churchyard, especially ones like him.

'I mentioned you to my father after meeting you in the churchyard on Saturday,' she tossed over her shoulder, leading him through a gleaming hall with tasteful antique furniture that smelt of polish. 'I'm sorry I had to dash off like that. My father was very curious to know why you were asking after Bradley. I'd hoped you'd return. He said he's always felt a little guilty over Bradley and George's deaths although he has no reason to, but reason doesn't sit well with emotion.'

The name George was a new one on Marvik. Was it relevant to his and Strathen's mission? Maybe. On the other hand, possibly not. He'd soon find out.

'It might do him good to get things off his chest,' she added, pausing outside a door and lowering her voice. 'The past gets a lot closer as you get older. Physically he's not in very good shape but his mind is crystal clear. It's rare he gets visitors these days and he'll be delighted to talk to you.'

Marvik was shown into a pleasantly appointed lounge populated with tasteful antique furniture, totally in keeping with the house. There was a very large brick inglenook fireplace and a log burner that wasn't functioning but the very modern central heating was, hidden behind covered radiators or possibly even under the floor, he thought as he followed her across the pale blue carpet to the lattice bay window that overlooked an extensive and very pretty cottage garden.

Sitting in the window in an expansive wing-backed chair was a frail, elderly man who looked up as they entered. His body was so thin that Marvik thought it might break in half but the eyes that observed Marvik were keen and intelligent. Irene Templeton made the introductions and invited Marvik to take the armchair opposite her father, across the small table. She then tactfully retreated after saying she would make him a coffee.

Marvik began by apologizing for disturbing him, but Warnford waved that aside with a thin, bony hand. Marvik thought he must be in his late eighties.

'So you want to know about Bradley?'

'Yes. Your daughter said he was raised on a farm but he went to sea — why?'

'Because his best friend George Gurney did. And they're buried together, next to one another.'

The picture of Bradley Pulford's gravestone flashed before Marvik like a photograph and next to it the one of George Gurney who had died three days before Bradley.

Warnford said, 'They were inseparable as kids and then as men. They'd been thrown together because of the war — both were evacuees on Sir Ambrose Shale's estate. Do you know it?'

'Yes.' He didn't see the need to mention he had been on exercises on the land adjoining it.

'He used to own half the properties in the village but they've all been sold to second homeowners. The local people couldn't afford to buy them so most have moved out. And the farms have been sold but then Cedric Shale, Sir Ambrose's only child, doesn't have any heirs and he's elderly like me. I've heard he's housebound now, much like me. But you want to know about George and Bradley.'

Marvik nodded.

Ralph Warnford continued, 'I was a teenager when they both came here as babies, evacuated with their mothers from London. But both boys lost their parents during the war. George's mother died of pneumonia and his father in a Japanese prisoner-of-war camp. Bradley's parents were killed in the Blitz.'

'Your daughter told me about Bradley's mother meeting her husband in London. He had a forty-eight-hour pass.'

Warnford nodded. 'After the war and over the years, I'd come home on leave from the navy and we drew closer. Bradley was plucky, a bit of a daredevil, while George was quieter, but they both had a restlessness about them. They settled to working on the land but it was always as if each was searching for something else. When George's adoptive mother remarried a man he couldn't stand the sight of and vice versa after her first husband, George's adoptive father died, George decided he'd take off. Bradley got even more restless without his buddy and when his adoptive parents died there was no need for him to stay. I'd persuaded George to join the navy but I've often wished that George hadn't taken my advice. And if he hadn't gone to sea then perhaps Bradley wouldn't have done and both might have been alive today. They couldn't even be parted in death because they both died in the same place and within days of each other. I made sure they were buried close together.'

Marvik sat up, keenly interested. 'What happened, sir?' Was this relevant? Surely it meant something. But what?

'I was a chief petty officer on board the same ship as George. Maybe that's why I felt even more responsible. It was in Singapore.' Warnford paused as Irene entered. Marvik curbed his impatience. She set the tray down on the small table between them. On it was one large coffee, milk, sugar, a plate of biscuits and another mug of hot water with a slice of lemon in it which she handed to her father.

'Caffeine doesn't agree with me. Not very good for the bladder and at my age my bladder doesn't need any extra aggravation,' Ralph Warnford explained with a smile. Then, nodding towards the pictures on the cabinet, he added, 'That was taken in Singapore.'

Irene Templeton crossed to the cabinet and returned with a photograph. As she handed it to Marvik the phone rang and she left to answer it.

Marvik's mind was swirling with thoughts about the deaths of the two men in 1959 and if they were somehow connected with two deaths in 1979 and the death in January on the Isle of Wight, but out of politeness he curtailed his eagerness and studied the picture. He found himself looking at a tall, good-looking, dark-haired man in a summer naval uniform of white shorts, white socks and a crisp white shirt. Little of the man in the picture remained in front of Marvik. He suppressed a shudder, secretly vowing that he'd burn every photograph he had if he ever reached Ralph Warnford's age. He'd hate to be reminded of what he had once been.

Although the chances of any visual record of his time in the armed services were nil, thank goodness.

Warnford said, 'That was taken in 1958 at the Sembawang Naval Base, Singapore. Our ship, *HMS Ternly*, was stationed there from February 1957 to January 1959. It's hard to believe now but in those days we did a tour of two years. That's a long time to be away from home and the family but you accepted it. It was part of the job. I was thirty-one and it was before I got my commission. I was a chief petty officer, supply, what they call logistics these days. I liked it out there, despite the heat, or perhaps because of it.' He smiled and Marvik caught a brief glimpse of the man in the photograph. He put the photograph down and picked up his coffee.

'I didn't spend that much time at sea either,' Warnford continued. 'Most of it was spent in the barracks at HMS Terror while the ship was being refitted and repainted. *HMS Terror* was originally an Erebus Class Monitor, which was based in Singapore before the war — until the last day of 1939, actually. The barrack block was called HMS Sultan before it was renamed, but I don't suppose you want a lecture on naval history.' He gave a smile and Marvik returned it.

After taking a sip of his drink and replacing the cup on the table, Warnford resumed. 'The British left Singapore in 1971 and handed over the base to the Singapore government. It became a commercial dockyard and a thriving port. I went there many more times and each time I did I was reminded of George and Bradley. They said that Bradley slipped and fell into a cargo hold — maybe he did because his mind was distracted by thoughts of George's death. He would have been very upset. Or maybe he decided to end it all and threw himself into the hold.'

'Would he have done such a thing?'

'No. I think it was just a tragic accident.'

Or was it? wondered Marvik. 'Was George's death mentioned at Bradley's inquest?'

'I don't know — we had left Singapore by then. But I doubt it. I'm not sure anyone knew of the connection between them. I didn't even know Bradley was in Singapore.'

'So he might not have known about George's death unless it was in the newspapers or on the radio.'

'It might have been but again I'd be surprised if it had been. The navy played things very close to their chest in those days, especially when we were overseas. And it was at the end of all the trouble in Malaya. Perhaps Bradley had arranged to meet George and he didn't show up and Bradley then heard he'd died.' Warnford shrugged his bony shoulders. 'I didn't find out about Bradley's death until my wife wired the ship and told me. The authorities notified the vicar here at Steepleridge. I said I'd make sure that Bradley was flown home to be buried beside George, whose body we brought back on board ship.'

'How did George die?'

'He and another sailor were detailed to collect some cargo from the British High Commission in Kuala Lumpur to bring back for loading on board ship. The lorry they were travelling in hit a rock and came off the road, leaving the driver, Able Seaman Ken Travis, unconscious. George was unscathed. He went for help. Travis ended up in hospital. Two days later George was posted AWOL. It was totally unlike him to go off and not return for duty. Then his body was found in one of the less salubrious districts, which was why it was probably hushed up. He'd been stabbed and robbed and the post-mortem found a large amount of alcohol in his system, which again stunned me because George was teetotal. All I could think of was that he'd got in with the wrong crowd, or a woman had plied him with drinks or laced them and then lured him away and robbed him. It's a sordid end and George didn't deserve such a death. Neither did Bradley.'

Marvik was interested in the fact that the circumstances surrounding George Gurney's death were out of character, but did it connect with what had happened to his buddy, Pulford? And was it linked to Oscar Redburn's disappearance?

'Have you ever heard the name Redburn?' he asked.

Warnford considered it for a moment then shook his head. 'It doesn't ring any bells.'

'How about the name Joseph Cotleigh or Jack Darrow?'

'No, sorry.'

Marvik took a sip of his coffee. Irene Templeton hadn't returned so he guessed she'd been called away to do something or had tactfully left her father to reminisce in private. 'What was the cargo they collected from the High Commission?'

'I don't know. We weren't told. It was loaded on board ship and transported back to Portsmouth, then unloaded and sent up to London. You didn't ask questions — you did as you were told, but then you'd know that being a serviceman.'

'Ex-serviceman,' Marvik corrected lightly. 'You can tell?'

'You called me sir. Not many outside the services do that and there's your bearing and physique and the scars. Army or Marines? Marines, I'd say.'

'Correct.'

'I'm not completely ga-ga then.' Warnford grinned mischievously and continued. 'All I can tell you is that there were two not very large crates, each about the size of a travelling trunk. They were marked fragile and confidential and were sealed. I oversaw the unloading of them in Portsmouth dockyard. They were collected by two soldiers in a lorry who had all the correct authorization but where they went after Pompey I have no idea.'

'Was it usual for the navy to take cargo on board?'

'If it had military significance or was of a delicate nature and couldn't be trusted to a merchant vessel, yes.' Ralph Warnford eyed him keenly. 'Are you wondering if whatever it was had something to do with those two boys' deaths?'

Marvik didn't know but the timing was interesting, and the thought had occurred to him that George Gurney had discovered what was in at least one of those crates when the lorry had hit the rock and he'd helped himself to it. He could have been robbed for what he had stolen but that didn't explain why Pulford had died. It would be interesting, though, to discover what had been in those crates, except he didn't know how he was ever going to be able to do that.

'Were you responsible for Bradley's headstone?' he asked.

'Yes. I thought he deserved something decent and the quotes sum up his love of the sea, a very short-lived love as it turned out. George's adoptive mother was obviously responsible for burying George. I feel sad he was given such a bland gravestone. She and her second husband died some years ago.'

'And Bradley's personal effects?'

'There wasn't much. Some photographs of both his biological parents and his adoptive ones, a couple of letters, some clothes and that was it.'

Marvik reached for his phone and, bringing up the photograph of the five men, he held it out towards Warnford. 'Do you recognize any of these?'

Warnford reached for a pair of spectacles on the table and, donning them, peered at the picture. 'No.'

Marvik rose and stretched out his hand. 'Thank you, sir, you've been a great help.'

'I'm not sure that I have but it's polite of you to say so.'

Marvik also thanked Irene Templeton, who told him he was welcome to return any time.

Outside and well away from the house, Marvik switched on the mission mobile phone, as Strathen had christened it. He'd bought two in Poole — cheap basic phones which they could ditch as soon as this was over. He rang Strathen but there was no answer. He must be at the inquest.

Marvik returned to the church and gazed down on the graves of George Gurney and Bradley Pulford. Their deaths so close to one another had to be more than a coincidence and the fact that a man had shown up in Swanage in 1989 claiming to be Pulford and not George Gurney also had to be significant. Pulford had died after Gurney, so had Gurney given something from one of those crates to Pulford to bring home, only Pulford had been deprived of it because Ralph Warnford hadn't discovered anything unusual or significant in his personal effects? Marvik didn't think the old man was lying. If both George Gurney and Bradley Pulford had been killed because of this item, had it been brought back to England by the killer? But if so, what had happened to it? Did it have anything to do with

Redburn's disappearance or the fact that *a* Bradley Pulford had shown up in Swanage in 1989 and a man claiming to be him had been washed up on the Isle of Wight in January?

Marvik needed a blast of sea air to help clear his thinking. He struck out across the graveyard into the fields and headed in the direction of the coast, taking pleasure in pushing his fitness levels on the steep inclines of the hills and trekking across the rolling fields until he was on the edge of the army ranges where walks were only permitted on certain days. This wasn't one of them. But that didn't worry him.

Ignoring the signs that told him to keep clear of Ministry of Defence property, he climbed over the low, dry-stone wall topped with barbed wire and headed over the rough undergrowth, catching the fresh scent of the sea in the cold breeze and remembering the night manoeuvres he'd carried out here. He saw the shelled buildings ahead, the remains of cottages and outhouses and the tower which was all that was left of a small private church. He remembered that these had all belonged to the Shale estate at one time. The lost village of Tyneham was situated further west. The buildings had deteriorated since he was last here. There were more bullet holes and more debris from mortar shells.

Soon he was on the cliff edge looking down on to the small shingle and sandy bay protected either side by an outcrop of black rock that fed down into the sea. The bay was off limits to the public and fossil hunters. The signs still declared he was on Ministry of Defence land but he knew this bay. He'd come into it several times under cover of darkness on exercises. The memories pricked at him, making him feel nostalgic, an emotion he despised. Angrily he pushed them aside and headed east towards Swanage, bringing his mind back to their assignment. There were so many fragments, snatches of information and disjointed items that didn't add up to anything except that Sarah was dead and someone had tried to kill him and Bryony Darrow. They might try again.

He rang her mobile phone using the mission mobile, wondering if she'd ignore the call as she wouldn't recognize the number. Even if she had recognized it, though, she might still have ignored his calls. From her point of view he'd caused her nothing but trouble. She didn't answer. He didn't leave a message. He rang the hospital and asked to be put through to the ward where Ben was. Bryony might still be with him. It took him a while to get an answer and when he did he asked after Ben Darrow who, he was told, was improving. He asked if Ben's sister was there.

'No, she left this morning.'

'Did she say where she was going?' Marvik asked, wondering if she might have left a contact address.

'No, sorry.'

He rang off. She couldn't stay at the hospital all the time and as Ben was improving she'd obviously used the opportunity to take a break. Perhaps she was staying locally in Chichester with an acting friend or perhaps she'd taken the train to London to stay with friends there. He hoped she was OK. He felt uneasy about her and uncomfortable not knowing where she was. If she was in peril and he failed to protect her that would be two deaths on his conscience, and on Crowder's, he thought with anger, cursing the fact that he and Strathen were given so little help. It was like trying to make progress in heavy mud. Had they got bogged down with this strike of 1979? Maybe, but there was still the fact that Bryony had teamed up with Sarah and Bryony *had* been targeted. There was also the fact that Bryony's grandfather, Jack Darrow, had worked on the docks and had died on a cargo ship in the same manner as Bradley Pulford and that had to mean something — a thought that he was keen to run past Strathen.

Marvik walked back to Wareham and caught a train to Poole. By the time he reached the boat Strathen had returned from the inquest. He reported that, as expected, the inquest had been opened and almost immediately adjourned and that he'd learned precious little except that Sarah had not been booked into any guest house or hotel as far as the police could find, and no one had yet come forward to say she had been staying with them. That puzzled Marvik because Sarah had not unpacked her belongings at the cottage at Eel Pie Island — not even her toiletries — and she'd already given up the flat in Eastbourne. Had she travelled to Swanage by train that morning? If so, she'd had a very early start. She had looked tired but she'd told him she'd arrived the previous day and had contacted the local vicars and priests to find out if they knew the relatives of Bradley Pulford. Was that a lie? Had someone driven her there? If so then why hadn't she or he come forward? The same applied if she had been staying with someone. The reason, he said to Strathen, as they discussed this, was because that person was the killer.

Strathen agreed and suggested they move the boat in case the police decided to wonder who he was and why he'd been at the inquest. It was as they were heading east to Lymington Marina that Marvik relayed what he'd got from Ralph Warnford and the thoughts that had occupied him on his way back to Poole.

'Could Darrow have worked in Singapore at the same time as Bradley Pulford?' he ventured. 'Perhaps Bradley gave whatever he'd got from George Gurney to Darrow to bring back to the UK, but if he did bring it back in 1959 what did he do with it?'

'Well, he didn't sell whatever it was otherwise he wouldn't have been working as a stevedore, living in a council house and striking for the rights of his fellow workers.'

'Maybe he didn't realize the value of it, or perhaps he heard about Bradley Pulford's death or was there when it happened and, scared the same thing would happen to him, he got rid of it.'

'But the same thing did happen to him,' Strathen insisted. 'OK, twenty years later. Perhaps that's a coincidence, perhaps not. I'll find out if Darrow was in Singapore in 1959. I'll also see if I can discover what was in that cargo collected from the British High Commission, but don't raise your hopes.'

Marvik said he wouldn't.

Strathen continued, 'I couldn't find much on Joseph Cotleigh except that he was born in 1953. Both parents are dead. There could be relatives but there's no one with that surname listed in Southampton, and even if we found someone who knew him, I don't think we'd get much from them.'

'But I might from Brampton. With a little bit of gentle or not-so-gentle persuading he might even want to tell me who was after us last night.' And tomorrow morning, first thing, Marvik said he would return to London and ask him.

CHAPTER FIFTEEN

Friday

'Mr Brampton's been called abroad on business,' his secretary announced in the modern chrome-and-glass reception of Front Line Economics the next morning. Marvik had caught an early train to London from Lymington. Strathen was taking the boat back to Southampton.

'When?' Marvik asked sharply, causing her to blink. He was disappointed and frustrated but not surprised. He stared at the petite blonde who the receptionist had summoned on his arrival. She was nervous; he didn't think that was her natural demeanour but that she had been warned about his possible visit and told to lie if he or anyone came asking for her boss. As she'd emerged from the lift and tapped her way across the tiled floor on her high heels she'd studied him warily and seemed to be priming herself to break the news to him.

'He was unexpectedly called away last night,' she answered, avoiding his eye contact.

I bet he was. 'Where?'

'I, er . . .'

'Where?' he barked, causing her to flinch.

‘Frankfurt. A client requested an urgent meeting. He won’t be back for several days.’

‘The client’s name?’

‘That’s confidential.’ She swallowed and pushed her hair off her face. ‘Anyway, I don’t know who it is. Mr Brampton didn’t say.’

She flushed under Marvik’s hard stare. Maybe she didn’t know. She’d been told to say that and no more. Had Brampton spoken to her or simply sent her an email or text? She was obviously frightened. He wondered what Brampton had told her about him. It couldn’t be the truth because Brampton didn’t know that. Perhaps the scars on his face also worried her. But Brampton’s impromptu absence meant to Marvik’s mind that he was either running scared or someone, possibly the same people Brampton had met on the South Bank and who had been sent to silence him and Strathen, had ordered him to leave or assisted him to go into hiding. And that had been triggered by his questions about that dock strike in 1979 and Oscar’s disappearance.

Marvik turned as though to leave then spun around in time to witness the relief on her face, followed by a flash of fear.

‘I’m sorry I can’t help you,’ she gabbled before turning and hurrying towards the lift. The doors slid open and as she entered it a woman stepped out: the same one Marvik had seen at the conference in the red jacket. This time she was wearing a light-grey jacket over black trousers and a brightly patterned multi-coloured scarf around her long, slim neck. Marvik watched as she exchanged a few brief words with Brampton’s secretary, who tossed a glance at Marvik. Then the lift doors closed and the dusky-skinned woman looked directly at him and then addressed the receptionist. ‘Just going for a coffee.’ Marvik knew the message had been intended for him. He followed her as she walked briskly along the road and turned into one of the chain coffee shops a few yards down. Maybe she just fancied him. But Marvik knew that something more than a coffee was on offer. He hoped it was information.

'Let me,' he said.

'Make it a take-out.' She glanced around. 'But we'll drink inside.' She gave her order and although the café was busy she managed to secure a table towards the rear, giving them a certain degree of privacy. The music would do the rest.

He placed the coffee in front of her and took the seat opposite. She unravelled her scarf to reveal a loose-fitting cream blouse and smiled at him. It was a very nice smile, full of promises that sent a man's pulse racing and his blood surging, and he was no different from any other man.

'You were asking Amy where Donald has gone,' she said. She spoke without an accent, her voice low and even-toned.

'Do you know where he is?'

'Not in Frankfurt, that's for sure, because if he was he'd be at one of two places — the European Central Bank or with Deutsche Phillipe, the German headquarters of one of our major pharmaceutical clients, and he's with neither. I checked. And I also checked the airlines. He didn't catch a flight to Frankfurt.'

'Why would you do that?'

'Because I don't trust him and I don't like him, but that's not the real reason, although it helps.' She swallowed some coffee.

Marvik rapidly read between the lines. 'You had an affair with him?'

'Briefly. It wasn't one of my better decisions.' She pulled a face, then added, 'And no, this has nothing to do with a woman scorned. But he did threaten to sack me. I said just try.'

She was about twenty years younger than Brampton, not that the age gap mattered when it came to lust. She sat forward with a serious expression on her soft-featured face.

'He's still trying to get rid of me and I'm still compiling my evidence so that I can blow the whistle on him.'

'About what?' Marvik asked, deeply interested.

'Collusion, falsifying information, taking bribes.'

'That's a pretty big allegation.'

'Isn't it just?' she said with relish, grinning. 'And I was hoping you might have more information that can help me, Art Marvik.' She'd been beside Donald Brampton when he'd introduced himself at the drinks party. 'I'm Melody Everley, by the way.'

'What kind of information?' he asked casually, though his mind was racing.

She shrugged. 'Anything that can help me to expand my dirty dossier on him.'

'Why do you trust me? I could be in collusion with Donald Brampton. I could be his friend or a crook out to blackmail him.'

'You're neither because I overheard Donald talking about you on Wednesday after I saw you at the drinks reception. I went into the ladies', remember.'

Marvik did. And she'd invited him for a drink before doing so.

'When I came out Donald was outside the conference room along the corridor to the right. He was on his phone. He didn't see me. I eavesdropped.'

'Go on.'

'Donald said, "He's sniffing around, wants to know what happened during that strike. For Christ's sake, get him off my back. You owe me, remember. Neither of us can afford this coming out." Then he said something about dirty secrets — I couldn't quite catch it, and that he'd be there in five minutes. He rang off and I thought he was going to head back to the conference drinks but he didn't. He got his coat and left.'

'Did he know you'd overheard?'

'I doubt it. I made as if I'd just come out of the ladies' and was heading back to the conference room.'

'And you followed him.'

'Yes.'

Marvik recalled seeing the flash of red jacket. 'You saw me watching him and the man he was with on the South Bank.'

She nodded and sipped her coffee. 'I'd like to know what dirty secrets. What happened in the strike — which strike? Why are you interested?'

Marvik certainly wasn't going to tell her. 'Did you recognize the man he was talking to on the South Bank?'

'No. Did you?'

'Have you seen him before?'

She shook her head. 'Do you know who he is?'

'No.'

She looked as though she didn't believe him. She sat forward. He could smell her musky perfume. 'I'll tell you what I have.'

'In return for what?'

'Anything you can give me — now, preferably, but I'll settle for later.' She again tossed him a flirtatious smile. This time he thought she was overdoing it a bit.

'How do you know that I won't use your information to blackmail him?'

'I hope you do — it would serve the bastard right. But I'd prefer to have him exposed in the media. I've almost got enough ammunition to ruin him and his precious reputation but a bit more wouldn't hurt. OK, I know it sounds vindictive and it is but it's no more than the little shit deserves.'

Brampton must have really pissed her off. She took another sip of her coffee and seemed to be weighing him up. He said, 'I'll help if I can but no promises, and it will have to be later.'

She studied him for a moment, then shrugged. 'Suits me. That's something I can look forward to. Where did you get those scars, by the way?'

'I'll tell you that later too.'

She gave a small laugh then her expression became more serious. Marvik was keen to hear what she said even though he wasn't sure how much of it would be the truth.

'I'm an economist, but you've probably already gathered that. I head a team of four in the competition section of the company. Companies who have strong market power can find it difficult to merge with other companies or to create joint ventures because of the constraints of competition policy. My job is to help them find a way through the competition legislation by compiling reports on the markets involved and to determine the financial losses that could arise for customers and competitors associated with mergers and anti-competitive behaviour. I produce expert reports, give oral evidence and assist with appeals against the competition authority decisions if it goes against my client.'

'Sounds complicated.' Marvik couldn't see how this was going to help him but he'd hear what she had to say.

'It can be but essentially it's about understanding how markets work. I report directly to Donald as head of the company. We've worked very closely together on several client reports and I know for a fact that some of the reports have been massaged in favour of the merger or acquisition and that Donald has been taking bribes in order to come down heavily in favour of one side or the other.'

'How do you know?' Was it true? Recalling his encounter with Brampton, Marvik thought that maybe it was and maybe Brampton, worried he was going to find that out, had called in some favours, as Melody had claimed, in the form of the heavies who'd come to Strathen's apartment. It made sense. His interest deepened.

'Because the figures I've compiled and the ones he's presented are not the same.'

'Have you faced him with this?'

'Not yet. I'm waiting until it's rock solid and I've handed it over to a financial journalist I know, *then* I'll tell Donald. It's something I am very much looking forward to.' She consulted her watch. 'I'd better be getting back.' She rose and picked up the paper cup containing her coffee. 'You won't forget what you said about helping when you can?'

'No.'

'How can I get in touch with you?'

'I know where to find you.'

She eyed him steadily and with an air of puzzlement. 'What will you do now?'

He held her stare and after a moment picked up his cup. 'Finish my coffee.'

She smiled. 'Thanks.'

'For what?'

'The coffee.'

'Of course.'

He watched her leave and then, a few seconds later, headed outside. He saw her turn into Brampton's offices. The streets were crowded. His eyes locked on a heavy-set man in dark clothes wearing earphones doing something with his phone. He might be an innocent passer-by but Marvik wasn't taking bets on it.

He turned and headed in the direction of the Strand. How much store could he set by what Melody Everley had told him about Brampton? It could be a complete pack of lies. Why had she told him? Was she in danger? From Brampton? Maybe. But Brampton wasn't around. Or from the men protecting Brampton? Possibly. But Marvik believed Melody had her own protectors and one of them was tailing him now — he could very well be another of Brampton's contacts. Perhaps she was still having an affair with Brampton and he'd given her instructions to probe him to find out how much he knew if he came asking again. But she'd got nothing from him and hadn't seemed too bothered that she hadn't. No, Marvik knew what her role had been and that was to delay him until someone could be put in place to follow him.

He crossed the road, catching sight of the man behind him. He was keeping his distance and didn't look at all interested in where Marvik was going. Anyone inexperienced or untrained in surveillance wouldn't have thought anything of it but Marvik knew differently. Would he try something here in London? It would be easy enough in a crowd: a gentle shove, a push, a knife in his back or a poisoned blade. Marvik would have to avoid crowds, which was impossible given that he was in a heaving capital full of humanity. Or would it be a push under an underground train? As he climbed the four stone steps into the pillared entrance of an impressive building he glanced to his left. The man was still there behind a crowd of Japanese tourists.

Marvik postponed thoughts of Brampton and entered the plush, highly polished interior of the private bank where he announced himself to a smartly dressed clerk and requested access to his safe deposit boxes. After a lengthy but necessary process of confirming his ID he was shown to the vaults where in privacy he pressed his hand on the electronic plate, entered a code and opened one of the four large safe deposit boxes that contained his parents' private papers. Inside on the right were stacked a number of small hardcover notebooks labelled by his father. With his heart racing a little faster he extracted the notebook he'd taken from Sarah's room. It was the same size as those in the box, and yet as he made to put it with them he thought that it felt unusually lightweight. With curiosity he opened it. The pages at the front were blank. Those in the latter half of the notebook had been torn out and in their place, taped to the inside of the rear hardcover was a three-and-a-half-inch computer disk with his father's handwriting on it and just one word, 'Vasa'.

He hesitated, his fingers twitching over the disk. Did he rip it off and take it with him? But what good would that do? He had no computer device that could read these old back-up disks. Shaun would have, though. He took a breath, pushed the notebook into the box and locked it. He didn't have time, he told himself, returning to a member of staff who was waiting for him by the lift. But even then he heard the excuse. He didn't even want to silently acknowledge the real reasons for his reluctance to face up to the past.

He blocked it out and focused on the mission. Crisply, he asked a staff member if he could use a private phone and was shown into a small but modern furnished room equipped with a phone, computer and a fax machine, the latter experiencing a resurgence in popularity because it guaranteed greater security than the Internet. Again he was left alone, and although there was the possibility that his conversation could be taped, he thought it highly unlikely in a bank whose reputation had been built on privacy, exclusiveness and discretion.

He called Strathen using the mission mobile they'd purchased and relayed what had happened at Brampton's. 'I think he's been told to lie low until this is over. His secretary was very nervous.'

'So you're expecting company.'

'I've already had it,' and he relayed what Melody Everley had told him.

Strathen echoed Marvik's thoughts. 'She seems to have been very quick off the mark and ready to trust you,' he said suspiciously.

'Maybe it's my boyish good looks or charm.'

Strathen scoffed. 'I've looked into Brampton. He's done very well for himself. Freynsham wasn't lying when he said that Brampton worked for the Adam Smith Institute, one of Margaret Thatcher's favourite think tanks, and she was hardly a champion of strikes or strikers. Quite the opposite. After that he acted as a special policy adviser to the Conservative MP James Beeding and then at the Target Policy Centre, another Conservative think tank, where he became Executive Director before setting up his own company in 1990.'

'So not the type to stand on the picket line with his union comrades, championing the working classes.'

'You wouldn't have thought so. His business, Front Line Economics, has expanded considerably and the accounts show a very healthy profit. Brampton takes a hefty dividend each year. He's single — no hint of sexual scandals or embittered lovers.'

'Not unless you count Melody.'

'If that's true. He has an apartment in Kew Bridge, Riverside, London. Very expensive and very flash. He could have gone to ground there. There's a concierge though and he probably wouldn't let you in.'

'Brampton's probably instructed him to call the police if I show up.'

'But then he'd have to give them a reason and getting involved with the police is the last thing he wants. Too public. And that kind of media coverage wouldn't be good for business or his profile. He is, as Freynsham said, quite often in the press and on TV commenting on economic matters. The apartment fronts on to the Thames. There are some houseboats moored there but there's also a pontoon and landing pier. He could have left by boat, especially given that the people you saw him meeting on the South Bank left the Festival Pier by boat. He has access to government ministers and industrial and professional organizations at top level. He was born and raised in Southampton, the son of a newsagent. Both parents dead, an only child.'

'So he could have been playing a dirty game in the strike of 1979, pretending to be solidly with the strikers and yet all the time feeding information to the port owners and shipping companies.'

'Yes, who in turn were feeding it to the government who gave the information to the media to disgrace the strikers and undermine the strike.'

'Is revealing that enough for him to run scared?'

'If it involved murder — Darrow's and possibly Cotleigh's. He might even be responsible for Oscar Redburn's disappearance and possible death.'

'He'll lie low then until you and I are dealt with.'

'Which we should have been the night before last.'

'Freynsham can't know anything otherwise he'd have been dealt with a long time ago. But if Redburn wasn't killed then he could have returned in 1989 to blackmail Brampton and when someone decided to deal with him he took off again. Perhaps they got the wrong man and dealt with Joshua Nunton instead and that scared Redburn. And if that's the case then George Gurney and Bradley Pulford's deaths in Singapore aren't connected to it and Darrow didn't bring any valuable cargo back with him.'

'But he could have done,' Strathen said.

'You've got something?' Marvik asked, excited.

'Darrow *was* in Singapore in 1959. His son told me. It didn't take me long to track him down in Hartlepool. I rang his home and his wife gave me his mobile number when I said it was about his son, Ben, who was ill. I spun Darrow a story about being a doctor at St Richard's Hospital where Ben had been admitted, and that I needed to know if either he or his parents had suffered from any inherited genetic conditions as Ben was exhibiting symptoms of a form of inherited malaria that can be contracted from living in the Far East and passed on between generations. I reassured him that if Ben was tested positive we'd let him know, but he seemed more concerned about himself than his son. He's probably down at the doctors now and they're scratching their heads, never having heard of such an illness.'

Marvik laughed.

Strathen continued, 'He said he hadn't been in touch with his son for a year. He had been with his daughter about a month ago when she asked him if he had any photographs or papers belonging to Jack. He said he didn't. He knows his son is a junkie and says he's washed his hands of him. He told me that his father had worked as a stevedore in Singapore dockyard from late 1958 to early 1959.'

'So Darrow *must* have known Pulford.'

'Probably as they were both ex-pats. But Jack wasn't there long before he was summoned home. His wife became seriously ill after their second baby was still born in November 1957. Nigel Darrow was eighteen months old then.'

'So Jack buggered off to work abroad leaving his wife to cope with a toddler and to recover alone from the death of her second child. Doesn't sound like the act of a caring or compassionate man to me.'

'Maybe not but times were different then. They didn't talk about that kind of thing — stiff upper lip, put it all behind you and get on with life, only Audrey Darrow couldn't. She had a mental breakdown and was admitted to a psychiatric hospital where she stayed for two years and was in and out of for much of her life. And it could explain why the package, *if* there was one, got overlooked by Darrow, *if* Pulford gave it to him to bring back. The man had more pressing things on his mind.'

'But he must have known about Pulford's death, working in the docks.'

'Yes, but if he mentioned the package it could have delayed his passage home. He'd have had to stay for the inquest so he kept quiet.'

Marvik thought that made sense. 'Then in 1979 he remembers it and tells someone.'

'And that someone could have been Gordon Freynsham.'

'You've got more?' Marvik said, catching the keenness in Strathen's tone.

'Fossils.'

Marvik caught the sound of a distant telephone ringing.

Strathen continued, 'A team of palaeontology researchers from the University of Malaya and the Japanese universities, Waseda and Kumamoto, found dinosaur fossil teeth in the rural interiors of Pahang, reputed to be the first known discovery of dinosaur remains in Malaysia following field expeditions which began in 2012. They were identified as the teeth of a spinosaurid dinosaur, a carnivorous fish-eating dinosaur found from sedimentary rock strata of late Mesozoic age, most likely Cretaceous circa 145 to seventy-five million years ago.'

'I'm impressed.'

'So you should be. In the interior of Malaysia, Jurassic Cretaceous sediments are known to be widely distributed. It's believed that large deposits of dinosaur fossils still remain there and could become a target for illegal excavations by private fossil collectors or robbers.'

'But that was recent. We're talking about 1959.'

'Patience. In the seventies Mount Gagau, at the Kenyir Lake National Park, was found to have fossilized remains in its hills and Freynsham would have read about that. What if one or some of these rare fossils had been found earlier, in the forties or fifties and stored or put away by the British alongside other fossils and cultural artefacts, and Gurney found them when that lorry crashed on its way to transporting them out of the country? He recognized what he had, because after all he did come from the English Jurassic Coast. He gave them to Pulford because someone else was after them and Pulford gave them to Darrow before he was killed. Darrow, knowing Freynsham's area of expertise, remembered this package and asked him about them. Freynsham told him they were worthless when he knew bloody well they were worth a fortune. Brampton overheard and so too did Redburn, or all three of them conspired to steal them. Freynsham could sell them and they'd split the proceeds.'

'But they needed to kill Darrow and one of them did, only Cotleigh witnessed it so he had to be dealt with.' Marvik's mind grappled with this. 'Redburn took off with his share which ran out in 1989 when he returned. He saw how well Freynsham and Brampton were doing and decided to blackmail them. He took the name of Bradley Pulford to rub it in, knowing from Jack Darrow that Pulford had given him the package to bring back.'

'It makes sense.'

'But eventually they weren't having it so they either conspired to kill him or called his bluff and off he goes again until earlier this year when he decided to have one last try at extracting money from them and ends up dead on the shore on the Isle of Wight. And if that body is Redburn then the DNA taken from the remains will match with Sarah's.'

'Yeah, but would Crowder sanction that?'

'No, because it's all theory. Unless I can get a confession out of Brampton, which is unlikely now that he's gone to ground, but Freynsham's a very different matter. I'll head there now.'

Strathen said he would continue his research. Marvik rang off and had reached the bank's exit when his pay-as-you-go phone rang. He thought it was Crowder but it wasn't. It was Bryony. He answered it, making sure to keep inside the bank.

‘I’ve just come from Ben’s bedsit. Someone’s been in there and trashed it and I don’t think it was the police looking for drugs,’ she quickly announced.

And if the surveillance equipment was still working then someone would have seen her and been detailed to follow her.

She sounded scared. He didn’t blame her.

‘I don’t know what to do. Look, you’ve got to help me.’

‘Head for Waterloo station. Wait for me under the clock inside. I’ll be there as soon as I can.’ And that meant he’d have to shake his tail.

CHAPTER SIXTEEN

He was about half a mile away from Waterloo station which meant a fifteen-minute walk across the Thames via Golden Jubilee Bridge or five minutes on the Northern Line, which ran to Waterloo every three minutes. But if he went there directly his tail might guess his destination and it would be difficult to shake him off. There was the chance he could lose him in the crowd on foot. It depended on how good the man was. Marvik thought he'd see.

As he left the bank, he caught a glimpse of him standing at the bus stop. Marvik set off at a rapid pace. He turned right at Villiers Street, hurrying down it, weaving his way among the crowds, and then another right towards Golden Jubilee Bridge. He didn't look back but knew he was still being followed.

He ran up the steps and broke into a jog until he was about halfway across where he stopped suddenly, and, imitating Brampton, reached for his phone. He spun round and began talking into his phone while looking down the river towards Whitehall, Big Ben and the Palace of Westminster. His tail had no option but to either turn back or continue. He continued, averting his gaze to the other side of the river but Marvik would recognize him again. He could have been the man who had been on the motorbike outside Ben's bedsit — the build was right.

Marvik cut short his imaginary conversation as the man disappeared from view down the steps. Marvik turned and ran along the bridge in the direction he'd come. Tearing down the steps, he darted into the Embankment underground station. By now his tail would know he'd been tricked and be rushing back. But maybe he didn't need to because all he had to do was relay to his control what had happened and someone else would pick up the job — someone who was close by or who had also been following him, because there could have been two of them, maybe more, just as there had been when they'd come for them in Strathen's apartment.

He spotted the second man as he was making a pretence of studying the underground map. He was younger and leaner, dressed scruffily and sporting the same headgear: wires, earphones and a phone to make it look as though he was listening to music.

Marvik swiped his card on the ticket machine and made for the Bakerloo line and the platform that would take him to Charing Cross. He let the swarms of travellers push and bustle around him. From the corner of his eye he saw the man loiter in the entrance to the platform. Marvik caught the sound of an approaching train and the soft whoosh of hot air that pre-heralded its arrival. He moved towards the platform, took out his phone and made as though to consult it, looking around and behind him as though puzzled. He let the commuters jostle him, blocking him from sight.

The train rushed in and slid to a halt. He climbed on. The man tailing him did the same. Marvik stood by the doors. His pursuer took up position along the carriage to the right of him. He was fairish, unshaven, late thirties, with a lean face and a blank, vacant expression as though engrossed in his music or audio book. It was going to be a close-run thing and even then he didn't know how successful he'd be. He prepared for action. Timing was everything.

The train pulled away. Within seconds it seemed they were approaching Elephant and Castle, where Marvik knew he could get a train to take him to Waterloo. The train slid into the station. A few people alighted. Marvik had seconds before the doors shut. His eyes were peeled on the woman on the platform with her high-visibility customer service jacket and the paddle-shaped board in her hand that signalled all was clear for the doors to close. There was also that flashing of lights around the door switch that heralded they were about to close and a fraction of a second before they did. Marvik had a split second for action and he took it. He was off the train; the doors hissed closed behind him within a hair's breadth. The train moved away, carrying the man who had been tailing him.

Marvik hurried out with a grim expression. He was counting on the fact they wouldn't think he was heading for Waterloo station. He wished now he'd told Bryony to wait anywhere but on the station platform but it was too late for that. The train to Waterloo pulled in and he climbed on board. A few minutes later he was running up the escalator into the vast chasm of Waterloo station and crossing the heaving concourse, his eyes skimming the crowds for signs of either of the men who had tailed him or for someone who had taken over. He couldn't see anyone but someone might have been detailed to watch this end; they might have followed Bryony, in which case his tactics had been a waste of time. He'd soon find out.

She was where he'd told her to be, looking anxiously around her, shifting impatiently from foot to foot and glancing at her phone. She was wearing a three-quarter-length grey coat still with the same black dress underneath, so a friend hadn't lent her a change of clothes but she'd got the coat from somewhere. As Marvik headed towards her he scanned those who were eyeing the departure boards while he also registered the time of the train he needed.

'At last,' she cried, relief flooding her face and anxiety in her tired eyes. 'I thought you'd never come.'

The strain of the last two days was etched on her forehead and around her mouth. She'd managed to find some make-up and had applied lipstick, blusher and mascara. Her blonde hair was once again straight and clean. She'd probably freshened up in the hospital while with Ben, but he wondered where she had stayed last night. Perhaps with a friend who had loaned her the use of make-up and a coat but not a clean dress. She looked exhausted.

He grabbed her arm and swung her round. 'Walk. Don't say anything.' The Southampton train was leaving in ten minutes, which gave him time to buy their tickets from the machine. They couldn't get through the barriers without them. That accomplished, he steered her towards the platform at such a pace that it forced her to run beside him. The guard looked as though he was about to whistle the train's departure. Marvik almost threw her on the first carriage and as he did the doors slid shut, the whistle blew and the train moved off. No one else jumped on immediately before or after them.

The train wasn't busy, it being the middle of the day. Instead of taking the first available seats Marvik indicated for her to walk on. In the narrow space between the third and fourth carriages, he stopped. They were alone.

'Why did you leave the hospital?'

'Why shouldn't I? I wasn't compelled to stay there.' She flushed slightly, looked away then back at him with a mixture of defiance and sheepishness. 'I wanted to see if I could salvage my career. I missed the recall for that part and I contacted my agent and told her about the house fire and Ben being ill and asked if she could get me another slot. She said she couldn't. It's been cast. It's OK, I didn't mention you. But she told me the police had been in touch trying to contact me. They got her details from my website. I said I'd contact them but I haven't yet.'

'Why not?'

'Because I don't know what the hell to tell them.' She rounded on him. 'I don't want them messing about in my life and Ben's. I've had a lot of time to think about what's happened and being on a boat immediately after my house was torched and Ben being a heroin addict is probably enough to make the police think I'm a drug dealer or something equally ludicrous. The press only have to get a sniff of that and it could be my career ruined for ever.'

'I thought there was no such thing as bad publicity,' he muttered.

'Don't you believe it! You got me into this — you have to get me out. I'm not going to the police unless you and your friend come with me.' She looked away and then back up at him. 'And you won't do that, will you?' she added, resigned.

'Not until I know who killed Sarah and why.' He was glad she'd avoided the police. She had a point too. The police might think he and Shaun were drug dealers. Perhaps it had been the drug squad after all who had come in the very early hours of the morning to Strathen's apartment. And the police would certainly be inclined to believe he was a killer. Crowder could get him out of that but it would mean he'd failed and Marvik wasn't going to countenance that. Strathen wouldn't either. Marvik knew that the police would catch up with Bryony eventually unless she could lie low for a while until this was over. Marvik didn't know how long for, though. She'd have to stay with Strathen. They had to complete this mission — and soon.

'Where did you get the coat?' he asked.

'From a friend. I stayed with her last night.' She undid it to reveal the black dress. He could still smell the smoke on it.

'What made you go to Ben's bedsit?'

'I thought I'd stay there until things could be sorted out but when I saw what someone had done I got scared.' She looked dejected and tired. She'd had a tough time. 'Where are we going?'

'Southampton, to a boat in the marina there.'

'The same one that Ben got sick on?'

'No. We'll stop off in the town and you can buy what you need. You'll be safe with us.'

'You and your Marine friend?'

'Yes. Let's find a seat.'

No one had gone past them into the adjoining carriage, and glancing behind he couldn't see anyone loitering or taking an interest in them. They walked through the train until they came to two vacant seats in the first carriage. Marvik still couldn't see anyone following or watching them. Bryony took the window seat. She remained silent, preoccupied, staring out of the window. He didn't intrude on her thoughts. He rang Strathen and told him he had a guest and that they'd meet him at Southampton in the marina.

As the train sped south, his mind flicked back to the notebooks in his safe deposit box and the one he'd placed there. Did any of the other notebooks contain a computer disk? he wondered. How had Sarah come by it? Could it have been overlooked by the solicitor, Michael Colmead, when Marvik had given him instructions to make sure all his parents' papers were collected and despatched to the bank? Had someone taken it from their boat or the house? But why should they? And that didn't explain why or how it had come to be in Sarah's possession.

Then there was the name 'Vasa' which his father had inscribed on the disk. It was the Swedish version of Vaasa, a city on the west coast of Finland, his mother's native country but he didn't think his mother had originated from that city. Time to consider that later, *if* he chose to. He closed his eyes and let his mind go blank, yet he didn't sleep.

The train slid into Southampton Central just before two thirty. No one alighted who looked as though they were following them and as they crossed the road towards the shopping centre, Marvik checked again. They were OK.

He gave Sarah enough cash to buy what she needed from one of the chain stores, adding that it was there or nowhere. They didn't have time for shopping or for her to try on the clothes — she'd have to take a chance they would fit. While she purchased what she needed he headed for the food hall to stock up. He then bought some toiletries and towels. It meant losing sight of Bryony and he was relieved when he saw her at the checkout. As they walked towards the marina she told him she'd bought some make-up, two T-shirts, a jumper, a pack of black tights, underwear and a knee-length skirt.

'I'll pay you back out of the insurance money,' she added. 'My landlord must have been insured.'

Marvik didn't like to tell her that he wouldn't have been insured for her personal effects and clearly she'd had no insurance herself. 'Has he been trying to get hold of you?' He must have been told by now.

'No, but then that's hardly surprising as he's up the Congo or somewhere equally obscure and remote. He's a documentary filmmaker. He has the same agent as me. We met at a drinks do. The house belonged to his father and he inherited it.'

They turned into the marina. She nodded a greeting at Strathen who was in the main cabin, his laptop computer in front of him, the lid down.

'Take the aft cabin,' he instructed.

'Can I ring the hospital?'

Marvik answered, 'Not from here and not on your mobile. You can call them from the marina office later.'

'OK.' She went below and Marvik, stepping into the cockpit with Strathen so as not to be overheard, quickly brought him up to speed with what Bryony had told him. The wind was rising.

'I've got some interesting information,' Strathen said.

'Better save it for later,' Marvik hastily said as Bryony appeared.

'I'd like a shower.'

Marvik thought he could do with one too. There were two showers on board but Marvik said he'd walk with her to the marina showers. He waited outside while she entered. Strathen joined him a few minutes later. There was no one watching them.

Strathen relayed what he'd discovered. 'I've been doing some further research. While we could be right about rare fossils from Malaysia being in that package that Gurney got hold of, it might have contained something else just as valuable. Amber.'

'And Freynsham would have recognized that too.'

'Yes.'

But something else nudged in the back of Marvik's mind. 'Brampton's ring and tie pin were both made of amber. OK, so maybe it doesn't mean much,' he quickly added.

'But on the other hand it might.' Strathen continued, 'The Merit Pila lignite field in central Sarawak is the most important coal deposit of Malaysia. Much of it is close to the surface and can be mined by opencast but it also contains frequent long, thin seams of amber. The largest pieces of amber have been found there and if that was what was in the package then it would have fetched a fair sum of money if sold in 1959 or 1979.'

'And if there was lots more of it in that cargo then someone was making sure that it was taken out of the country before full independence came into being in 1960. Someone with access to sources at the highest level in government, or who was high up in the government at the time, who could utilize the navy to bring it back to Britain.'

'Yes, and the fact that Gurney and Pulford were so speedily eliminated means that this person must also have been in Singapore at the time, possibly overseeing the loading of the cargo on to that navy ship.'

Marvik rapidly considered this. 'He knew exactly what was in those crates and what was missing, which means he must have checked them either before they were loaded or while they were on board. I need to talk to Ralph Warnford again.'

'Want to head back to Poole marina?'

'Yes.'

'And Bryony?'

'Comes with us unless she changes her mind and decides to stay here or head back to Chichester, but I don't think she will. We'll tell her as little as possible, and not necessarily the truth. The less she knows the better.'

Strathen agreed. He took Bryony to the marina office to call the hospital while Marvik quickly showered. He joined them as they were heading back to the boat.

'Ben's recovering but the hospital said they need to discuss his future treatment with me,' Bryony relayed. 'I expect they want shot of him because they need the bed, but being a heroin addict they can't just throw him out on the streets and he can't go back to the bedsit, not only because it's a wreck, but because of what you said about Sarah's killer coming after him and me. I fobbed them off for now, saying I couldn't get there but I'll call them tomorrow.'

She climbed on board with Strathen but Marvik didn't follow; instead he went to the aft and made to cast off.

'We're leaving?' she asked, startled.

Strathen answered, 'Yes. There's no point in staying here.'

'Where are we going?'

'Poole.'

'What's there?'

Marvik replied, 'Possibly the answers to who killed Sarah and why.'

CHAPTER SEVENTEEN

Saturday

It was eight twenty when Marvik knocked on the door of Irene Templeton's thatched cottage in Steepleridge. Within a few seconds it was opened by a florid-faced, balding man in his mid-sixties who regarded Marvik with open hostility. His brown eyes flicked to Marvik's scars and the door closed just perceptibly.

Marvik recognized him as the impatient husband who had been tooting his horn in the car outside the church. Quickly he introduced himself and was relieved to see Irene Templeton appear behind her husband. Marvik apologized for the intrusion but said he had another question to put to Mr Warnford and that it was quite urgent that he spoke to him.

'It's a good job you've come early,' she said brightly, admitting him. 'Gerald is taking my father to the golf club. Dad likes to sit in the club room and chat to some of the older members he knows, having been a member there himself, while Gerald plays golf. Come through.'

Gerald looked as though he'd liked to have refused Marvik entry. Marvik heard him huff as he followed Irene into the lounge, where he found Ralph Warnford dressed smartly in a dark grey suit, shirt and tie, sitting in a wheelchair. His eyes lit up as he greeted Marvik. Quickly he dismissed Marvik's apology.

'It's about that cargo, sir,' Marvik began, taking the seat in front of the elderly man. 'Did anyone come on board to check that it was loaded?'

'No. I oversaw that.'

'But you didn't open the crates.'

'No. I wasn't authorized to. They were labelled strictly confidential.'

'And they were both sealed.'

'Yes, and there was no evidence they had been tampered with.'

'What did you do after they were loaded?'

'I signed the documentation and reported to my commanding officer that they were secure on board.'

'Did he inspect them?'

'He might have done later but he didn't immediately after I'd handed him the paperwork.'

'Was there anyone else travelling on board with you, a government official or diplomat?' Marvik asked.

'No, only the crew and some soldiers we were taking back to England. No one had clearance to go to the hold where the cargo was.'

That didn't mean they hadn't, just that Warnford wasn't aware of anyone doing so. And there was still the possibility that someone could have accessed the crates after the lorry crash and before they had been put on board the ship. How they would discover who that person was, though, was probably as impossible as discovering what the cargo had been.

Disappointed, Marvik made to take his leave when Warnford said, 'The captain dined ashore with some people from the High Commission before the cargo was loaded. He could have been told what was inside the crates but he'll have died a long while ago so you won't be able to ask him. His name was James Ethelton. He was Scottish and a very good friend of Sir Ambrose Shale's. In fact, he and Sir Ambrose had dinner on board ship the day before it sailed.'

'Why was Shale in Singapore?' Marvik asked, suddenly alert to this new information, hardly daring to hope it might take them a step forward.

'His ships often put in there and he had other business interests in Malaya. He owned mines and plantations. In fact, it was on one of Shale's ships that Bradley died. But as I said before I didn't know that Bradley was dead when we set sail for home.'

Marvik swiftly sifted this new information, recalling what Irene Templeton and Ralph Warnford had previously told him. Ambrose Shale had owned most of the land around here and both Pulford and Gurney's adoptive parents had managed farms belonging to him. Sir Ambrose Shale had been a wealthy man — influential, too — with connections. He was dead, though, so he couldn't be the man Crowder was interested in. But there was a connection.

'What was Sir Ambrose like?' he asked.

Warnford didn't need to think about his answer. It came immediately. 'Brave, tough, clever, highly respected and a very astute businessman. He was also very religious, a legacy from his father who had been a renowned and respected clergyman in Bath. But Ambrose wasn't interested in going into the church. Much like me — my father was the vicar here. I never intended following in my father's footsteps. Ambrose had a love of the sea the same as I did but there our paths diverged.'

Gerald Templeton cleared his throat noisily and said, 'Dad, we should be making a move.'

Warnford nodded but continued, 'Sir Ambrose built his shipping business from scratch. He was too young to be in the Great War and he escaped the terrible flu epidemic after it. At the age of twenty he started by chartering sailing vessels from Bristol but very soon turned to motor ships and cargo when he saw the returns were greater. By 1925 he'd raised money from investors to purchase the Portery Shipping Line, a fleet of eighteen ships which he expanded to twenty-seven, sailing from various ports around the UK but primarily the south.'

'Southampton?'

'Yes, and London and Bristol. His cargo ships were soon on regular runs to Australia, in fact, transporting building materials for the building of the Sydney Bridge which opened in 1932, and on runs to Canada and India and then the Far East. By 1939 he owned thirty-three ships. Thirteen of them were lost during the war. Unlucky for some, eh?'

Marvik heard Irene's husband sniff impatiently. 'Go on,' he encouraged.

'Ambrose bought the Wellmore estate and Kingston House, where he came to live with his wife in 1933. I was only seven at the time but my father used to take me to the big house when Sir Ambrose wanted to see him and to the farm cottages to visit his tenants. There were also services held in the private church for the family and servants — the one that's crumbling to ruins on the clifftop which the army pump shells into.' He smiled knowingly at Marvik, who smiled back. Warnford quickly continued before his son-in-law could interject. 'Sir Ambrose was delighted when his son, Cedric, was born, but his joy soon turned to sorrow when his wife died shortly after giving birth. I remember my father telling me about the private christening in the church. During the war we didn't see a lot of Sir Ambrose or the family and servants because the house was given over to the army for the duration and the American army were based there in preparation for D-Day. But you know that, being a veteran. By then I'd joined the navy. It was right at the end of the war, so I didn't get to see much action.'

His son-in-law looked set to interpose but Ralph Warnford, as though sensing this, promptly continued. Marvik thought there was a wicked twinkle in the old man's eyes.

'Ambrose Shale returned to Kingston House just after the war. I think it must have been about 1946. The family spent the war years in Scotland, except for Ambrose Shale, who spent most of it travelling on board his ships. He was called up in 1941 but was deemed medically unfit — a weak heart, it seemed. So he decided to travel on his ships as an example to the men. He was said to be a very good seaman and earned a great deal of respect from the men. He faced the same dangers as them — weak heart or not he never showed fear and he came through the war unscathed. No one saw much of Cedric Shale — he was away at school and then overseas. In fact, no one saw much of him until he inherited the estate and his father's business in 1965. My father was very ill by then. I had compassionate leave and my father died that same year. I don't know who buried Ambrose Shale or where he was buried.'

Irene Templeton answered, 'He's in the family plot in Salisbury.'

'Dad . . .' Irene's husband tapped at his watch.

Marvik said, 'And after 1965, did Cedric Shale spend much time on the estate?'

'I think he preferred London, or at least that's what people around here said, including my mother, who I used to come back to visit. My wife and I were living in married quarters by then, first in Plymouth and then in Portsmouth. Cedric left the management of the estate and the house to estate managers and they came and went once Frank Leyton retired fourteen years ago. Leyton managed the estate when Cedric inherited it after Sir Ambrose's estate manager retired, having been left a legacy by him.'

Irene said, 'I met the existing estate manager, Greg Audley, two years ago. I went to Kingston House to ask if Mr Shale would donate something for the raffle for the church fete. Mr Audley said he'd ask him. I was left waiting outside and he returned within a few minutes with one of Cedric's paintings — apparently he does a lot of them. Even by then he'd become reclusive. Well, quite frankly, it was dreadful. I think it ended up on the tip. No one wanted it.'

'Why not?' Marvik asked, curious.

'It was just daubs of black and red paint.'

'Are there any heirs?'

Irene again answered, ignoring her husband's black looks, 'Not family ones. Cedric never married. We've often wondered who will get the estate when he passes on. When I say "we" that's mainly me and the vicar. We're hoping that some of the local charities and the church will be benefactors but I'm not counting on it.'

'Will there be much to leave?' Marvik mused.

'Who knows? He's been selling off the farms and property.'

Ralph Warnford said, 'Cedric, although a successful businessman, never seemed to rise to his father's heights. He didn't even get a knighthood.'

'He might have been offered one and refused,' suggested Irene.

Her father shrugged his bony shoulders.

Marvik thanked Warnford and his daughter and took his leave, much to her husband's relief. Sir Ambrose Shale was dead. If he had been in collusion with someone in government to steal precious fossils, amber and artefacts from Malaya and benefit from the sale of them then the revealing of that knowledge couldn't harm him or anyone else who had collaborated with him. They'd all be long gone, but someone might be desperate to protect their father's reputation. Cedric Shale. Would he care, though? He was elderly and reclusive. He had no heirs. He was selling off the estate, according to Irene Templeton. Why? Because he could no longer manage it? Marvik doubted he needed the money — not unless he had gone through the vast fortune his father had left him and that was possible. Marvik recalled what Warnford had said about Sir Ambrose's business interests in Malaya. Maybe he or his managers had discovered the fossils or a rich seam of amber on his property, but if so, there was surely no need to get them out of the country in the manner Warnford had described. He rang Strathen and asked first where Bryony was.

'In her cabin.'

Marvik relayed what Warnford had told him, asked Shaun to get whatever information he could on Sir Ambrose Shale's business empire and then struck out west for Kingston House.

CHAPTER EIGHTEEN

The large Georgian manor house lay beneath Marvik as he emerged from the small copse on the hill. Arranged over three storeys the white-stone building, with two elegant bays at either end, sat in splendid isolation in the valley. A high wall surrounded it, punctuated by a pair of wrought-iron gates, probably electronic. They were closed. The western flank gave on to a hilly wooded area, which Marvik knew was part of the army range, as was the land to the immediate south of the house. The gently rising fields led to the cliff edge and the jagged bay where he had stood two days ago in among the ruined buildings. The magnificent coastline spread out before him, dipping into bays and rising in grass-covered cliffs. The red flag was flying which signalled that the army were on manoeuvres, and he heard the sound of gunfire above the bleating sheep in the fields around him.

He extracted a pair of powerful binoculars from his rucksack and focused them first on the gated entrance. Above the gates were two video cameras at either end of the stone pillars. There were also cameras on the boundary walls. Shale obviously liked his privacy. Nothing wrong with that. There was an intercom system to the right of the gates. He could ask to see Cedric Shale but if he was as reclusive as Irene claimed then Marvik doubted he'd be permitted entry. And saying he wanted to talk about the late Sir Ambrose Shale wouldn't grant him an audience either.

He trained the glasses on the house. The ground-floor windows were shuttered, so too were those on the middle floor, but he paused to study the triple bay window on the left-hand side of the house. The window was open at the bottom on the right and one of the curtains was half draped across it. Beneath the window was a narrow ledge and to the right a drainpipe that led from the top of the bay to the ground. In the sloping roof above was a small window and another was above the centre of the house, with the pattern of the left-hand bay repeated on the right-hand side of the house. There were cameras above both drainpipes facing out across the front grounds. The paintwork on the windows was flaking and the plaster work in disrepair.

He swung the binoculars over the grounds. Weeds were growing around the porticoed entrance and in the long, sweeping gravel drive. The grass hadn't been cut in a long time and the shrubs had spread. Shale had locked himself inside and didn't seem to be worried that the place was falling down around him. Marvik wondered how many staff he employed. A cook and housekeeper, probably, but not a gardener by the look of things and probably not a driver if the man never left the house. But someone must operate the electronic gates and be linked up to the surveillance cameras. Was it the estate manager, Greg Audley, whom Irene Templeton had mentioned?

He swivelled the glasses to see a van approaching the house along the private road. It bore the name of a national supermarket chain. Stuffing the glasses into his rucksack, Marvik broke cover of the woods and ran down the hilly slope, keeping low. He didn't want to be seen and ejected before he got the chance to meet Cedric Shale. As the van pulled up in front of the electronic gates Marvik darted behind it, still keeping low and out of sight of the driver and of the security cameras. He was counting on them and the boundary ones pointing outwards.

The driver leaned out, pressed the intercom, announced himself and was permitted entry. Marvik jogged behind the van as it slowly travelled up the driveway and headed left along the western flank of the house towards the rear. In a glance, Marvik registered the stretch of grass to his right in front of the weed-strewn path bordering the ivy-clad walls. There were two long sash windows that reached to the ground and a set of French doors. There was no sign of any security cameras. Breaking cover from the rear of the van, again keeping low, he ran to the windows, noting with satisfaction that the framework was crumbling. Retrieving his keys from his pocket, he extracted a thin strip of metal and inserted it under the catch. The window slid open with a screech that he thought could have been heard a mile away. He froze, expecting an alarm to sound, but if it did it was a silent one. No one came running.

He climbed in and surveyed the room. It was empty. He noted the faded patches on the walls where once pictures had hung. The mantelpiece was devoid of ornaments and the built-in bookshelves bare of books. It looked as though it had once been used as a study. There was no carpet on the wooden floor and no infrared sensors.

He crossed to the door and eased it open. It gave on to a wide black-and-white tiled hall; on the right was a sweeping staircase. Again there was no furniture in the hall. Cobwebs hung from the two chandeliers and from the corners of the ceiling but the floor was swept and clean. Marvik stood and listened. He could hear voices from the rear of the house to his left but the two doors that led to it were both closed. Again he noted the absence of sensors and cameras.

From his perusal of the house earlier there was, he suspected, only one place to find the elderly Cedric Shale. Taking the stairs two at a time he noted that the carpet was grubby, the brass stair rods pitted and stained and the banister unpolished. Again, there were faded patches on the walls where pictures had once hung. Only two remained — one of a steamship circa the twenties and the other of a man in scarlet robes and gold chains of office. The pitted brass plaque beneath it claimed it was Sir Ambrose Shale, a narrow-faced fair man with a solemn expression. Maybe he didn't like having his picture painted, Marvik thought, coming out on to the landing.

It might only be a matter of minutes or seconds before he was noticed and intercepted. He had little time to spare. But there were no alarms or cameras in the corridor, and still no one came to apprehend him. As he made his way to the bay-windowed room he'd seen from the binoculars he threw open the doors to a couple of rooms on his way. Both were empty. The corridor, too, was bare and grubby and the whole floor smelt of dust, decay and disinfectant, the latter of which emanated from the room which was his destination.

The door opened silently to his touch and Marvik found himself in a large room decorated in pale blue faded wallpaper. It was clean but even the disinfectant couldn't disguise the smell of sickness and urine. Sitting in the window in a wheelchair was a lean figure, half bent over. At first Marvik thought the man must be asleep but as he approached he lifted his head. Wild, frightened eyes greeted Marvik from behind a gaunt, lined face. Marvik quickly held out his hands in an open, friendly gesture. It made no difference. The man shouted: 'Don't kill me. Don't kill me.' He put his hands to his ears and threw his scrawny body from side to side, screaming and shouting.

Marvik cursed. Surely this would summon whoever he'd heard talking in the kitchen.

'I won't harm you,' he said moving forward. But the elderly man wasn't going to be convinced.

'The devil. The devil!' he screeched, putting his hands over his ears and thrashing his body about wildly in the wheelchair.

There was nothing for it. Marvik could hear a door slamming and running footsteps. Time to leave. He raced to the open sash window, thrust it open wider and climbed out on to the thin ledge, pushing the window down as much as he could behind him. Reaching for the drainpipe, his fingers gripped it and nimbly he scaled down it, expecting to see security officers below him and one above him leaning out of the window. But dropping on to the gravel and looking up there was no one peering out of the window and no one rushed to detain him. The screaming continued, rising hysterically, yet still no one came for him.

Keeping close to the wall, he retraced his steps to the side of the house and once again entered through the sash windows. Stealing to the door that led into the hall, he opened it a fraction and waited. He could hear voices from above, a man and a woman's. He crept out into the hall and up the stairs, his pulse beating fast. As he came on to the landing he could hear the voices more clearly. The door to the old man's room was open slightly and Marvik drew closer to it, peering through the crack. Inside were a man and a woman in their fifties. Both were standing over the bed where Cedric Shale was now lying, slipping into sleep.

'Will he be OK?' the man asked somewhat anxiously.

'He'll be fine now. Stop worrying, Greg. I've just upped the dose a little.'

'Not too much, I hope.'

'I know what I'm doing,' she snapped. 'What set him off?'

'Who knows? Anything can, you know that. Hallucinations are part of the dementia he has, poor soul. He's convinced that he's going to be killed. And you know how deluded he is, thinking we're all out to kill him, when it's quite the opposite. He can't help it.'

'Should we tell the boss?'

'Tell him what?' she scoffed. 'There was no one here. He didn't see anyone. Do you want to get us the sack?'

'No.'

'Then keep your mouth shut.'

She turned away from the bed. Marvik stepped back and pushed open the door to one of the empty bedrooms he'd checked earlier. He saw them exit. Both were stoutly built. The man, Greg, had grey hair and a rumpled, ruddy countenance; the woman had short brown hair and a squashed, round, lined face.

Marvik heard their voices on the floor below fade into the back of the house. He was now convinced they were the only occupants. There had to be a servants' staircase in this house, probably at the far end of the corridor. As he headed along it he checked the doors to the bedrooms and bathrooms — all of them were empty with the exception of the last room facing the front with the matching bay window. It was lavishly and comfortably furnished in gold and blue, with clean drapes at the window, a king-sized bed which was made up and modern bedroom furniture. It opened up into another room which had been made into a shower room. Everything was clean. The fabrics and bed linen were of a high quality. There were no female toiletries or clothes but there were men's toiletries and some casual expensive designer clothes in the wardrobe. Studying them, Marvik noted they fitted a slim man of about six foot.

He tried the door opposite, knowing that it would lead to the servants' staircase, and it did. As he descended the grubby wooden stairs to the ground floor he could again hear the couple talking. The door was ajar and Marvik could see that they were in a large, modern kitchen. Greg Audley was sitting at the island in the middle, while the woman, probably his wife, was at a coffee machine. Marvik stealthily headed past the door and into the hall where he turned into the room he'd entered by and made for the window.

Once outside he ran across the grass to the western edge of the boundary wall towards the woods and the army range. The cameras must have picked him up, but Audley was in the kitchen and he was all the security this place had except for an alarm which was obviously switched off during the day. There was a chance the cameras were hooked up to someone's computer or phone and he was being observed but Marvik was no longer worried about that.

He reached the wall and within seconds had found a place where he could easily scale it. Soon he was in the cover of the trees and heading south, his mind spinning with what he'd just seen. A sick, elderly, deranged man, Cedric Shale, living in fear and alone, except for the paid help. His possessions all but gone. What had become of his wealth? He must have made considerable money from the sale of his business empire and his farms. Had someone blackmailed him over the years because of something his father had done and when the money had run out Shale, through his carers, had been forced to sell his possessions? His money couldn't have been spent on his care because all he had was two people looking after him and the house hadn't been heated, only the rooms that were being used, such as Shale's bedroom, which had been warm. The radiators had been switched off in the other rooms. Had the Audleys exploited Shale? But the woman had mentioned the 'boss'. So, who was the 'boss'? Could it be Donald Brampton? But why would he be fleecing Shale? The answer could be connected with the cargo that Ambrose Shale had brought back to Britain from Malaya via the navy and Marvik wondered if that cargo had been on the navy vessel unofficially. Perhaps Captain Ethelton had been doing his old friend a favour. The two army guys who had shown up in Portsmouth dockyard to transport it to London could have been phoney with fake papers, and instead the cargo had been transported to Sir Ambrose Shale's home here and he'd sold the looted cargo over the years. Brampton had discovered this via Jack Darrow and the package he'd got from Pulford.

Brampton had been benefiting from the sale of Cedric Shale's belongings. And he was keeping him alive because he wasn't going to kill the fatted calf. Once everything had been sold and every penny Shale owned had been transferred to the 'boss's' coffers, then there would no longer be any reason for Shale to live. The devil indeed would come to kill him. And Brampton might not be in this alone because if Marvik could believe what Melody had told him he had phoned someone and demanded their help. He recalled what she claimed to have overheard: *He's sniffing around, wants to know what happened during that strike. For Christ's sake, get him off my back. You owe me, remember. Neither of us can afford this coming out.* Then she said she'd heard him say something about dirty secrets.

Marvik looked up at the heavy, dark grey cloud building from the west and out to sea, heralding the approach of rain. Getting wet was the least of his preoccupations. He wanted to know who was keeping Shale imprisoned and alive.

He negotiated his way around the ruined buildings towards the cliff edge, listening to the sound of the gunfire and knowing it was too far away to trouble him. Once again, as he'd done on Thursday, he stared out at the grey, choppy sea. There was a yacht with its sails down making for port before the weather worsened and a fishing boat heading east in the same direction. Not the Killbecks', though. He gazed down on the bay. It was difficult to enter given the rocks on either side but not impossible. Both he and Strathen had done so not only in daylight but at night. Something stirred at the back of his mind but, try as he might, he couldn't retrieve it.

He rang Strathen, hoping he'd get a signal. He did. He asked if he could talk. Strathen said he could. Bryony was in her cabin and he was on the pontoon well away from the boat. She would have to pass him if she wanted to get off.

'How is she?'

'Restless and anxious.'

Marvik relayed what he had discovered at Kingston House, his thoughts about the cargo on board the navy vessel and on Donald Brampton.

'Ralph Warnford was right,' Strathen said. 'Sir Ambrose Shale owned mines and plantations in Malaya and he was a very influential businessman with contacts in all the right places. He used to entertain politicians at Kingston House in the fifties and early sixties including the then Prime Minister, Harold Macmillan, so it's certainly possible he could have used the navy to bring out rare fossils, amber and artefacts he'd managed to purloin while operating there. As to Cedric Shale, I've been searching the financial news archives. There are no pictures of him. He kept a very low profile in the business community earning the nickname of the "shy tycoon" but he expanded the business very successfully until it was sold to Pentland in 2000 for millions. The acquisition was referred to the Competition Commission but it got through all right.'

'Now I wonder who did the economic reports and the representation,' Marvik said cynically.

'I won't give you three guesses because you'll get it in one. Front Line Economics. So we have another connection. Shale succeeded his father in 1965 and according to the financial press the company ran through a number of general managers who oversaw the business operations over the years. I've run their details through my databases and four of them are dead.'

'Sounds like a high-risk business!'

'Maybe working for Shale gave them all early heart attacks. The fifth general manager was James Deacon. I've spoken to him on the telephone. He was quite happy to talk about Shale when I said I was writing a book on the Shale family, although he claimed he didn't have much to tell. But when I prodded him, he said that Cedric Shale was so changeable that he was almost impossible to work with. He'd agree to one thing and then the next moment claim he hadn't. It was often difficult to get hold of him and when they had meetings he'd conduct them as though on autopilot. He said he often used to leave the meetings wondering what the hell they had agreed. I said that despite that, the corporation was highly profitable and successful. He had to admit that it was, and that Shale could be ruthless when required. If a division wasn't performing, then either the management would be sacked or the division sold off. He claimed that Shale had a nervous kind of energy, like a man always on tenterhooks — restless, as though his mind was constantly jumping about but he had a knack of seeing into the future. He shed some businesses and acquired others at the right time. He said, and I quote, "He had nil people skills and always seemed vague and weak, as though he didn't have a clue what he was doing, but underneath he must have been clever and astute — one of those boffin types. Boffins don't always make good business leaders but this one did, though God knows how." His secretaries came and went — none of them stayed longer than a couple of years and he often used temps. It's an unusual profile for a corporate executive. Deacon said that Shale hated photographs and would never have one taken. There was never any talk about romantic entanglements of any kind. He once told Deacon in a rare moment of confidence that he'd much preferred to have been a painter but it hadn't been an option. Makes you wonder why he didn't just sell it all when he inherited it.'

'Well, it's all gone now,' Marvik said. 'Someone's selling it and it's not the Audleys.'

So what next? Did he return to Kingston House and confront the Audleys? Did he travel back to London, gain access to Brampton's apartment and see if he could find out where he had gone? Or should he confront Freynsham again and ask him what was in that package that Darrow had given them? But they didn't even know there was a package, he thought with exasperation. It was all theory.

He rang off after Strathen said he'd continue probing as best he could with Bryony on board, but at present she seemed remarkably disinterested in what he was doing and hadn't even complained that she was stuck on a boat.

'Did she ask where I was?' Marvik had said.

'Yes. I told her you were making enquiries. She looked annoyed at the fob off but she didn't press me.'

Marvik gazed out to sea, feeling frustrated and, if he admitted it, a little defeated. What were they missing? He tried to pull together the various strands of what he'd seen, heard and learned over the last few days but it still didn't add up. The yacht had gone from his sight but the fishing boat was still heading east. It focused his thoughts back on the Killbecks and from them to the Pulford who had shown up in Swanage in 1989. Why had the phoney Pulford, possibly

Oscar Redburn, latched on to the Killbecks? There had to be a reason and maybe that was the critical point — not why he had taken off but why he had picked on them when he could have returned anywhere along this coast and latched on to another boatowner. And why a boat?

His eyes dropped to the bay then out to sea at the fishing boat as his brain teemed. The thought that eluded him a moment ago took shape. Was it possible? Had Pulford approached the Killbecks in 1989 because he had known or seen them in 1979, not at any strike but on the coast? And perhaps he'd had a hold over them, which was why Leonard Killbeck had let Pulford live with him and why Leonard and Matthew had given Pulford a job. Had Pulford witnessed them doing something illegal? Had the Killbecks been smuggling? And perhaps in 1990, Matthew, with the aid of his brother, Leonard, his son, Adam, and even Joshua Nunton had killed Pulford, or rather Oscar Redburn, as Marvik was convinced he really was, and had dumped his body in the Solent. If so, then the body washed up on the beach on the Isle of Wight in January was someone else, possibly Joshua Nunton, who had taken off after the murder unable to live with what he had done. It still didn't explain everything — far from it — but if he worked on that basis then there was a great deal more that Matthew Killbeck could tell him, and this time Marvik was not going to be fobbed off.

CHAPTER NINETEEN

Marvik had been banking on finding Matthew at home, knowing that he rarely left Mary, but for the second time he was greeted by Abigail. 'Matthew's had to go out on the boat with Adam. Jensen's still claiming he's on his death bed and there's little chance of him picking it up and walking, let alone working, and they're behind with the catch.'

That meant he'd head to the bay. Marvik made to leave but Abigail's words nudged something at the back of his mind . . . death bed, dying, the dead rising and Mary's frightened words the last time he had been here. What was it she'd said, yes, *has the devil got him?* meaning her husband, Matthew. And Shale had accused him of being the devil. Was the devil Mary was so afraid of the same one that Shale was also terrified of? Did the devil have a scarred face like him? If so it certainly wasn't Brampton or Freynsham but it could be the man Melody had heard Brampton contact. He asked if he could speak to Mary. Hopefully this time she wouldn't be so petrified.

Abigail raised her eyebrows at the request. 'I'm not sure you'll get much sense out of her. But you're welcome to try.' She stepped back and Marvik walked into the room where the frail and fragile Mary was sitting close to the electric fire.

As she looked up Marvik steeled himself for the same reaction as he'd had previously but she just stared blankly at him.

'I'm a friend of Matthew's,' he said, perching on the armchair opposite, trying to reassure her. 'I wanted to ask you about the dead rising up.' Abigail eyed Marvik, agog. Gently, he continued, 'You said something in the churchyard and in the pub about Jesus dying and rising again.'

She shrank back, fear now creeping into her eyes. 'The devil.'

'Where did you see the devil, Mary?' Marvik gently urged.

'He's coming to get me,' she cried, her paper-thin skin turning pale.

Marvik hastily rose. He didn't want to upset her. 'It's all right, Mary. He won't get you. You're quite safe,' he said gently.

She looked as though she didn't believe him.

Abigail showed him out. 'I did warn you.'

'Do you know who she's talking about?'

'I've no idea. What she sees is the past mixed up with the present and sometimes what she might have imagined as a child or young woman.'

Maybe, but Marvik was convinced she was talking about someone real. And he was growing even more certain that the 'devil' Mary saw was the same one that Shale saw. Abigail's words reverberated around his head, *the past mixed up with the present.* Mary had seen 'the devil' in the past and she'd also seen him recently, otherwise why was she so agitated and frightened?

Marvik pulled up the collar of his jacket against the rain and instead of heading for the bay he detoured through the sodden streets towards the church where the funeral service for the phoney Bradley Pulford had been held. Within ten minutes he was retracing his footsteps of eight days ago. What was it that Mary had kept saying in the pub — something about the dead rising up? Had she seen someone she believed was dead? Had Mary seen someone from the past standing in the distance, at the lych-gate perhaps? But Marvik was certain there had been no one except the Killbecks, himself and the vicar in the churchyard, unless he counted the undertakers and he didn't think any of them was Mary's devil.

He studied the gravestones. Many of them were ancient. But behind the church, just as there had been in Steepleridge, there were more recent ones including that of Leonard Killbeck who, as Matthew had told him, had died in 1995. There was also a headstone for Albert and Lillian Killbeck and, looking at the dates, Marvik knew they were Matthew and Leonard's parents.

He turned and made for Swanage Bay and the lifeboat station. His mission mobile phone rang on the way. It was Strathen. Marvik could hear the wind down the line, which meant Strathen was in the cockpit or on the shore.

'Bryony's gone,' he said without preamble.

'When?' Marvik asked sharply.

'Twenty minutes ago. She went to the marina shower block. I kept my eyes peeled on her but after a few minutes she didn't come out. I asked the marina staff to check the showers. Empty. She didn't go out the front but there's a door at the rear that gives on to the refuse area. It's kept locked only this time it wasn't. It had been forced open. I've checked the marina CCTV — the cameras don't extend to the rear but they picked up a black van leaving the marina at the same time as when Bryony was inside. The registration number was obscured. I fobbed off the staff, saying she was my girlfriend and we'd rowed.'

'So he's finally got her.'

'Looks that way. I also called Crowder after our earlier discussion and your idea that Bradley Pulford might have seen Matthew and Leonard Killbeck along the coast in 1979 engaged in some illegal activity which was why he'd thought he'd found a safe billet with them in 1989. I asked him if Matthew, Leonard or Adam Killbeck had a police record. Matthew Killbeck has one for violent assault in 1971. He was in a pub brawl. Nothing since.'

'If Mary really believes she saw someone who she thought was dead then it could be Pulford who has returned and the body discovered in January which was cremated is Joshua Nunton, as you said earlier. I don't think Leonard Killbeck has returned from the dead unless his headstone is a fake.'

'I'll check if he really is dead.'

'And with Bryony missing it might be a good idea if you moved the boat.'

'Already have. I'm at sea heading towards Swanage. I'll anchor off the pier.'

It wouldn't be a very pleasant journey in the rain and wind but Strathen was experienced enough to easily handle it. Marvik said he was heading there now in the hope of seeing the Killbecks. They might have called an earlier halt to their fishing because of the weather and he could have missed them.

The fishing boat was on the shore along with the pick-up truck but there was no sign of either Adam or Matthew. Marvik made to cross to it but as he did he caught a movement out of the corner of his eye. He tensed and spun round in time to see a figure lunge at him. In an instant Marvik grabbed the upraised arm and in one fluid movement twisted it up high, locked his foot around Adam Killbeck's ankles and brought him crashing down on to the hard concrete, almost wrenching Adam's arm from its socket. Adam screamed in pain and Marvik, wasting no time, grabbed him roughly by his dark jacket and hauled him up. He made to smash his fist into the face when a cry rang out from behind him.

'No!'

Marvik ignored it. Through gritted teeth, he addressed the body on the ground. 'No motorbike this time — makes it much easier for me,' he said, and made to strike when the voice again came from behind.

'It's not him you want, it's me.'

Marvik paused. Then he thrust Adam Killbeck back so hard that his head knocked against the concrete. He cried out in pain. Marvik could see that he'd dislocated Adam's shoulder. Well, tough. He spun round to face Matthew Killbeck. Abigail must have called Matthew on his mobile phone as soon as he'd left the house; they'd cut short their fishing and had laid a trap knowing that he'd return here at some stage to find them. Abigail had probably also told Matthew that Mary had been rambling on about the devil and the dead.

With a worried expression on his weather-beaten, sodden face, Matthew addressed Marvik. 'I need to get Adam to hospital.'

'First the truth — no bullshit this time.'

Matthew hesitated. Adam hauled himself up, his face ashen. He looked dazed and he was groaning with pain. Marvik said, 'The quicker you talk, Matthew, the quicker your son gets medical attention. Who are the dead rising up?'

'No one. Mary gets confused.'

'Who did she see in the churchyard at Pulford's funeral service?'

'There wasn't anyone, only us — you know that. She's got dementia.' Matthew's troubled eyes glanced at his son and then back to Marvik.

'So why did a man pretending to be Bradley Pulford latch on to you and your brother, Leonard, in 1989? What was it he had over you? What did he see you doing in 1979 along the coast?'

Matthew visibly started. His skin paled. Marvik knew he was on the right track. 'Why would you let him stay with your brother and sleep with your niece?'

Matthew's fists clenched. His mouth set in a tight line.

Adam groaned. Matthew's eyes flicked to him and back to Marvik, full of fury.

'You have a police record for violence. You got caught once but how many times have you got away with it? How many times have you killed?'

'I haven't killed anyone.'

'No? What about Leonard? Maybe he was the killer?'

Adam was moaning with pain as he lay on the wet, hard concrete. Marvik had to hurry. There were no boats anchored in the bay but someone might see them from the pier, although thankfully it was wet and the light was dim.

'Leonard would never kill anyone,' Matthew maintained.

'But you were on the coast in 1979 and Pulford saw you doing something illegal. He threatened to tell.'

'Dad.' Adam stirred himself and looked up at his father with pain-wracked, haunted eyes. It was, Marvik interpreted, a plea for him to keep quiet rather than to get him medical help.

'What happened, Matthew, in the bay below Kingston House?' Marvik persisted. The last was a guess but not such a wild one given that the Shales were involved in this as far back as Singapore in 1959.

'Nothing,' Matthew vehemently declared.

But Marvik knew that at last he had another piece of the puzzle. Whatever it was, it had been enough for Oscar Redburn to return as Bradley Pulford in 1989 and live off the Killbecks, occasionally putting in a day's fishing when he felt like it.

'I must get Adam medical help.'

'Not until I get the truth.'

'Dad, say nothing,' Adam groaned, trying to raise himself, but the effort was too much. He slumped back.

Matthew made to go to him but Marvik blocked the way. He held the elderly man's hostile and frightened stare. Suddenly Matthew's body slumped. Marvik held his breath in anticipation.

Matthew addressed Adam. 'No, son, it's no use.' Then to Marvik: 'I knew you'd find out the moment you came to the funeral. I could see you wouldn't let it go. I thought at first that you must be working for the police but you didn't act and talk like a copper. Then I thought you might be related to Joshua except the only relation he had was his mother and she's dead.'

'What did Pulford see, Matthew?' Marvik repeated. He could see Strathen's boat edging into the bay.

'The same as me, or rather more than me.'

Marvik eyed him, puzzled.

Matthew continued, 'I heard it first. The army were on exercise. I was walking along the coast, I was trespassing on army land, but then I often did. I know my way around there enough not to get shot at. I saw the motorboat making out to sea, very fast, and as I drew near to the bay and looked down a man came out from behind the outcrop of rocks on the other side of it and stared after the boat. He turned and looked directly at me. He was as white as a sheet. He scrambled up the cliff towards me in a right state, gabbling on about how this man had been shot on the beach and how his body had been bundled on to the boat. He said he'd been looking for fossils. He knew that it was prohibited there so when he heard someone come down the cliff path and then the boat approach he hid out of sight behind the rocks. He said he had recognized one of the men and knew he was a powerful man with influence and wealth, who had dangerous friends.'

'Cedric Shale.'

'I don't know if it was him. I didn't see him.'

But he had seen the boat and a man like Matthew would have recognized it if it had been local or if he saw it again.

'What kind of boat?'

'I don't know.'

Oh, but Matthew did. Marvik let that go for now as Matthew continued, 'He asked me what I was going to do and I said . . .' He paused.

'You said forget about it. That it was none of your business.'

Matthew nodded. 'It wasn't that I was afraid, just . . .'

'You don't like the police and you had a record for violence. They might have believed you were the killer.'

'He said it was for the best. He'd clear out and say nothing. Besides, the man they shot might still be alive. He went west and I headed home in the opposite direction. I forgot about it.'

'Until 1989 when he showed up on the quayside as Bradley Pulford.'

Matthew nodded, his expression haunted. 'That's who he said he was. I didn't ask for his papers.'

'Dad.' Adam's face was contorted with pain. He looked as though he was going to throw up. Matthew pleaded with Marvik with his eyes but Marvik said, 'Go on.'

'He'd come looking for me and asked me to give him a job. He knew I was a fisherman because I must have let it slip on the cliff path and it wouldn't have taken long for him to find me anyway. He said he needed a job. I took him on.'

'But he didn't really want to work.'

'No.'

'Did he say why he'd come back?'

'No.'

'Or why he was using a false name?'

'I didn't know it was false.'

Marvik saw that was the truth. 'He blackmailed you with what you'd witnessed.'

'But I'd witnessed nothing.'

Marvik didn't believe him.

Matthew Killbeck said, 'Pulford was clever and cunning. He sort of got under our skin. I hadn't killed anyone — I'd only half witnessed something — but he made me feel as though I'd seen more and been involved in more. He said I'd be charged by the police as an accessory after the fact, or even as a killer — there would be so little evidence left to say otherwise.'

Marvik heard Adam being sick. He was groaning with pain. Matthew reached for his phone. Marvik stepped forward. 'In a moment.'

Matthew took a breath. 'What made things worse was that Stacey took a fancy to him and he thought he was in clover. Adam and I lied when we said he was a good worker — he wasn't. He was a lazy, idle bugger who thought he was better than he was. He was a sponger. Then he asked for a share of the business and I told him to piss off. But he kept on about how the police would think I was a killer, and about my police record. Then Stacey got pregnant. So I agreed. Adam went nuts. He hated Pulford and couldn't understand why I was always giving in to him. Adam thought Pulford could do no wrong in my eyes and Stacey thought the sun shone out of his backside. He asked for money and I kept bailing him out.'

'And Joshua Nunton got increasingly jealous and angry.'

'Yes. Please let me get help for Adam?'

Marvik gave a curt nod. Matthew retrieved his phone, dialled the emergency services and explained that Adam had a head wound and was being sick. He gave their location. When he came off the phone, Marvik said, 'Joshua Nunton wanted shot of Pulford and so did Adam.'

'Yes. And I did.'

'You all conspired to kill him.'

'We agreed to take him out in the boat and dump him at sea, but when we reached the boat the morning we planned to do it, Joshua was on board, dead. And Pulford had disappeared.'

Marvik wasn't sure that was the truth. Perhaps they had all gone out on the boat and Pulford had been killed. Joshua, unable to live with what he'd done, had gone on the run and, as he and Strathen had discussed, he'd returned a month ago and ended up dead. Perhaps it had been Joshua Nunton's DNA that had matched Jensen's because Stacey had been sleeping with both men. But he'd accept Matthew's version for now.

'So you dumped Joshua's body in the sea and let everyone think he'd taken off.'

Matthew nodded miserably. He crossed to his son stretched out on the ground.

Marvik caught the sound of the ambulance approaching. 'Then I came asking about Pulford and a man called Oscar Redburn. Did Adam try to run me down on a motorbike?'

'No. He hasn't got a motorbike and he can't ride one.'

The ambulance drew to a halt and Marvik saw two paramedics jump out. There were just a couple more questions he needed to ask.

'Did you or Adam kill Sarah Redburn?'

'No. Why should we? We don't know her.'

Marvik scrutinized Matthew's tired and drawn face. 'You said that Pulford wasn't in the photograph I showed you of the two men.' It was the one that Gordon Freynsham had given him.

'He wasn't.'

'Are you certain?' Marvik looked for the lie and couldn't see it. But Matthew was distracted by the paramedics attending to Adam. Marvik took out his phone and showed Matthew the photograph that Bryony had given him.

'Which one is Pulford?'

Matthew's eyes screwed up as he gazed down at it, then he started physically and his eyes widened. 'My God! That's him. That's Pulford.'

Marvik stared at where Matthew was pointing. It wasn't at Oscar Redburn, as he'd expected, but at a man who had died in 1979. Joseph Cotleigh.

CHAPTER TWENTY

'Leonard Killbeck *is* dead,' Strathen said as they sat in the corner of a pub in the town. 'Or certainly someone bearing his name was registered as having died of a stroke in 1995.'

Marvik had showered and changed into some dry clothes and they'd gone ashore because Strathen's connection to the Internet in the bay had been practically non-existent. It was still raining heavily.

Marvik said, 'But Joseph Cotleigh wasn't dead in 1979 if Matthew can be believed and I'm certain he's telling the truth, which means either they didn't bother to check dental records and just assumed it was his body—'

'Sloppy.'

'Or it suited someone for it to be Cotleigh washed up in Chale Bay on the Isle of Wight in February 1979 in order to be able to spin that yarn about him running off with union funds. They took a chance on Cotleigh not showing up and saying hey, I'm not dead.'

'Not much of one if they knew he had been in that bay and had witnessed the shooting. And they knew he'd buggered off. Cedric Shale could have told them.'

'But who are *they*? Who is behind the cover-up with Cedric Shale, if it was him in that bay the day of the shooting?'

'Intelligence? The government? The opposition party?'

Marvik took a swallow of his beer. 'If Shale *was* party to the murder, or guilty of committing it, and someone has covered up for him then his motive has to be connected with his father and Malaya in 1959. And the man who actually got shot in Kingston Bay and turned up dead on the Isle of Wight in 1979 has to be Oscar Redburn. It ties in with when he went missing.'

Strathen nodded. 'Looks that way.'

'So which of them had the package that Darrow brought back, Cotleigh or Redburn?'

'Has to be Redburn because he ended up dead.'

'And the fact he chose that location for a meet means that whatever he had was enough to blackmail Cedric Shale with.'

'And it might not have been either amber or fossils.' Strathen took a swig of his lager. His laptop computer was in front of him on the table.

Marvik sat forward. Four men entered the pub and went to the bar.

'I've been looking a bit deeper into Ambrose Shale. He got into Malaya very quickly when the Japanese left there after the war. The country was in a shit state. Ambrose Shale and other British businessmen were eager to exploit the valuable minerals there such as coal, bauxite, tungsten, gold, iron ore, manganese and tin. Also rubber. Malaya became practically owned by British businesses, especially the rubber estates, and after the war the government were very keen to protect their business interests. But they failed to protect the rights of the Chinese in Malaya, who'd already had a raw deal under the Japanese. The government were scared there might be a Chinese revolution in Malaya like the Chinese Revolution of 1949. So an insurgent movement was formed out of the Chinese who, as you probably know, Art, had been trained by the British army during the war because they were the only resistance to the Japanese occupation.'

Marvik did. He took a pull at his beer as Strathen continued.

'Most of the Chinese were employed in the tin mines and on the rubber estates at the time of the Japanese occupation and they were very soon deprived of their normal employment. The Chinese couldn't return to their homeland so they were left to scratch for a living in the jungle clearings. They made up almost forty-five per cent of the population. But the British government favoured the Malay community over and above those of the Chinese and, in a nutshell, the colonial powers, that is us, the British, tried to suppress the resulting unrest by banning some trade unions who were protesting against the unfairness and inequality and by imprisoning some of their members and harassing those of the left wing.'

Marvik thought of Jack Darrow and Joseph Cotleigh in that 1979 strike.

'Of course, as we know, that didn't work,' Strathen continued. 'The unrest escalated.'

'And British business interests thought that would mean the end to trade with the West. And for people like Ambrose Shale that would mean a huge loss of wealth.'

'Yes. The disaffected Chinese received considerable support from the Chinese and the Malayan Communist Party, the backbone of the insurgency. The British declared an emergency in 1948, as you know. The Malayan Emergency. Not just to defeat the armed insurgency but also to crack down on workers' rights. The Malayan Emergency ended in 1957 but there were still skirmishes after Malaya got independence in 1957. The state of emergency wasn't actually declared as being over until July 1960.'

'And the interests of British businesses were protected no matter what the cost.'

'I would have thought so, wouldn't you?'

'And did Ambrose Shale come out of this clean?' Marvik mused as more people piled into the pub, laughing and shaking off their wet clothes. It was group of six women in their forties who looked intent on a good Saturday night out.

'He got a knighthood.'

'For services rendered,' said Marvik, full of cynicism. 'Making sure that any sensitive documentation — correspondence, reports, details about meetings that took place between those with powerful British business interests and the High Commissioner in Malaya — were taken out of the country. According to Ralph Warnford, Ambrose Shale was in Singapore when that cargo was shipped out in 1959. When that lorry crashed and spilled some of its contents George Gurney saw Ambrose Shale's name mentioned in a not-too-honest light. Ambrose might have obtained his business interests in Malaya in a corrupt way. Gurney recognized the value of what he had. And the same goes for Bradley Pulford. They had both worked on the Shale estate. And Darrow, working in the docks, would have recognized the name of Shale, the ship owner, except he didn't remember the package or know what was in it until he came across it again during the strike in 1979. Then he realized he could use the information to smear Cedric Shale and promote his workers' cause. He told Cotleigh or Redburn or both and maybe asked for their advice. One or both of them killed him because they realized the documentation could bring them personal wealth and sod the workers. They arranged to meet Cedric Shale to blackmail him but Shale had other ideas.'

Strathen agreed. 'And from what I've researched of Cedric Shale, his character and what you found at Kingston House, plus what Matthew Killbeck told you, Shale wasn't working alone and hasn't been ever since. The "boss", as you heard the Audleys call this other man, has been systematically blackmailing him and is stripping that house of everything valuable and selling it off.'

'And when it's all gone Shale will die.'

Strathen nodded.

'Why would Cotleigh return in 1989 as Bradley Pulford? What was in it for him aside from an easy billet by blackmailing Matthew Killbeck? And why assume the name of Pulford, unless it was adopted to blackmail Cedric Shale? Bit dangerous, though, given that he'd witnessed the previous blackmailer, Oscar Redburn being murdered.'

'Timing,' said Strathen.

Marvik sat forward. He caught the eye of a woman at the bar waiting to be served who smiled fleetingly. Marvik didn't return it. A couple in their twenties came and sat at the table near them.

Strathen threw them a glance and continued in a low voice, 'There was another dockers' strike in 1989 and a pivotal one based on the proposed scrapping of the National Dock Labour Scheme. I did tell you I hadn't been idle.'

'Wouldn't have thought it for one moment.'

'The government announced it was to abolish the National Dock Labour Scheme which guaranteed work for more than nine thousand dockers. It was introduced by a Labour government in 1947, giving dockers the legal right to minimum work, holidays, sick pay and pensions. Not much to ask, you'd have thought, but the government of 1989 didn't like it and neither did the owners of the ports.

'The National Dock Labour Board was made up of union and employer representatives. Registered dockers laid off by any of the companies bound by the scheme had to be taken on by another or be paid off. The Employment Secretary of the day, Norman Fowler, said that the scheme stood in the way of a modern and efficient ports' industry. Those involved in the scheme said they were losing business to other ports in the UK and Europe because of the restrictions it imposed. Fowler said there would be generous compensation for men laid off as a result of the scrapping of the scheme and that there would be no return to using mass casual labour. Pressure was put on the politicians and port users to use their influence on ministers to end the scheme. They did on the sixth of April 1989. The dockers went on strike in July 1989 but by then it was too late. There was a big media campaign against them of a similar ilk to the one in 1979, portraying them as bloody-minded, selfish, greedy, holding the country to ransom — all the usual stuff. And there were a couple of economic studies commissioned which proved that by scrapping the dock labour scheme more jobs would actually be created than the number lost.'

'Don't tell me — Brampton was behind them.'

'He might well have been. His business was set up a year afterwards, perhaps on the financial proceeds of a favourable report for the government. Cedric Shale's ships were port-bound. He was solidly on the side of the government and made no bones about it.'

'So Cotleigh reckoned Cedric would pay up to keep his father's shady past quiet and to stop him from revealing what happened in that bay in 1979. And someone did pay up from 1989 until 1990 when he took off again.'

Strathen frowned, puzzled. 'Yeah, but why did Shale let it go on that long? Why not summon help from his previous accomplice? The person who had been with him in the bay when Redburn was murdered.'

'Maybe he thought he could handle it alone and when he finally realized he couldn't he summoned help.' Marvik frowned, troubled. 'Whoever this "boss" is he's a ruthless bastard and clever. Is Bryony still alive?'

Strathen looked grim. 'If she's served her purpose, then no.'

'And that purpose was to report back to the "boss" how far we'd got with our enquiries and where we are. But she can't know that you've moved the boat.'

'No, but having relayed where we were it won't be that difficult to ask around the harbour masters in the area and locate us. Don't worry, I've rigged the boat so that I'll know if so much as a bird shits on it. I called the hospital. Ben was discharged this morning. Someone came to collect him. The nurse I spoke to didn't know who it was, or where Ben's gone, but the tiny tracking device I sewed into the hem of Bryony's coat last night while she was sleeping gives her location as Godalming, near Guildford. There's a private rehab centre there. I think she's safe for the time being until we can be dealt with.' He swivelled the computer around to face Marvik. 'I thought you might like to see this.'

Marvik was staring at a black-and-white photograph of a Fred Parker classic motorboat. Underneath the picture was a caption: 'Sir Ambrose Shale on board his boat *Amber May* June 1955 with his son, Cedric.'

Cedric would have been just seventeen. He looked more like fifteen and clearly hadn't been a very confident youth. He was fair and not as tall as his father but lean like him. They were both dressed in classic casual clothes of slacks and open-necked polo shirts, but where Sir Ambrose carried his off, Cedric looked as though he'd be more at home in a school uniform. They were standing in the cockpit beside one another. Marvik recognized the small Isle of Wight town of Cowes behind them and, judging by the number of yachts around them, it was August and Cowes Week, a major regatta in the sailing calendar. Sir Ambrose was smiling into the camera and appeared very satisfied with life, while Cedric was staring down and frowning. Maybe the sun had been in his eyes. Or perhaps his father had ordered him to be in the photograph, obviously against his will.

'Here're some more recent pictures I got from the newspaper archives.' Strathen handed across his mobile phone. There was one taken at Sir Ambrose's funeral in 1965. Cedric, dressed in a sombre black suit, was climbing out of the funeral car in front of Salisbury Cathedral. It was ten years after the picture on the boat had been taken and he looked more like early thirties than late twenties. He was still lean and fair and there was still that slightly bewildered, surly expression on his face but he had more lines in a furrowed brow. The other picture was a corporate head and shoulders shot of Cedric with an accompanying article in the *Financial Times* about him succeeding his father's business. The date was a year after the funeral. He was still frowning but this time Marvik thought he looked confused, as though he couldn't quite understand how he'd got into such a position.

Marvik handed Strathen back his phone.

Strathen said, 'I found a few more articles about the Shale Corporation over the years but no more photographs of the reclusive businessman. I did find one in the sailing press from 1998.' He pulled up a picture on his computer.

'Nice boat,' Marvik said, eyeing the sleek and expensive modern motor yacht.

Again Shale had that same edgy, troubled expression. He was still the lean man of his youth. His hair had got thinner though and his face more gaunt. Behind him at the helm with his back to the camera was a man. Marvik couldn't see who it was and yet something about the figure struck him as being vaguely familiar. He couldn't place why. Either side of Shale were two people — a smiling woman in her mid-thirties and the other a man in his fifties, both with champagne glasses.

'The brokerage staff he purchased the boat from,' Strathen explained. 'They went out of business two years afterwards.' He drained his lager and continued, 'Cedric Shale left his public school when he was seventeen in 1955, the year that photograph with his father on the boat was taken. Then there's no record of him that I can find until 1965 when he took over the business. He could have been working abroad for his father. Or he could have been travelling or in hospital.'

'You think he might have been mentally ill?'

'Maybe but not enough to stop him from taking over the business and running it successfully for thirty-five years.'

There was a burst of laughter from the group of women. The bar was filling up as more people spilled in and the music seemed to be getting louder.

Thoughts were running through Marvik's mind. Many troubled and puzzled him but one was bugging him, which he voiced to Strathen. 'Would Cotleigh's threat that Matthew could be construed as an accessory to murder have been enough to blackmail him? The Matthew I've met would have told Cotleigh to sod off and not allowed him to worm his way into their lives. There has to be more. There has to be a reason why Matthew put up with Cotleigh for two years.'

'Then perhaps we'd better ask him.' Strathen packed away his computer.

Marvik rose. 'He'll be at the hospital if Adam has been admitted. They'd have taken him to Poole. It's got the nearest accident and emergency department.'

They called a taxi from the pub, after Marvik had checked with the hospital that Adam Killbeck had been admitted. Within forty-five minutes they were heading towards the ward. Marvik knew that Strathen, like him, was recalling his own stays in hospitals and reliving the memory of the frustration, anger, pain and occasionally the despair they'd felt, impatient to be out and back on duty. Only both had found that eventually duty was no longer theirs to return to. Crowder's missions filled a gap but was it enough for him? Strathen could and would resume his intelligence security business in between missions, but as for him? Marvik didn't know. He knew that neither of them wanted to report in to Crowder yet, not just because they had nothing concrete but they had a point to prove to both Crowder and themselves. But as they weaved their way through the corridors Marvik wondered if they had handled this well enough. Doubts crept in and he hated that.

The nurse at the station outside the ward pointed out Adam's bed but even before they reached it they could see Matthew wasn't there. Adam had been sedated. There was no point in trying to talk to him and the nurse had no idea when the elderly gentleman who had been with the patient had left.

'He must have returned home, anxious about leaving Mary for too long,' Marvik said as they headed for the exit.

They picked up a taxi outside the hospital and remained silent on the journey back to Swanage. Within an hour Marvik was once again knocking on the door of the small house. It was almost ten o'clock but a light was showing in the downstairs window. He was again surprised when Abigail answered it, but that turned to concern when she said that Matthew hadn't returned.

'Has he contacted you?' Marvik asked as Abigail ushered them into the small lounge. There was no sign of Mary. Marvik assumed she must be in bed.

'No.'

Marvik asked for Matthew's mobile phone number and rang it. He exchanged a worried glance with Strathen. 'It's on voicemail.' He rang off, then addressed Abigail. 'Has Matthew ever gone away before without contacting you?'

'No. Never. Do you think he's had an accident?'

'Have you tried Jensen?'

'I'll try him now.'

She went out into the kitchen, where Marvik could hear her talking. She returned with the phone in her hand. 'Jensen hasn't seen or heard from him. I'm not sure what to do. Adam's not answering his phone either.'

He wouldn't. So Matthew hadn't even contacted her to tell her Adam was in hospital.

'Shall I call the police, only if I do and they find he's left Mary they might notify social services? I can stay with her tonight. I'll let my husband know. But I can't look after her all the time. I wouldn't want her moved, though. It would upset her too much. I can't see Matthew leaving Mary for too long. He must have had an accident. The fishing boat . . .'

'We'll go and look for him and make inquiries.'

She looked relieved. She gave Marvik the landline number and her mobile phone number. As soon as the door closed behind them, Marvik said, 'I think Matthew knows who the killer is and he's gone to have it out with him.' They had no idea where that was. 'Let's check the boat.' Marvik wished they'd kept the taxi waiting.

'It's only just over a mile,' Strathen said, reading his thoughts and setting off. 'We can walk it. Good opportunity to test out this new leg of mine. It's meant to be all singing and dancing — well, walking, at least, and now we'll find out. Maybe I should have fitted the running prosthetic.'

They set off at a brisk enough pace. Even if Strathen was in pain or experiencing discomfort, Marvik knew he wouldn't show it and he'd never admit it.

At least the rain had stopped and the wind had eased. Marvik heard a clock strike ten thirty and a squeal of car tyres. The streets were deserted, as was the bay by the lifeboat station when they reached it. There was no sign of the fishing boat.

Marvik exchanged a glance with Strathen, who said, 'I don't think Matthew Killbeck's gone out for a spot of night fishing.'

'Perhaps being at sea is the only place he can think,' Marvik answered. Strathen would identify with that.

As though to confirm it, Strathen said, 'Or the only place he feels truly at rest.'

'Suicide?'

'Either that or someone has forced him to go. Either way he could end up being fish bait.'

'Then we'd better find him before the killer does.'

CHAPTER TWENTY-ONE

There were two places where Matthew could have gone. One was out to sea and the other was where this had begun for him — the bay where he had witnessed what had happened in 1979. Returning to the latter might be a symbolic gesture or perhaps Matthew had told the killer that was where he would meet him. Matthew was an experienced sailor but sailing alone on the small trawler in the dark would prove testing enough for the best of them. Even with a depth sounder, spotlights and GPS it would be very treacherous negotiating the water into that bay.

Strathen, after checking over the boat despite his rigged alarms, verified that no one had broken into it or had planted a device of any kind on or in it. He plotted a course for the bay and headed towards it. Marvik knew they should alert the coastguard but that meant explaining why they were concerned about Matthew and giving their details. Being visible to the authorities was the last thing they wanted.

There was now a smattering of stars and a glimpse of a moon behind fast, scudding clouds. Visibility had improved but Marvik couldn't help wishing he was on his boat or Strathen's, both of which were equipped with powerful search lights. This boat, though, had a light and Marvik also had a handheld one, which he now swept over the dark sea as his eyes searched for the lights of the fishing boat. There was no sign of the trawler — not even on the radar — and there was no call from Abigail to tell them that Matthew had returned home. Marvik didn't think there would be. He tried Matthew's number again using his mission mobile phone. It was still on voicemail. Marvik didn't think anyone would hear from Matthew again.

When they reached the mouth of the bay there was no sign of the trawler. 'Better call it off,' Strathen said. 'We'll moor up out here and grab a few hours' sleep.' They wouldn't be disturbed.

The seagulls woke Marvik. There was a pink light in the sky to the east. The March morning had a biting edge to it but the sea state was calm. Strathen was awake and making breakfast. Marvik wondered when the coastguard would find the trawler. Whether they would find Matthew Killbeck was another matter. Marvik again considered Matthew's motives for taking off into the night. Had he killed whoever was behind this? Or maybe he'd just grown tired of it all and killed himself.

He trained the binoculars on the bay in front of him. It was good to study it from the seaward side because this was how Shale or his accomplice, or both of them, on board a boat had approached it in January 1979. His eyes travelled the small stretch of curving sand and the black rock that bled off from it at either side. He could hear the tide washing on to the sand and shingle beach in a gentle, slow, rhythmic motion. The seagulls circled overhead, cawing, piping and bleating, dipping and diving on to the shore and the sea. It must have been a calm day in 1979, much like this, he thought as he trained the glasses up the cliff face and then at the grassy bank at the top of the cliff. He swung them to the left and could pick out the ruined houses, the small church and outbuildings used by the army for exercises. There was no one in sight and no sound of gunfire this morning.

In 1979 two men had met here, one with the intention of blackmail and the other to kill. The bay was difficult to navigate with its underwater rocks and granite shelves. It needed an experienced sailor to know when and how to approach and to depart, taking with them a human cargo. But then the bay belonged to Cedric Shale and he knew how to handle a boat — perhaps the other man with him had also been an experienced sailor. Was it the man who had been hunched over the helm in the photograph Strathen had shown him last night? Again something nagged at the back of Marvik's mind but, try as he might, infuriatingly he couldn't grasp it.

His thoughts returned to Matthew Killbeck, here, as a witness, on that fateful day in 1979. Perhaps Matthew Killbeck had lied to him when he said he'd seen the boat take off. Marvik only had his word for it. Perhaps Matthew had met Redburn on the beach and killed him and Cotleigh had witnessed it. That would have been a powerful weapon for a blackmailer. And perhaps Leonard Killbeck had been in the boat that had taken Redburn's body away, which was why Cotleigh had managed to get himself a billet with Leonard in 1989. He voiced his views to Strathen as he tucked into his breakfast, adding, 'But if Matthew and Leonard killed Redburn, I can't see what their motive could have been unless it was the fact they'd been smuggling and had hidden an illicit cargo here.'

'You're forgetting that Cotleigh came back in 1989 calling himself Pulford and as far as I can ascertain neither Matthew nor Leonard Killbeck were in Singapore in 1959. And if Matthew and Leonard killed Redburn why didn't they kill Cotleigh aka Pulford as soon as he showed up? Instead they let him live and work with them for over a year.'

'You're right and Matthew is not the "boss" the Audleys referred to who is keeping Shale alive.'

'And he's not the man Crowder is after.'

Marvik agreed. He bit into his toast and after a moment said, 'Matthew could have recognized Shale as being on that boat but how would he have known him? They hardly moved in the same circles or had the same interests, except for the sea, but at opposite ends of the scale: one a professional fisherman the other a leisure sailor.'

'Perhaps he recognized the other man.'

'Which means it could have been someone he'd seen in the news, someone in a powerful position, and he knew that his word about what he saw wouldn't be taken over that of Shale and this accomplice.' But Marvik frowned as he considered this and recalled Mary's words and frightened countenance. 'For Mary to be scared, though, it has to be someone she also knows and that means it might be someone from Matthew's own circle. But who?' Marvik said, frustrated, his mind trying desperately to pull together all the information they'd gleaned. 'It's got to be someone close to Matthew, someone he'd do anything to protect.'

'Let's return to Swanage,' Strathen said. 'He might even be there. Yeah, I know, unlikely,' he added in response to Marvik's sceptical look.

Even before dropping anchor, Marvik could see that Matthew hadn't returned. As he looked through the glasses, though, he saw two figures on the shore heading towards a motor launch: Adam and Jensen Killbeck.

They quickly launched the tender and headed towards them. Adam stiffened as he saw them approach. His arm was strapped up, his face ashen and his expression set and grim. Jensen Killbeck looked his usual bored self.

'Want to beat me up again? Then go ahead — I can't stop you,' Adam snapped as they drew level with him.

Steadily, Marvik said, 'I want to know why your father is protecting Cedric Shale.'

'Who?'

Marvik could see that Adam knew exactly who he was talking about. He continued, 'Especially when Shale isn't a risk anymore. He has dementia. Even if he told the police that Matthew helped him kill a man they wouldn't believe him.'

Adam's expression darkened. His fist balled. 'Dad's killed no one.'

'Are you sure?'

'Fuck off.'

Adam made to turn away but Strathen blocked his path.

'Takes two of you to beat me up now?' Adam sneered.

Jensen was now eyeing them apprehensively, his phone in his hand.

'Well, go on, I can't fight back with one arm,' he taunted.

'No one wants to beat you up. We just want the truth,' Marvik calmly replied.

'Truth!' Adam spat. 'Who gives a fuck about the truth?'

'We do.' Marvik rounded on him angrily. 'One woman has died because too many people have lied. She was innocent and another innocent woman might be dead. How many more deaths do there have to be before you and your father tell the truth?'

'I don't know what you're talking about. Jensen, get the boat ready,' he commanded.

'You're going to look for Matthew?'

Adam remained silent.

'He might already be dead.'

'I know that,' Adam hissed, his eyes blazing with pain and anger. 'And if he is then you killed him so before you start spouting off about others killing take a good hard look at yourself.'

Stiffly, Marvik said, 'If Matthew didn't kill anyone then he's protecting someone and if it's not Cedric Shale then who is it, Adam?'

'No bloody idea.' But it was bluster.

'We can help find him. There might still be time,' pressed Marvik. He could see Adam was in pain, he was upset and he was scared, not for himself but for his father. 'Who is Mary talking about when she said the dead had risen?'

Adam's skin blanched. Marvik watched the expressions race across his troubled face: anger, fear, despair.

'Dad didn't kill anyone,' he repeated but the rage had gone.

Marvik's mind continued to race. 'But he is protecting someone?' And why would he do that? Out of loyalty or fear? 'Who is your father afraid of?'

'No one,' Adam declared defensively and with pride.

'But your mother is. Mary is terrified because she's seen this man come back from the dead and she's afraid for Matthew.'

Marvik's mind dashed back to the church and afterwards to the wake in the trendy pub where Mary had kept saying something about the dead rising and Matthew had apologized and tried to quieten her. A pub that at the time Marvik had thought wasn't the Killbecks' natural habitat. They'd never have chosen voluntarily to drink inside it but it had been close to the church, which was why Marvik thought they had suggested it. But perhaps there was another reason why it had been chosen and suddenly what had been nagging at the back of his mind snapped into place. He knew exactly where he'd seen that hunched figure at the helm on Shale's expensive new motor cruiser of 1998. It was the same posture of the man at the bar with his back to them. The man hunched over his phone drinking a glass of wine.

'Who was the man in the bar, the day of the funeral service, Adam? The one your father met afterwards?' Marvik pursued, catching Strathen's eye.

Adam glanced away and shook his head solemnly but his whole body language was that of defeat.

Marvik continued, 'After I'd left, Matthew told you to make sure Mary got home safely and that he had someone he needed to talk to.' Marvik didn't know that for certain. It was a guess but not much of one. It's what Matthew would have done. Matthew had been told to stay behind and he'd been instructed to invite Marvik for a drink to find out why he was at the funeral. And the next day Marvik had called on Matthew Killbeck and Mary had again talked about the dead rising up and she'd uttered a name. Marvik conjured up her petrified face and along with it the name, *You're not Mr Howard* and Killbeck had quickly answered, *She thinks you're the plumber who's come to fit a bathroom.* But Mary had other ideas. *Have you come about the dead?*

Evenly, Marvik said, 'Where's Howard?'

He didn't think Adam could get any paler but he did. His body swayed. He shouldn't have been out of hospital but Marvik was betting that having heard the news that his father was missing he'd discharged himself.

'We need to find him,' Marvik persisted.

'I don't know where he is.'

'But you do know him. He's the man your father is protecting.'

Adam inhaled and dashed a fearful glance at them. He let out a long, slow breath and nodded. His troubled eyes swivelled between Marvik and Strathen. Marvik said nothing. Strathen beside him kept silent. After a moment he continued, his voice full of anguish, 'I didn't even know dad had another brother. No one spoke about him, not even my grandparents. There was only ever Matthew and Leonard. Dad said that Howard hated being a fisherman. He was never going to take to the nets. He left home at fourteen and they never saw him again.'

'Not until that day of Pulford's funeral.'

Adam nodded but Marvik knew that wasn't the truth as far as Matthew was concerned. He'd seen his brother before, in 1979, and he'd seen him since the funeral nine days ago.

Now that Adam had decided to tell what he knew he couldn't get the words out fast enough. 'It's like you said — dad told me to take mum home. He said he had some business to attend to. I didn't know what he meant until I heard him talking on his mobile phone, when we were fishing, when Jensen was sick. He said it had to end and he mentioned you. He said you were asking too many questions and that you'd get to the truth. Dad looked ill and old when he came off the phone. I asked him about it. He tried to bluff it out but he couldn't. He told me to look after mum if anything happened to him. I made a joke, saying he had years left but he said, "Not if Howard has his way." I asked who Howard was and he said, "My brother" then he clammed up, said it was best I didn't know. I wish to hell you'd never come here stirring things up. We were all right. You should have left us alone. Now piss off and let me find Dad.'

He marched off towards Jensen. They let him go. There was nothing either of them could do to stop him. Marvik understood why he had to try. He turned to Strathen. 'Howard's the man on that boat with Cedric Shale in the photograph you showed me. It's the same hunched figure I saw at the bar in that trendy pub. I didn't see his face. He has to have been the man with Shale in the bay in 1979. He and Shale killed Redburn and Matthew recognized his brother. I'm betting Cotleigh knew that. Matthew might have hurried down into the bay to remonstrate with his brother and Cotleigh saw and overheard it. Cotleigh took off scared, thinking that Howard and Shale would come after him, but after ten years he thought it was safe to return and blackmail Matthew Killbeck, and through him also blackmail Cedric Shale and Howard Killbeck. It's Howard who is keeping Cedric Shale alive in Kingston House while he systematically sells the contents and siphons off the proceeds. He's making sure that Cedric stays locked away with his ramblings about the devil and blood. He won't kill him — not until he's got all the money he needs because he's obviously not mentioned in any will. *If* there is a will. But how did Howard get to know Shale so well?'

'Perhaps he went to Singapore on one of Ambrose Shale's ships, just like Bradley Pulford, and got a job on one of Ambrose Shale's plantations or in the mines and met Cedric through it.'

Marvik watched Adam and Jensen launch the boat. Adam was wincing in pain. Their search was pointless and perilous but it was no use telling Adam that, as they'd seen.

He said, 'Howard might have hated fishing but he's a man with the sea in his blood, like Matthew and Adam. He'd take to the sea like his father and grandfather.' Again, something nudged at Marvik.

Strathen said, 'He can't be far away because he'll need to silence us.'

'Then it's time I left a calling card with the Audleys.'

CHAPTER TWENTY-TWO

This time Marvik had no need to hide from the electronic surveillance devices. On the contrary, he wanted his approach to be fully visible. He'd taken a taxi from Swanage to Steepleridge and from there had walked across country in the late afternoon to Kingston House, leaving Strathen in the town in a café on the Internet trying to find out what he could on Howard Killbeck. He'd already called to report that Howard Killbeck had been born on the first of June 1938 and there was no register of his death. Neither of them knew what name he'd taken over the last sixty years but Strathen was looking for it. The Audleys might give that to Marvik.

He approached the electronic gates wondering if Greg Audley was watching him from behind a monitor, or perhaps Howard Killbeck was. There was no vehicle parked in the grounds so why were the gates open? Perhaps a trade van had made a delivery and Audley had forgotten to close them. No one came out to accost him and the intercom remained silent. He could have pressed it but there didn't seem to be any point when he only had to walk in.

He jogged up the weed-strewn gravel driveway, glancing up at Shale's bedroom window. The curtains were pulled across. The windows were closed. As before, he made his way around the side of the house with an uneasy sensation pricking between his shoulder blades. He could sense that something was wrong. His body tensed and his pulse beat a little faster.

At the French doors he halted. Last time he'd come here he'd effected an entry through the sash windows beside the doors but now he walked on around to the rear of the house to the kitchen. The door was open. That surely wasn't usual. His senses on full alert, he stepped inside as the adrenaline surged through his body. He was ready for action if or when needed, but no one came to assault or challenge him because the room was empty.

A chill ran down his spine as he surveyed the ultra-modern large kitchen. The central island was littered with used crockery. There was a pot of coffee. He touched the side. It was stone cold and on the two plates were the congealing remains of a fried breakfast.

Swiftly, he crossed to the door, keeping alert for the slightest sound or movement. Only silence greeted him. Entering the narrow corridor and ignoring the door to his left, he headed for the door in front of him which led into the expansive hall. To his left and just ahead was the wide, sweeping staircase. Still no sound and still no one came to confront him.

As he ran up the stairs he wondered why the Audleys had cleared out in the middle of their meal, which was a strange time to choose but then Howard Killbeck might have ordered them to do so. Was Howard Killbeck already here, having anticipated Marvik's arrival? Howard couldn't have known for certain this was where he had been heading because nobody except Strathen knew that and there was no tracking device on Marvik. He didn't even have any of his three phones switched on.

The upper hall was dimly lit, the dark afternoon clouds making it gloomier. A spat of rain hurled itself against the window behind him as he picked his way along the corridor to the room with the bay window where he had previously found Cedric Shale in a wheelchair. His ears strained for any sound. Again only silence greeted him, that and the smell of disinfectant and something else. A smell that he was all too familiar with.

Steeling himself and taking a breath, Marvik pushed open the door. It gave a slight creak. There was no sound from inside. He entered. The room was dark but his eyes quickly registered the bay window opposite while his senses prepared for an attack if it came from behind the door, but he knew it wouldn't. There was no demented elderly man in a wheelchair this time. He turned towards the bed. There he picked out the shape of a body. Approaching he saw at once that it was Cedric Shale and that he was dead, but he'd known that almost the moment he'd stepped inside the house. It had the stench of death about it. He had smelt and seen enough of it to know when he was in its presence.

Shale's skin was icy cold to his touch. He'd been dead for some hours. Running his small torch over the body in the dim light of the room, Marvik noted that there were no physical signs of violence and no smell when he sniffed close to the gaping mouth, so poison was probably out of the equation. Shale could have died of natural causes but if he had, his timing was immaculate. Marvik thought it more likely he'd been injected with an overdose of morphine. Had Greg Audley or his wife done that or was it Howard Killbeck's work?

Howard was cleaning up. He knew that Marvik was close to the truth and he couldn't leave any loose ends, which didn't bode well for Bryony or Matthew and the Audleys. Had they really taken off? Marvik liked to think so.

He turned and ran down the stairs, but in the corridor between the hall and kitchen he paused at the door on his right. Thrusting it open he found, as he had expected, that it led to the cellar. Descending the stone steps, he played his torch over the dusty cobweb-ridden wine racks. They were empty. Howard had cleaned that out too.

Standing stock-still, he swung the torch's beam around the freezing cold echoing cellar until the light picked out the gruesome spectacle he knew he would find. The Audleys were on the stone floor in the far corner. Dead. But Marvik crossed to make sure. There was nothing he could do. Both had been shot at close range. There was no sign of a gun. A break-in? A robbery? Marvik knew otherwise but Howard Killbeck hoped it was what the police would conclude.

Fury knotted his gut at the senseless slaughter. He had to stop Killbeck but how when he didn't know where to find him and he didn't even know what he looked like? But maybe he did. He'd said to Strathen earlier that Howard was a man of the sea. And his mind sped back to his breakfast with Sarah, recalling everyone he'd seen — the stocky man in his forties who had entered the café after them, as had the man in his fifties who had read his newspaper. Sarah had shown no reaction to either of them and they were the wrong age for Howard Killbeck. The jogger on the promenade was in his late thirties, which left the silver-haired man in his seventies wearing a sailing jacket who had smiled as he'd leaned over and ruffled the fur of a dog a woman had been walking.

Marvik made his way up the driveway, his mind racing. Sarah hadn't been booked into any bed and breakfast accommodation or hotel. No friend had come forward to say she had been staying with them and she hadn't arrived by public transport. No, because she'd arrived by boat, and she'd stayed overnight on that boat before showing up on the shore by the Killbecks' fishing boat. Marvik remembered there had been a handful of boats anchored up on the opposite side of the pier to where he had been anchored. And among them a boat that he was betting belonged to Howard Killbeck, the silver-haired man he'd seen on the promenade, a man she had trusted. Marvik's fists clenched. Howard, using a false name, had befriended her. Marvik didn't think it would have been difficult. He'd probably feigned an acquaintance with Oscar or an interest in funding a future marine exploration project — maybe both. If only Sarah had trusted him enough to tell him. But Howard had probably sworn her to secrecy with some cock and bull story.

Marvik turned in the direction of the bay, oblivious of the rain beating against him, his mind considering why Howard had befriended Sarah. Was it because Cotleigh had made contact with her before he was killed and Howard badly wanted to know what Cotleigh had told her? The fact that Sarah then began to ask questions about her father's disappearance alerted Howard to the fact that she might just get to the truth, especially when she had shown an interest in talking to the Killbecks. And that, along with his own sudden appearance at the funeral and then seeing him deep in conversation with Sarah at the café, had been enough to sign her death warrant. Fury surged through Marvik, tinged with sadness at her memory as he traipsed on towards the bay, automatically picking his way over the rough terrain in the diminishing light as he continued to pull the threads of what he'd learned, heard and seen, together.

Joseph Cotleigh had witnessed the murder of Oscar Redburn in the bay that lay ahead of him. Cotleigh had taken off immediately after it but he'd returned in 1989 and he had been allowed to live in Swanage for just over a year. Why? Why hadn't Matthew told Howard about him? Why hadn't Cotleigh blackmailed Shale? He hadn't because Shale would have told Howard and Howard would have killed Cotleigh. Maybe both Cedric Shale and Howard Killbeck had been out of the country and had returned in 1990, and that was why Cotleigh had suddenly disappeared again. Why risk coming back here though if he wasn't blackmailing Shale and when he knew that Shale and Howard Killbeck were men capable of murder? Why had he returned this year? This time, though, he *had* been killed. Perhaps that was Howard's work. Perhaps it was Matthew and Adam's. Perhaps it was an accident. But Marvik didn't believe that for one minute. Something had driven Cotleigh to return and to contact Sarah and, judging by what Marvik had heard about his personality, he didn't think it was out of the goodness of his heart. No, he thought that he'd benefit financially. And Marvik knew why he'd thought that. He'd been hoping to find the package that Redburn had got from Jack Darrow. And Cotleigh believed that Sarah either knew where that was or could help him find it. She couldn't and perhaps Howard Killbeck had discovered that and that was why he had killed her. She was of no use to him.

Cotleigh had returned in 1989 and stayed for so long because he had been looking for it. It was why he'd walk the coastal path, as Matthew had told him, or more specifically come here to the bay. When Shale and Howard had killed Oscar Redburn they hadn't found the package on him. And it was what Crowder wanted — the dangerous cargo from 1959. A cargo that had resulted in six deaths — no, nine — there was Cedric Shale and the Audleys. But if Cotleigh couldn't find it and Howard Killbeck didn't know where it was, how the hell could he and Strathen locate it? And why was it still important? With Cedric Shale dead there was no longer the threat that the documentation from Malaya could expose his father to corrupt business practices after the war. The answer was because it also implicated highly influential key public figures, and it was Howard's passport to more riches through blackmail. Crowder's remit was to protect them.

Marvik came out on the top of the bay but the wind was pushing at him and the rain was driving off the sea. He needed shelter to call Strathen. He turned, saw the tower of the small, ruined church which had once belonged to Shale and hurried there along the clifftop. He climbed nimbly over the low, dry-stone wall and barbed wire fence of the Ministry of Defence land and soon he was inside its ruins. At a push it could only have housed about thirty people, enough for Sir Ambrose Shale's estate workers, he thought, recalling Ralph Warnford's words about the services that used to be held there. There was no roof now but the walls were still erect and, with his back to the one that faced out to sea, which afforded him some protection from the elements, he called Strathen, praying he would get a signal. He did. He explained what he'd found at Kingston House and his thoughts.

Strathen said, 'If the documents were wrapped in cardboard they'll be rotted by now and if they were stashed in a cave in the bay they'll have been destroyed or washed out to sea.'

'Perhaps they were put in something sturdier — tin, for example.'

'We can hardly get out the metal detectors and comb the entire coastal path. Time's running out, Art.'

'I know.'

Where was it, for Christ's sake? 'Oscar Redburn came to the bay to meet and blackmail Shale. He wasn't expecting Howard Killbeck, and neither was he expecting to be killed. He'd have brought the package with him. Maybe he showed Shale some of its contents, to prove he had it, and said that the rest would be delivered on payment, only Cedric Shale lost his nerve and shot him before he had got it.'

'Howard Killbeck must have searched that bay rock by rock in case Redburn stashed it in a crevice and Cotleigh would have done the same. It can't be there.'

Strathen was right.

Marvik looked up at the dark sky, letting the rain cascade over him to where the bell had once been — the bell which had called the family and estate workers to worship and had sounded when there was a wreck. He put himself in Oscar Redburn's shoes and assumed Oscar's personality, recalling all he'd heard about him from Sarah, Freynsham and Brampton. They'd all described him in the same manner.

'From what I've been told about Oscar Redburn he was arrogant, clever and manipulative. He was two-faced, claiming to be on the side of the working man when what he really craved was money and what it would give him. He had contempt for authority. Sarah said he protested against racism, war, the government, anything to do with capitalism or what he viewed as capitalism, and we believe he had in his possession documentation which was proof of deceit, corruption and dishonesty at the highest level of government and business, which struck at the heart of capitalism and implicated one of its finest examples, Sir Ambrose Shale and his son, who had inherited the business and continued to follow in his father's footsteps. So if he didn't hide his cargo in the bay he'd have stashed it somewhere close at hand, somewhere he could easily retrieve it, where he thought it would be safe, where no one was allowed to go except . . .' His words tapered off as he gazed around him. Excitedly, he continued, 'Army land. The church where I am now is the first building you come to on the right of the bay. And the fact it's on army land would simply have added to Redburn's sense of irony given that the army had been in Malaya assisting in putting down workers.' Yes, Marvik could see Redburn being very smug and pleased with himself for being so clever and artful. 'And Matthew said he didn't think anything of the gunshot he'd heard that day in 1979 because the army were on exercise. Howard Killbeck and Cedric Shale had thought the same when they killed Redburn. What was one more gunshot? They never considered then or since the possibility that Redburn could have trespassed on to Ministry of Defence land before meeting them and risked being shot. And Redburn was too conceited and cocky to believe he would be caught by the army or wounded. It has to be here. I'll start searching for it.'

'Art, that'll take an age.'

'I know.'

He heard Strathen take a breath. 'I'll head over to the bay in the boat.'

Marvik shrugged off his rucksack and retrieved his torch. The day was drawing in earlier because of the weather. He swung the torch over the ruined building, imagining what it might have looked like in 1979. There would have been more of it left then and Redburn would have entered, stood inside the small, empty nave and quickly surveyed it for a suitable hiding place. Marvik didn't think he would have looked for long or explored the small chapel. He'd been counting on returning within a short space of time and retrieving the package, so he would have hidden it behind some rubble or underneath some bricks and earth close to the entrance. That was where he'd begin. But even then the package could already have fallen down the cliff and been washed out to sea.

He must be mad, he thought, as he took the right-hand side of the ruins. He could be wildly wrong. Why hadn't Cedric Shale or Howard Killbeck reasoned this out the same way he had? Perhaps because they didn't know enough about Redburn. They didn't understand what he was really like. They had misjudged his intellect and his arrogance. They had assumed he'd hidden the package in the bay and that it had been washed away. And they'd stopped looking after 1990 when Cotleigh had once again taken off. They'd thought they were safe — why? Because they thought Cotleigh aka Pulford was dead but he wasn't. The dead man had been Joshua Nunton. And the reason Howard Killbeck would think that it was Cotleigh who was dead was because his brother, Matthew, had told him that.

Methodically, he moved the bricks and rubble on the ground, thinking he was crazy to do this alone. He needed help. He should wait for Strathen but he was filled with a desperate sense of urgency. As Strathen had said, time was running out. It already had for many. Three people had been killed in the last few hours. Bryony's life probably hung in the balance. His might too. Howard Killbeck could have been watching him enter the house from behind a monitor. He could have seen him set off towards the cliff.

Marvik shone his torch into the crevasses. The wind howled through the ruins and he could hear the scurrying and shuffling of animals. He was thankful the army weren't on night exercise otherwise he might have been at risk of being shot. He listened for any sound of movement outside that might alert him to the presence of Howard Killbeck.

He wasn't sure how long he lifted and replaced bricks or dug down into the earth, but the afternoon turned to evening and darkness. Then his fingers struck against something. It didn't feel like stone. It could be a clod of earth covering stone. He moved a brick carefully out of the way and stretched his hand inside a small recess. With eager anticipation while trying to steal himself for disappointment, he reached in and withdrew an oblong-shaped tin covered with dirt and grit. It was three inches thick, six inches wide and eight inches long. He felt an overwhelming sense of anti-climax and frustration. It wasn't big enough to contain documentation. It had probably been left by a squaddie and had once contained tobacco. Nothing was here. It was back to square one.

Nevertheless, he slipped his fingers under the lid and prised it open, expecting to see only dirt but, shining his torch on the contents, his heart stalled and the breath caught in his throat. Inside were a number of small black-and-white photographs. As he flicked through them the blood froze in his veins. A tight, hard ball of wrath gripped him. Now he knew how Cedric Shale and Howard Killbeck had met. And he knew why so many people had died. He was indeed looking at a treasure, to use Redburn's words. A treasure of a particularly evil and deadly kind.

CHAPTER TWENTY-THREE

Strathen arrived in the bay on the high tide and came ashore in the tender. It was dark, the rain had ceased and the clouds had rolled back far out to sea, leaving a sprinkling of stars and a full moon.

'Will he come?' he asked as they walked towards the cliff face.

'For these he'd go to the end of the earth.' Marvik handed Strathen the tin. The moon was strong enough to bathe the bay in light but Strathen shone his torch on the small black-and-white photographs. He gave a low whistle, his expression grim as he examined them.

'So that was how they met. Doing their National Service during The Malayan Emergency.'

Marvik nodded. 'It's easy to recognize Shale from the photograph you showed me of him on the boat with his father despite the fact in these pictures he's in army uniform.' The eighteen-year-old Shale, lean, sun-tanned and fair-haired, had a gun pointing at a man's head as he knelt, clearly pleading for his life. In another picture the man was dead and Shale was standing victoriously over his body, smiling.

'It's hard to believe it's the same man James Deacon, Shales' general manager described to me, although maybe not,' Strathen added after a moment. 'Looks as though he was always a bit mentally unbalanced.'

'And Howard Killbeck took advantage of that when those pictures were taken and over the years he's exploited it. That's Killbeck.' Marvik pointed to three other pictures Strathen was holding. 'There's no name on them but I'd swear it's him. There's a likeness about the shape of the face to Adam and Matthew.' Marvik stared with disgust at the dark-haired, lithe man beating a prisoner, and there was one where he was smiling into the camera, which Shale must have been holding. In his hand was his trophy — a man's severed head. Marvik recognized the smile despite the years — it was the same one he'd seen from the café window on the beach-front at Swanage when he'd had breakfast with Sarah. Cedric Shale had been ranting on about blood and the devil — so too had Mary. Howard Killbeck *was* the devil, and along with him, Cedric Shale.

Strathen said, 'There's no register of those who did National Service. Both men were born in 1938 so if they started their National Service when they were eighteen that would mean they served from 1956 to 1958. But if Shale and Killbeck were in Singapore in 1959 maybe they both deferred their National Service, which was permitted.'

'And if that's the case then when Ralph Warnford's ship sailed with its dangerous cargo, which might have included other evidence of brutality and sensitive documentation, it ties in with the fact that both Gurney and Pulford were killed by them. Neither of them, though, could retrieve the evidence of their brutality because Pulford had already given it to Darrow to bring home. Alternatively, Ambrose Shale's visit there was to make sure this evidence of his son's brutality was destroyed and he ordered the killing of Gurney and Pulford. Maybe Ambrose Shale's job was to make sure that anything that showed up the British government and business interests in a bad light got loaded on board *HMS Ternly* and brought back. The government wouldn't have wanted anything like this coming out.'

'Not then or now,' Strathen said. 'But some of what went on in Malaya and during the Mau Mau uprising in Kenya *has* come out and it fits with Cotleigh's return earlier this year.'

'How?'

'In November last year some of the relatives of the Malayan victims brought a case against the British government for compensation for suffering torture during the Emergency. Cotleigh must have read about it and thought he could cash in on it. He decided to come back and got himself killed as a result.'

Marvik caught the sound of a powerful launch heading towards them. 'We'd better take up positions.'

He extracted one photograph and slipped the tin into his pocket. Strathen made for the rough-hewn cliff path and climbed a few yards while Marvik headed for the rocky outcrop to the west, where Matthew Killbeck said he'd seen Cotleigh emerge. Marvik had already explored the rocks and found exactly where Cotleigh must have hidden. It was a tall, narrow entrance. Big enough for one man to enter and to hide. And from here he could see the bay and any boat approaching it.

The sound of the motorboat grew louder. Marvik picked out the light on its bow and watched it draw closer. Howard Killbeck was making no effort to hide his approach but then he didn't have to: he believed that Strathen had what he wanted and was ready to bargain. It was what Strathen had told Bryony when he'd called her after Marvik had phoned through his find. Strathen had simply said that he thought she might like to know that he'd found what her grandfather had been killed for and that he was ready to sell. She'd claimed she didn't know what he was talking about but he'd answered, 'I'll be in the bay,' and had rung off and switched off his phone. He and Strathen had agreed their plan of action as Strathen had headed here.

Marvik picked out the figures on the RIB. Killbeck wasn't alone. Marvik hadn't expected him to be. At the helm was a bulky man whom Marvik instantly recognized as the man Brampton had met on the Embankment in London. It meant that Brampton was in Howard Killbeck's pay or rather in his debt, and Marvik knew why. It was as he and Strathen had discussed, and what Melody had told him: Brampton had manipulated figures and reports in favour of Cedric Shale's acquisitions and disposals, and the sale of his corporation to Pentland in return for Howard Killbeck's silence over the part Brampton had played during the 1979 strike. It seemed inconsequential, something that could have been put down to youthful exuberance, except that Brampton had been well rewarded by an incoming Conservative government for his treachery and probably had information about others who had engaged in dirty tricks to smear the dockers. Perhaps he'd foolishly mentioned this to Howard and Howard had tucked it away, ready to capitalize on it when he needed Brampton. Once Brampton was hooked, Howard Killbeck had built a powerful dossier on his corruption and he was in too deep.

Marvik watched Strathen descend from his position on the cliff with an awkward gait that he knew he was exaggerating.

Killbeck had come here with the same intention as he had in 1979: to kill the man in the bay and retrieve the evidence of his acts of barbarism in Malaya. Only this time Strathen was not Redburn and would not allow himself to be killed, and Marvik was not Cotleigh and would not look on while a man committed murder. There was a chance that Killbeck, or the burly bastard with him, would shoot Strathen as soon as they were within range — Marvik was certain they would be carrying weapons — and then would search his body for the package, but Marvik was gambling on the fact that Shale or Killbeck had made the mistake of shooting first and had then spent the next thirty-six years regretting it, not knowing where the package was. Killbeck was unlikely to make the same mistake again.

The powerful light on the RIB lit the bay and both men were carrying flashlights. They caught Strathen in their beams as he clumsily made his way towards them. Marvik thought he caught the sound of movement above and behind him. He swivelled his eyes to the clifftop but there was no one. Perhaps it had been a rabbit or a bird. Or perhaps not.

He emerged from the crevasse and, crouching low, eased his way closer to where he could get a clear view of the three men and hear the conversation. They wouldn't see him in the dark; their light was focused on Strathen. Marvik's body was primed for action; the adrenaline was coursing through him just as it must be with Strathen, and yet Strathen looked on his audience calmly and confidently.

Killbeck walked purposefully up to Strathen, his hand in his jacket pocket where Marvik knew there must be a gun.

'Bryony gave you my message,' Strathen said.

'That you have the package, yes. Where did you find it?'

'Does that matter?'

'No. I was just curious after all these years.'

'How long has she been working for you?'

'She doesn't *work* for me. She just trusts me.'

'Then she's a fool.'

Killbeck smirked. 'Yes, but then so are a lot of people. And Bryony is very fond of her little brother. You and Marvik taking him on the boat and him falling ill with severe sea sickness and heroin withdrawal was a godsend. I told her I'd ensure Ben got the best and most expensive treatment there is, abroad if necessary, to get him clean and keep him clean. And she could go with him. She cares about Ben a great deal, but then that's not surprising seeing as she practically brought him up while her father went from woman to woman and couldn't care less what his children did and with whom. I said they'd have enough money to start afresh in America and that I'd make sure they were OK. I didn't have to do much persuading. She left the marina willingly but you and your partner knew that. Where is Marvik?'

'He's been dealt with.'

Killbeck raised his eyebrows. 'I find that hard to believe.'

'Why? I might be a cripple but I can still kill a man.' Strathen continued, 'Didn't Bryony tell you we fell out over her? I see she didn't. Living on a boat is a very intimate experience and Marvik wasn't there all the time. She just preferred me — yeah, even with one leg. Marvik scared her. It's the scars and his violent temper. Another thing she didn't mention, I see, but then she is an actress and maybe a good one. She fooled you into thinking she cared about Ben but she'll be glad to get rid of him. Where is she?'

'Somewhere safe.'

Strathen shrugged as though to say he didn't really care anyway. 'Marvik and I knew you'd asked her to get back on board to find out how much we knew and to lead you to the package, *if* we found it. Well, I have. And I don't think Bryony will trust you after she's seen the evidence of your brutality.'

'But she won't see it, will she? Besides, it was a long time ago. It's ancient history. It was war. These things happen — you and Marvik know that,' Howard Killbeck said cockily.

Strathen looked unperturbed. Marvik eased forward a touch. The bodyguard's eyes swept the bay.

Howard continued, 'And nobody wants the dirty truth of what happened in Malaya to come out — certainly not the government who don't want to pay compensation to the relatives of the Malayans or Chinese.'

'The victims' relatives wouldn't agree.'

'But they're not in a position to buy the evidence from you. Oh, no doubt the media would cough up for it but it wouldn't be anywhere near the amount I'm willing to pay.'

Howard Killbeck gave a grim smile and in it Marvik caught the likeness between him and his brother, Matthew. Howard believed everyone had a price and so far those he had dealt with had. Marvik wondered how many other people Howard Killbeck had exploited and blackmailed over the years. Many, he guessed. He'd got away with it for so long that Marvik believed Howard had the dirt on some who had been at the very top of government who were still watching their backs, and that was why Crowder had called him and Strathen in. Why shouldn't Howard think that Strathen could be bought? He'd found both Bryony's and Sarah's weaknesses and exploited them for his own good.

'How much?' Strathen curtly asked.

'Fifty thousand pounds.'

Strathen laughed. 'Add another nought and I might consider it.'

'Five hundred thousand pounds is a lot of money.'

'We're talking about a lot of dirt.'

'I don't have that amount of money.'

But Strathen gave a harsh laugh. 'Bollocks. You've been living off the back of Cedric Shale for years.'

'He's done all right out of me. Cedric hated the business and he hated his father. If it hadn't been for me that business would have sunk years ago, excuse the pun. Cedric had no head for business and little heart for it. But he did as I told him and he made a fortune.'

'Which you've been busy spending over the years.'

'Cedric didn't begrudge me. The poor idiot worships the ground I walked on.'

'And of course you always had the evidence of his cruelty to wave under his nose if he stopped worshipping you. I understand he's senile.'

'Yes. And I'm still taking care of him.'

Not any more, thought Marvik, but he heard Strathen say, 'By incarcerating him in that house and stealing his paintings, furniture and belongings to pay for it.'

Killbeck's lips tightened. Crisply, he said, 'You want to sell the goods and I want to buy them.'

'That's my price. It costs a lot of money to live when you're disabled.'

But Killbeck hesitated.

'OK, the deal's off.' Strathen made to move towards the tender. The bulky man stepped forward, his hand in his jacket pocket, fingers no doubt curled around a gun. Marvik tensed.

'Hold on.'

Strathen turned back to Killbeck.

'OK, it's a deal.'

'When can you get the money?'

'Tomorrow afternoon. But I need to see the goods.'

'I haven't got it on me. It's where I found it, stashed away deep in a crevice in the rocks.' Strathen made towards them. Marvik stepped back.

'I searched them.'

'In 1979?'

'And since.'

'Not hard enough, it seems.'

'Is there anything of it left?' Killbeck said, moving after him.

'Enough.'

They rounded the rocks where Killbeck drew up sharply. His accomplice, with his gun withdrawn, made to rush forward to where Marvik was standing but Killbeck halted him with the raising of a hand and a sharp command. 'Wait.' His eyes were fixed on what Marvik was holding.

'Is this what you want?' Marvik held out one photograph. His torch was playing over it, the light from the RIB still shining on them, and the rocks bathed in moonlight.

Killbeck tensed. 'You have the rest?'

Marvik nodded. Strathen made to move forward to get to Marvik but at a sign from Killbeck he was immediately restrained by an arm lock around his neck and a gun in his back. Strathen could get out of that blindfold but he gave no indication of it.

Killbeck said, 'Hand it over, Marvik, or I tell Simons to shoot your buddy.'

'That will mean you can do a deal with me.'

'You'd let him die?' Killbeck said incredulously.

'He was going to double-cross me — why not.'

'Bollocks, you're in this together.'

There was a sudden movement behind Marvik and he swung round to find a leaner, taller man behind him. It was the man who Simons had met on the motor launch at the Festival Pier, the man who had tried to run him down with a motorbike, except he'd swapped the bike for a pump-action sawn-off shotgun. Three against one was not good, especially as they were all armed and he and Strathen weren't.

'You didn't think I'd come here unprepared,' Killbeck smirked.

'No. Not even in 1979 when Shale met you and you killed Oscar Redburn and bundled his body on your boat to ditch in the sea, which I take it is the fate planned for us.'

'Yes. But using the boat you've conveniently brought with you. Explosions at sea are so useful. Or perhaps you'll both be washed up on the beach and your boat found drifting.'

'Has Matthew's boat been found?'

'Matthew? No.' Killbeck looked put out for a moment.

'He took to the high seas last night.'

'That's his decision. Now the package or do I have to kill your buddy?'

Marvik hesitated then shrugged. 'I'll get it for you.' He turned.

'Careful,' growled the leaner man, aiming the gun at him.

'There's not room for two of us in there,' Marvik tossed over his shoulder at Killbeck. The flecks of white on the tops of the waves shone out in the beam of the RIB as they rolled on to the shore. 'Tell him to get off my back.'

'Wait outside, Creech,' Killbeck ordered. Then to Marvik: 'If you come out with anything but the package I will shoot Strathen.'

Marvik nodded and eased himself into the narrow crevice. He didn't have to enter it because the tin was inside his jacket pocket, but he needed Creech to come after him. The entrance widened out within a few paces. Marvik waited.

'What the fuck are you doing?' Killbeck called, irritated and clearly on edge. To Creech, he said, 'Go after him.'

Marvik stood in the depths of the small cave. It was pitch black but like Strathen he had excellent night vision. Their timing needed to be perfect, especially as there was one extra person and one more gun than they had bargained for. Marvik had thought one of them would stay with Bryony.

He tensed and stood motionless as Creech edged his way inside, the gun ahead of him just as Marvik had anticipated. As the gun and then the wrist came into view Marvik brought his heavy torch crashing down with such a force on the wrist that the man cried out, the gun tilted downwards, the barrel discharged in a deafening roar and in the spilt second that followed Marvik kneed Creech violently in the genitals which sent him stumbling to his knees, a karate chop on the back of the neck brought him to the ground and, for good measure, Marvik picked up the sawn-off shotgun and rammed the butt on the back of Creech's head.

'It's OK, he's down. I'm looking for the package,' Marvik mumbled, imitating Creech.

'You bloody idiot,' Killbeck edged forward and, as he did, Marvik stepped around Creech and repeated the action, this time delivering a violent chop to Killbeck's wrist and sending the gun flying. Swiftly, Marvik retrieved it and pointed it at Killbeck. 'Out,' he commanded.

'You won't use that.'

'Not to kill you but a bullet in the ankle will stop you from running.'

'Simons, kill Strathen!' Killbeck shouted as he stumbled on to the rocks, pushed forcefully from behind by Marvik.

'I don't think Simons is in any position to help you,' Strathen answered, eyeing the unconscious body on the shingle. 'Child's play, even with only one leg.' He smiled.

'Let's tie up these bastards,' Marvik said, reaching for the rucksacks they'd hidden behind the rocks.

Killbeck eyed him malevolently but there was still confidence in his grey eyes. 'I'll say that you attacked us, which incidentally is true,' he said as Marvik thrust his arms behind his back and tightened the twine around the wrists. Killbeck winced but the mocking tone continued. 'I came here with security because I needed protection against two trained killers who were trying to blackmail me.'

'Fine, then we'll tell everyone what we intended to blackmail you with.' Marvik caught the sound of a powerful motorboat out to sea. He registered Killbeck's flicker of concern and annoyance and a stab of victory shot through him. It felt good.

Strathen had tied up Simons. He was dragging the unconscious Creech from the opening in the rocks and proceeded to tie his wrists behind his back.

Marvik took the tin from the inside pocket of his jacket. 'You and Shale just couldn't resist gloating over what you were doing. You had to take pictures of it. Is this what you and he got off on?'

Killbeck didn't answer.

The RIB came into view, its searchlight sweeping the bay. Crowder was here with several officers on board. Marvik turned his attention back to Killbeck.

'How did these end up in the High Commission in Kuala Lumpar? Why not keep them on you?'

Marvik wasn't certain Killbeck was going to answer but after a moment he shrugged as though resigned. 'Cedric had them. He was detailed to gather up some reports and orders. He was looking at them when an officer came into the room to see why he was so long completing a simple task. The idiot panicked and thrust them in a folder.'

Marvik thought that perhaps Cedric Shale had been wondering if he should destroy them.

'The officer stood over him while he put the folder into one of those bloody crates.'

Marvik imagined what must have happened and voiced his thoughts. 'Then the lorry taking them to the ship crashed and a sailor from *HMS Ternly*, George Gurney, discovered the pictures when one of the crates split open and some of the documents fell out. He immediately recognized Cedric Shale, having worked on his estate in Dorset.' Perhaps his intention was to blackmail Shale or perhaps to confront him before going to the authorities. Marvik continued, 'Shale told you.'

Howard Killbeck said nothing. Crowder's RIB landed and six uniformed armed officers dashed towards them with Crowder following more slowly

Marvik continued, 'You killed Gurney but too late to stop him giving the package to Bradley Pulford. Gurney pleaded with you to be spared but you killed him anyway.'

'Try proving that.'

'That's not my job.'

Strathen hauled up Simons and thrust him at two uniformed officers, while another two crossed to Creech and dragged him up, groaning. Crowder drew level. Marvik nodded a greeting and continued to address Howard Killbeck.

'Then you killed Bradley Pulford but this time, despite battering him and threatening to kill him he didn't tell you what he'd done with the package and you had to embark for England or be posted AWOL. You returned on *HMS Ternly*.' Ralph Warnford had said that they had taken some soldiers home. 'You had no idea where those photographs were until Oscar Redburn contacted Cedric Shale to tell him what he had got from Jack Darrow.'

Crowder nodded at a uniformed officer who took Howard Killbeck's arm.

'But you bungled it, again,' Marvik sneered. 'You and Shale killed Redburn before he could tell you where he'd stuffed the package. And you didn't know that Cotleigh also knew about the contents of the package but not where it was and that he had witnessed you murdering Redburn and taking his body out to sea. Cotleigh had overheard Darrow telling Redburn about it. Darrow had given Redburn the pictures with instructions for him to give them to his left-wing contacts in the media. Darrow didn't want any part of it because although the media, instructed by certain interested parties of the then opposition and aided by Brampton, were smearing the dockers, Darrow didn't want to be seen stooping to their tactics. He foolishly trusted Redburn.'

'Like I said, everyone has a price.'

'And Shale was too terrified of you to do anything except what you told him. And that's the way it's always been, isn't it?'

'Not always. You've seen the pictures — he got off on it. Just as we all do, you included.'

Marvik balled his fist but the smirk on Killbeck's face and the mocking expression in his eyes made him slowly unclench. Marvik held the man's sneering countenance as he continued. 'Redburn told Shale that Darrow had the package, even though Redburn had it by then, and you arranged for Darrow to be killed.'

'No, that wasn't me. Cotleigh or Redburn must have done it.'

'And neither are alive to confirm or deny that.' But perhaps Cotleigh did kill Darrow and that was why he was late getting here. Cotleigh had come here with the intention of getting the photographs from Redburn, killing him and then blackmailing Shale.

'Your brother, Matthew, by coincidence, was here walking along the cliff and saw you. You ordered him to keep quiet about it, something he was only too willing to do. He didn't want to get involved with the law, but what he didn't tell you was that there was another witness to the murder, Joseph Cotleigh, who came out of his hiding place after you and Shale had left by boat. Matthew was relieved when Cotleigh said he'd keep silent about it and, afraid for his life, Cotleigh took off, but he returned in 1989 and sponged off Matthew until Matthew could stand it no longer and he found you and told you that Cotleigh had been there on that day, knowing that you would deal with him. Only you were too late, or rather you killed the wrong man — Joshua Nunton. Now Matthew was locked into another murder. He was mortified but he said nothing. He let you think that you'd got Cotleigh and together you disposed of the body.'

Killbeck addressed Crowder. 'I don't know what you can charge me with — there's no evidence.'

'There is in that tin.' Marvik handed it across to Crowder.

'The British government won't want that exposed.'

Crowder spoke. 'Times have changed.'

Marvik noted the flicker of surprise on Killbeck's face which was quickly followed by annoyance and then smugness. Even now Howard Killbeck was thinking of the favours he could call in from people in power and influence who could hush this up. Marvik addressed Crowder. 'There are three more bodies in Kingston House, murdered either by him or by his two thugs.' Then, turning to Killbeck, Marvik added tautly, 'And you finally killed Cotleigh when he returned to England in January. Did Matthew tell you he'd returned? That must have been a shock, knowing that your brother had lied to you in 1990,' sneered Marvik. 'Matthew warned you that Cotleigh had made contact with him and was going to try and blackmail him again. But Cotleigh had also made contact with Sarah Redburn and asked to meet her and that set her off on her own research and alarmed you. Then, when you thought she might join forces with me and get too close to the truth, you killed her.'

'Not me.'

Stiffly Marvik said, 'Which one of them then?'

'None of us. It was you she went to meet Sunday night. Maybe you killed her when she wouldn't let you have what you wanted,' he goaded.

Marvik stared at the lean, cocky elderly man and saw a trace of what Shale had put up with for years. The subtle bullying, the malicious mocking, the manipulation. He searched for the truth in the dangerous eyes, then with disgust he turned and headed towards the boat.

CHAPTER TWENTY-FOUR

Marvik broke the silence as they made for Poole in the wake of the RIB where Howard Killbeck and his accomplices were being transported. Crowder had joined him and Strathen on board. 'Whose idea was it to identify Oscar Redburn's body as Joseph Cotleigh in 1979?' he asked Crowder.

'The intelligence services of the day under orders from Her Majesty's opposition, the then Conservative party desperate to get elected with a majority. It suited their dirty tricks campaign to have Cotleigh running off with the union funds and being found dead.'

'Did Cotleigh steal the money?' asked Strathen at the helm.

Crowder shrugged. 'He was by no means a saint, and out for all he could get.'

'And what would they have done if Cotleigh had shown up?' asked Strathen.

'They'd have thought of something.'

Perhaps he would have mysteriously disappeared, thought Marvik. Whoever had authorized the cover-up hadn't cared that Linda Redburn would live the rest of her life wondering where her husband was, walking the coastal path looking for him and seeking the answers as to why he'd vanished. And a daughter wouldn't have grown up with a huge gap in her life and she might still have been alive, thought Marvik with bitterness.

Crowder said, 'So tell me what you've got.'

'And you'll fill in the gaps?' Marvik replied sceptically.

'If I can.'

Or more accurately if he wanted to, or if it was expedient for him to do so. Marvik didn't have all the facts but he could make a good guess at some of the missing pieces. He began.

'Cotleigh left the country in 1979 after witnessing the murder, scared that Shale and Killbeck would come after him. But he couldn't leave by traditional ferry to France from Weymouth because for that he'd need his passport, so he hopped aboard a private boat and was put off along the shore somewhere in France until he could create a new identity, and what better one than a man he knew was already dead: Bradley Pulford. He'd heard Darrow tell Redburn about his death. In 1989 he returned as Bradley Pulford. He thought the timing might be right to extract some money from Shale because of a new dock strike. But maybe the timing had nothing to do with the dock strike. Perhaps he was on the run from someone: an angry husband whose wife he'd been shagging and sponging off, or hiding from the police in Spain, Italy or France after tricking a wealthy widow out of her money, or maybe he'd just got bored with working.' Marvik recalled what Matthew Killbeck had said about him.

Crowder interjected, 'We don't have much background but we do know that Cotleigh worked in France, Italy and the Caribbean, crewing on yachts and delivering boats.'

Matthew had been right then. Cotleigh had been a drifter and had bummed off others for most of his life. He continued, 'Cotleigh also came back to look for the package — his passport to a life of idleness, retracing the route that Redburn had taken to the bay, but he couldn't find it. Matthew knew his brother wouldn't hesitate to kill Cotleigh. He kept quiet about Cotleigh's presence for as long as he could. Cotleigh was in no hurry to make contact with

Howard because he was still looking for the package. When it became clear that Stacey had fallen in love with Cotleigh and was pregnant and that Cotleigh intended staying on and becoming a non-working partner in the fishing business, Matthew tracked down Howard and got a message to him.'

Marvik didn't know how and they probably would never know unless Howard told them. Perhaps the brothers had worked out a code years ago. Perhaps Matthew had always known where Howard was and maybe the boat was the answer to that. Maybe Matthew had kept tabs on Howard's boat.

'Matthew didn't want another murder on his conscience but he saw no other way out. Not that he committed or was involved in Redburn's murder but Cotleigh had told Matthew he knew his brother was the killer and that he'd be named as an accessory to murder so best to keep quiet. Howard Killbeck came to kill Cotleigh but he was too late — Cotleigh had scarpered. He'd somehow got wind of the fact that Howard was coming. Perhaps Stacey had heard her father, Leonard, talking to Matthew about him or he'd said something that Stacey didn't understand because she had no knowledge of a third brother, but when she relayed it to her lover he knew exactly what it meant. He cleared out, leaving Joshua Nunton to be killed in his place. Perhaps he even set him up for it. Perhaps Howard Killbeck bungled this time whereas Cedric Shale did the first time with Redburn, but Joshua ended up dead and Matthew couldn't forgive himself for that. I'm guessing he disposed of the body at sea and that it was never found, or if it was, there was nothing left to make an identification. Cotleigh stayed away until January this year. Only when he returned this time he didn't know the intelligence services were alerted to the name of Bradley Pulford. What made them flag it up now?'

'In November certain documents from The Malayan Emergency were released under the Freedom of Information Act. But first they were screened and anything too damaging to the government — which had escaped incineration or being sunk deep out to sea, which were the orders back in 1959 — was extracted.'

Marvik saw what must have happened. 'In Shale's panic to hide the photographs, when the officer arrived to see what was taking him so long some got pushed into another file, one which travelled back on Ralph Warnford's navy ship.'

'Yes. There were only a couple of pictures but enough to alert intelligence, who were able to identify the two men in them as Cedric Shale and Howard Killbeck. Shale was suffering from dementia so he was no longer a concern but Howard Killbeck couldn't be traced.'

Marvik wasn't sure he believed that. If intelligence knew about Shale then all they had to do was put a watch on his house and wait for Killbeck to show. He had a suite there. And they could have asked the Audleys. Howard Killbeck had clearly assumed another identity but with careful questioning of the Audleys they could have found him. But perhaps time was against them. And even if they had located Howard Killbeck they still wouldn't have found the rest of the photographs. They must have known there were more.

Marvik brought his mind back to what Crowder was saying. 'It was possible that Howard Killbeck was dead, although there was no record of it. The trail was traced back to Singapore and to the deaths of George Gurney and Bradley Pulford and an alert was put out on both names, as a matter of course, even though both were registered dead. Then a Bradley Pulford showed up as having entered the UK in January.'

Strathen said, 'He was left to run in the hope he'd lead intelligence to the rest of the photographs or to Howard Killbeck. Or that Killbeck would kill him before he could stir things up.'

'Something like that.'

Marvik said, 'Do they know how Cotleigh died?'

'No. They lost sight of him.'

'Careless,' muttered Strathen.

'They probably don't have your level of expertise,' Crowder answered, which drew a grim smile from Strathen.

Crowder continued, 'Then the DNA tests confirmed he was the father of Jensen Killbeck. I was asked to handle the matter and I brought you in.'

'Will Howard Killbeck be brought to trial? Will the government want this coming out?' asked Marvik.

'He'll be charged with the murders of Greg and Jane Audley, and Cedric Shale,' Crowder answered evasively.

And Marvik didn't believe those pictures would ever see the light of day or that the relatives of Shale and Killbeck's victims in Malaya would get compensation.

Strathen said, 'And Donald Brampton? Is he alive?'

'I doubt it.'

So did Marvik.

After a brief pause, Crowder said, 'Matthew Killbeck's fishing boat was found two hours ago. There was no one on board.'

Marvik felt sorry for that. 'And Bryony?'

'She and Ben are safe.'

It was over, or almost. There were still questions. Marvik stared intently at the craggy, serious face. 'Was it one of your officers following me from Brampton's offices? It wasn't anyone connected with Bryony because there was no need for Killbeck to have me tailed as Bryony was already primed to tell him what we were doing and where we were heading. She called Howard Killbeck from the hospital and he told her what to do. He instructed her to call me from Waterloo station. I just happened to be in London, but even if I hadn't been she knew I would have gone there or instructed her to get on a train and agreed to meet her. Her instructions were to get into our confidence in order to find out what we knew and to tell him if we found the package, which was why Shaun called her when we did find it. We knew she'd tell Killbeck. She thought that Shaun and I were out to ruin her grandfather's reputation and destroy her career. She didn't *want* to believe ill of Howard Killbeck. He was an old man, much the age her grandfather would have been. He might even have told her he had known him and been a friend of his. And why should she trust us anyway, especially when I came asking about Sarah, who had been killed. Howard probably told her I was Sarah's killer and that Shaun had started the fire at the house at Eel Pie Island and it was all a trick to get her and Ben out of the way.' Bryony thought in movie terms, not reality. 'She used her mobile phone to enable Killbeck to track us and she contacted him on the boat and at the marina before disappearing. So who followed me from Brampton's offices?'

'I think you'll find they were members of the intelligence services.'

'They weren't very good.'

'We can't all be perfect.'

'And is Melody Everley working with or for them?'

'What do you think?'

But Strathen answered. 'Her job was to get close to Brampton because he was known to have associated with Oscar Redburn and Joseph Cotleigh. And he'd worked on some reports for Shale's corporation. He might have led intelligence to Howard Killbeck and he almost did except we got there first. Melody gave Art some information and waited to see if he had more to give her. They didn't know where Brampton had gone.'

'I'm not sure they know that now. He's not at his apartment.'

Marvik said, 'A boat on the Thames will have taken him out.' And it wouldn't be bringing him back. He reckoned the intelligence services would be relieved. Brampton's disappearance would be made to look as though he'd been a man suffering from stress. When his body was found, *if* it was found, no matter the manner of his death, it would be put down to suicide.

Marvik thought back to the motorbike riders who had tailed him. There had been two. One in London outside Ben's bedsit and the other at Swanage. The Swanage one was Howard Killbeck's thug, Creech, but the one outside Ben's bedsit must have been someone from intelligence, which Crowder confirmed.

'They were, as you know, listening in to Ben and Bryony's conversations in the bedsit and keeping track of her because of her connection with Sarah Redburn.'

'Who set fire to the house? Was it one of Howard's men?' But Marvik paused, puzzled. 'Howard had no need to kill Bryony then; he still didn't have the package and he knew that I might lead him to it.'

Evenly, Crowder said, 'Are you sure the arsonist wanted to kill Bryony?'

Marvik's eyes narrowed. He stared at Crowder's implacable expression. 'You mean I was the target? Because of Howard Killbeck.'

'I didn't say that.'

Marvik dashed a glance at Strathen, who eyed him quizzically.

'Then why?' But already his head was swimming with ideas. His heart was racing. 'I didn't meet Sarah on Sunday night as Killbeck claims.'

'She went to meet someone, though.'

'You believe Killbeck?' Marvik asked incredulously and puzzled. 'He must have killed her,' he insisted, his brain teeming.

Crowder said, 'It would have suited Howard Killbeck's purpose if she'd got close to you and you'd confided in her. You would have been assisting her in finding the truth behind her father's disappearance and she could have relayed what you discovered to Howard. He would have had no need then to use Bryony Darrow.'

Marvik took a breath. He hardly dared to think what he was. 'You believe Sarah was killed because of me.'

'Or because of your parents.'

Marvik started with surprise. He felt cold inside. 'Why because of them?'

'Only you might know that.'

'They were killed in a diving accident,' Marvik maintained, throwing a glance at Strathen at the helm, who returned it, perplexed. Crowder said nothing, forcing Marvik to add, 'You have information on their deaths?'

'No.'

But Marvik wasn't certain that was the truth. Crowder turned away and headed into the cockpit. Marvik stared after him then back at Strathen. His head was reeling. Could he believe Crowder? Howard Killbeck *must* be Sarah's killer. Perhaps he'd confess.

But as Strathen slowed the boat to the approach to the marina, Marvik knew that even if Killbeck did confess, there was still that fire and the notebook with the computer disk labelled 'Vasa' inside it, and because of that, and the fact it had been in Sarah's possession, Marvik had no option but to consider what Crowder had said. With that came the realization that he could no longer push away the past as he'd always done and hope it stayed there, because just as Abigail had said when she'd spoken of poor Mary Killbeck, the past had finally become the present.

THE END

THE JOFFE BOOKS STORY

We began in 2014 when Jasper agreed to publish his mum's much-rejected romance novel and it became a bestseller.

Since then we've grown into the largest independent publisher in the UK. We're extremely proud to publish some of the very best writers in the world, including Joy Ellis, Faith Martin, Caro Ramsay, Helen Forrester, Simon Brett and Robert Goddard. Everyone at Joffe Books loves reading and we never forget that it all begins with the magic of an author telling a story.

We are proud to publish talented first-time authors, as well as established writers whose books we love introducing to a new generation of readers.

We have been shortlisted for Independent Publisher of the Year at the British Book Awards three times, in 2020, 2021 and 2022, and for the Diversity and Inclusivity Award at the Independent Publishing Awards in 2022.

We built this company with your help, and we love to hear from you, so please email us about absolutely anything bookish at: feedback@joffebooks.com.

If you want to receive free books every Friday and hear about all our new releases, join our mailing list: www.joffebooks.com/contact

And when you tell your friends about us, just remember: it's pronounced Joffe as in coffee or toffee!

ALSO BY PAULINE ROWSON

THE ART MARVIK MYSTERIES

Book 1: DEADLY WAVES
Book 2: DANGEROUS CARGO

THE SOLENT MURDER MYSTERIES

Book 1: THE PORTSMOUTH MURDERS
Book 2: THE LANGSTONE HARBOUR MURDERS
Book 3: THE HORSEA MARINA MURDERS
Book 4: THE ROYAL HOTEL MURDERS
Book 5: THE ISLE OF WIGHT MURDERS
Book 6: THE PORTCHESTER CASTLE MURDERS
Book 7: THE CHALE BAY MURDERS
Book 8: THE FARLINGTON MARSH MURDERS
Book 9: THE OYSTER QUAYS MURDERS
Book 10: THE COWES WEEK MURDERS
Book 11: THE BOATHOUSE MURDERS
Book 12: THE THORNEY ISLAND MURDERS
Book 13: THE GUERNSEY FERRY MURDERS
Book 14: THE RAT ISLAND MURDERS
Book 15: THE LUCCOMBE BAY MURDERS
Book 16: THE SOUTH BINNESS MURDERS

Made in the USA
Monee, IL
05 January 2026

41028552R00156